Stranger On the Shore

Claire Highton-Stevenson

ISBN: 9798833345863

Dedication

Learning to love yourself is a process that takes dedication to ensure your happiness and fulfilment in life.

-Barbara Cain

Acknowledgments

Thanks Dor Howard and May Dawney for jumping in and saving the day!

Prologue

My name is Quinn Harper and for the most part, my life has been a steady existence. I went to college and got my degree, and then I headed to the West Coast and got my first job in Hollywood, waiting tables like every other young actor or screenwriter like me. I soon dropped the acting part, figuring I was better at putting words into other people's mouths than trying to convey them myself.

It worked out well for me. I got a big break when a studio hired me and the rest, as they say, is history, but this story isn't just about me. I just figured that I am the best person to tell it.

It's a story of love and loss, of heartbreak, and I'll be honest with you, there are some truly horrific moments in this story, but without telling them, you can't understand the pressure and intensity that surrounded me and my life during this time. And though it almost broke me, I'd do it a thousand times over again if it meant that I ended up where I am. Because I am happy, finally.

But love isn't always a Hollywood romantic comedy.

Sometimes it's a battle just to hold on for one glorious moment until the bad guy ruins it all over again. Sometimes the good guys lose, and the bad guy gets to do whatever the hell they want because there are no rules in life when it comes to love, ego, and power.

And in the end, the happy ever after is often whatever the main characters can salvage and grab for themselves. No matter how messy it gets.

So, brace yourself because my and Natasha's story is anything but uneventful, and some of you are going to be triggered by the events that follow, so be prepared. But I think it's a story worth telling. Proof that when you really want something, the dream can come true.

Now, sit back and let me tell you a story.

Part One

Chapter One

It was a Thursday in December, that much she definitely knew. Christmas was coming but Quinn wasn't that bothered. She had other things to be concentrating on. It was a much of a nothing kind of day where all that had happened of interest so far was that Quinn had gotten up, managed to get dressed, and was at her desk finally doing some work. Outside, the weather was doing a good impression of mustering up a storm. A dark and gloomy sky rebounding off the ocean to create a never-ending blanket of grey. It was cold too. California had a reputation for being a sunshine state, but those who actually lived on the beach knew that winter could be just as mean here as it was in a lot of other places.

Logs burned in the fireplace, a big marble mantle that was far too big for the size of the room, but Quinn hadn't cared. The fireplace had been the second biggest selling point when it came to buying this house over the one further along the beach. The first selling point had been the floor-to-ceiling windows and doors that looked out from the lounge onto the beach. It was a view that was worth every penny, and Quinn had fallen in love with it the moment she had seen it. She wasn't even really looking to buy a house. Content to rent the little condo she'd been in for years, but a big contract on a new TV show had meant her financial advisor did what she paid them to do and advised her. Buy a house. Put the money into bricks because it would be the best investment she could make. And he was right, this house was the best investment she could have made because she loved it.

And on this boring, nothing out of the ordinary Thursday morning, Quinn fell in love with something else too.

As she sat back in her chair, her pen stuck between her teeth as she considered the next part of her script.

Quinn glanced out of the windows as she always did. Sometimes just staring at the water ebbing and flowing was all she needed to clear her mind and let the story unfold in her imagination. But today her line of sight was obscured by a lonely figure sitting on the sand about a quarter of the way toward the ocean.

Honey blonde hair was tied neatly at her nape, the wind whipping it up would blow it into her face. The complete opposite of herself, with her short hair cut into the nape of her neck. Dark and brooding her look right now. She contemplated why she was there.

Quinn watched as the figure would reach up, her arm jerking slightly with the movement as she pushed the hair away or slid it back behind her ear. Other than that, she just sat there, still.

Intrigued, Quinn stood and walked to the window for a better look.

It was cold. Not the kind of day anyone would choose to sit on the beach, as was evident by the fact that it was completely deserted in both directions apart from the odd jogger or dog walker. The weather reports indicated several big storms over the coming days and some local residents had literally battened down the hatches and took off back to their more inland residences.

A frenzy of salty spray hit the windows. Grey swirls of angry waves crashed against the shoreline before racing backwards, sucked up once more before being spewed back against the sand, the water's edge inching ever closer inland with each turn. Quinn wasn't worried about that, the water never made it this far up the beach. It would take a mini tsunami to cause any issues like that, but she was concerned about the woman.

She wasn't dressed for this kind of weather. She stood out like the proverbial sore thumb in just a thin blue knitted cardigan that was wrapped around her and held tightly in place by thinner arms that hugged her knees to her ribcage. Her chin rested there, she seemed content to just stare out to sea.

Every now and then, there would be a jerky movement as one hand released its grip of her legs and wiped at her face or hair. She looked as though she were in pain.

Standing there, warm in her expensive mohair jumper and expensive chinos, Quinn was brought from her thoughts by the sound of *The A-Team* theme tune blaring loudly from her phone. She turned abruptly to pick it up and couldn't find it. The tune was coming from beneath the piles of paper, old scripts, and new contract offers that hung precariously on the edge of her desk. She knew from the ringtone that it was her agent, wanting to know if she had read the offers on the same pile that had hidden the phone.

"Well, yeah," she said in response to the question. It wasn't a lie, not really, she had skimmed through them briefly when they had arrived over a week ago. Currently, Quinn was working on a cop show, *Jackson & Jones*, and loving it, but her agent had other ideas and was constantly trying to woo her away to other, bigger projects.

But she had a healthy bank balance, her home was bought and paid for, and all in all, her life was good right now. And she could name-drop several now A-list stars as firm friends if she wanted to be the kind of person who name-dropped for a good impression, but that wasn't really who Quinn Harper was. Enjoying the backdrop of celebrity, without actually having to be one and live in that constant spotlight, was perfect as far as Quinn was concerned. She could attend all the big events, go to all the parties she wanted, and not once would the paparazzi even spare a second to take her photo. Living the dream, that's what they called it, right?

She could stroll around and be completely ignored, just like every other nobody in this town and that was just how she liked it.

With her agent still talking, Quinn turned away from the window and the woman on the beach and flopped down into the armchair nearest the fire. Letting the warmth of it soothe her. But as she sat there, half-listening, her mind kept being drawn back to the woman on the beach.

"I'm just not ready to sign up for anything else yet," she said into the phone as she leaned forward and added another log to the fire. "Because nothing really grabs me, you know? And I like this show. We're looking good for a TVSAA nom."

And that was the reason her agent was pushing for other things. The Television Screen Actors Awards were exciting enough for Quinn.

"Look, as soon as I find what it is I want, trust me, I'll be the first to tell you," Quinn assured. "Sure, okay. Bye for now." She closed off the call and got on her feet again. As she neared the window, she fully expected the woman to have gone, but she hadn't. Had she even moved?

The sight of her, sitting out there alone in the cold concerned her somewhat. The question 'why' kept playing on Quinn's mind. Firstly, because she was a human being who cared about others and this woman had her on high alert. But also because people watching was a master skill of any writer, and people didn't sit on a beach by themselves, in the cold, in the middle of winter, because they were happy.

Not to mention that this wasn't the part of the beach that generally attracted tourists. The houses that lined this stretch of Malibu beach were all privately owned, not hotels or places that people might visit. Each plot had its own area of the beach fenced off, but the rest was free to be used by anyone. The public walked past often, but mostly it was locals who used the beach, and you got used to seeing those regular faces. Nodding good morning or even waving a hello here and there. But just sitting there, in the damp and cold, by yourself, rang alarm bells for Quinn.

The clouds were darker now. The sky looking like a swirling marble of greys and black with the familiar blue of a Californian sky nowhere to be seen. Rain was needed, that much was true, so nobody was against a few storms. The previous summer had been a scorcher, so a little rain would be welcome in any other circumstance. The wind whipped up again, a little stronger this time, and sent sand and spray against the window with a hard rat-a-tat-tat.

Quinn hoped that the woman would go home before she caught her death, but at the same time, she felt strangely drawn to wanting to watch her. It had been a long while since she had been interested in anyone, but this wasn't quite the same thing, still, the woman already intrigued her by just sitting on the beach, more than anyone else had done over dinner and drinks recently.

It was usually around this time that Quinn headed out for a run, though she hadn't done so for a couple of days now. Laziness, the weather, and being absorbed in work had meant it had slipped off her radar of important things to do. Five kilometres along the shore then five back every day helped keep her fit and active. Rain or shine, she had no excuses not to get moving usually, and she decided there and then that she could kill two birds with one stone. Get back into the habit of exercise and take a closer look at the intriguing woman on the beach.

She ran up the stairs and changed into her running gear, choosing long sweatpants over her usual shorts, and a Lycra long-sleeved top instead of the usual sleeveless shirt. She strapped her iPod to her arm, connected the fancy wireless earbuds to it and pushed them into her ears, her feet pushing into comfortable shoes.

Stepping out into the cold wind was an experience. It wasn't just cold, it was bitter. The spray and sand stung her face as she took those first steps that led her into a slow jog past the woman. Quinn was surprised when the woman looked up at her and made eye contact. For a moment, Quinn almost lost her footing, she was stunning. Quinn nodded at her as a sign of acknowledgement before tearing her eyes away and gazing at the more familiar scene ahead, of sand, and more sand.

As Quinn ran, all she could think about were the woman's eyes. Green or maybe blue, marine, or sea foam, they deserved a fancy name like that. Quinn had never been so captivated in her life. Those eyes that were wet with tears, from sadness, or just the stinging coldness of the wind, she didn't know. What she did know however, was that she didn't want to run any further, and cutting it short, she turned and retraced her steps back towards her house, and to her. The stranger on the shore. But it was too late.

She had gone.

Chapter Two

Nothing much else happened over the weekend. Quinn actually read through all of the contract offers and politely declined them all. She had a reputation to uphold after all, and the next job that she took, be it for TV or film, needed to be something that a) she would enjoy, and b) added something to her already impressive CV. But every now and then she would glance out through the windows just in case. Something about the woman had stuck with her and now she wished she had stopped and talked to her, but then she reminded herself that privacy was often what most people wanted when they took themselves off somewhere quiet.

Saturday had become Quinn's roaming day, as her mother would have called it. Wandering around antique shops and flea markets, in search of nothing in particular, she just enjoyed it. Sometimes something caught her eye, and she imagined the backstory to it. Who had owned it, had it been a gift from a lover? Maybe that was why she liked antiques, they all had a history, stories waiting to be told. She didn't buy anything though, she rarely did. But from a young age, sitting on her grandfather's knee, to now, as a fully grown adult who ran, not to music, but to audiobooks, because she loved the stories. He had told her about the things he had brought back from the war, and his travels after, and it had all enthralled her growing imagination.

With music, she could never get the rhythm right and tended to run too speedily and tire too easily if the beat was fast; but a story? She could get lost in those, and she often did. Running much farther than she had planned to. So, stories were healthy as far as she was concerned.

The storm that had been threatening on Thursday had hit and lasted well into Friday. Thunder had crashed, and lightning forked and lit up the sky out at sea. On Sunday the heavens opened and a downpour to end all downpours burst from the sky.

Quinn had the fire burning almost continuously in an effort to keep warm. The house was nice and cosy, just how she liked it. It was a fair description of a lot of things in Quinn's life, herself included.

It wasn't a big house in comparison with some of her neighbors, but it was a home. Not a weekend getaway, or a summer vacation place, this was Quinn's home. The downstairs consisted of the large living room on the beachside of the house with its fireplace and floor-to-ceiling windows and doors that opened onto the beach and gave spectacular views. It was the room Quinn spent most of her time in. At the back, where the house backed onto the street, was the open plan kitchen diner and downstairs water closet and utility room.

Upstairs housed three double bedrooms, two with bathrooms attached, and a family bathroom for anyone else to use who might be staying. Not that Quinn had guests to stay very often, but the rooms were there just in case.

She didn't keep too much stuff around the house. An ex had liked to keep things tidy, and it had kind of rubbed off on Quinn, now, she'd probably be described as edging towards minimalist. There was a small cabinet on the wall in the living room that housed several awards she had received over the years, mostly for her work on some of the top TV shows of the time. *Gods on Top, The Cost of it All, and I See You,* to name a few. None of them were on air any longer, but the re-runs popped up here and there. They were still popular with the audiences at home.

She had one, though, that took pride of place in her heart, but she still locked it inside the cabinet along with the rest.

The golden statuette for Best Original screenplay that she had won for her part in creating the blockbuster *Euphoric*. It swept the board and catapulted all four of the writing team to the status of

Oscar winner, a coveted position that everyone in Hollywood endeavored to reach, and she had done at the age of twenty-eight She was thirty-six now, and still living off the glory of that one night on the red carpet, when her face and name was 'something' people recognized for about thirty-six hours.

Quinn sat down and began working on a few ideas that had been swimming around in her thoughts for a while now. Making use of her self-imposed sabbatical to see if she could come up with something all by herself was both exciting and terrifying.

Mostly for TV, you wrote episodes as a collective, sometimes one would take the lead and put forward most of the structure, but there would be input from everyone else, and those teams could be quite big on some shows.

It had been the same for *Euphoric*, except a smaller group of four writers all giving input to create a vision that could be moved from words on a page, to action on the big screen. So, it was a new concept for Quinn to try her hand at something as a solo writer again.

Occasionally, she would glance up from her desk and look out of the window to the sand, hoping to see the stranger. She had no idea why this woman had suddenly become so important to her, but something about her had struck her empathy. She wasn't there though, and so, Quinn stopped thinking about her and got on with the job at hand, her work. Because at some point, she would have to actually do something that paid her bills and got her out of the house and back into the real world, where other people existed and connected because she was definitely in need of that. She made a mental note to give some friends a call and organize something.

Chapter Three

Tuesday morning brought with it the much-needed sunshine that Californian residents were used to. It was cool, but not cold, and as Quinn was preparing for her daily run, she glanced out of the window, like she'd been doing every time she entered this room, and it wasn't just for the view. Every day, there was a small selfish bubble of hope that the woman would be back.

All weekend, she had been keeping an eye out, but she hadn't come. In some ways, she felt good about it, maybe the woman had just been having a bad day and needed some alone time. And now she was fine, and all was good in her world, but Quinn wasn't so sure that would be the case. The deep sadness that resonated from her was palpable, Quinn has seen it in her eyes.

So, when she looked out today and saw a figure sitting in the same spot, Quinn felt a sense of unease run through her, alongside a spark of interest.

Of course, she couldn't be 100 per cent sure that it was the same woman, though the likelihood was that it was her. What were the chances that, on two separate occasions, two different people would choose to sit in the exact same spot on the beach in the middle of winter and during some of the coldest weather for months? Quinn wasn't a gambling woman, but she considered these odds were in her favour. Also, her house just wasn't the one you'd pick to sit in front of and have a picnic with the kids. Most people who did that either lived in the house they were sitting in front of or they moved further down the beach and found a secluded spot away from the houses.

But just to be completely sure, Quinn pulled on her running shoes and left the house, bracing herself for the cooler air she would feel once she left the sanctity of her warm and cosy home, the fire lit and roaring, it would be perfect when she got back and stripped off for a shower.

As Quinn trotted past, she once again glanced at the person sitting on her part of the beach and once again, they made brief eye contact.

Sea foam eyes.

It was her.

She looked contemplative, Quinn thought. Clearly a woman with a lot on her mind. She also looked incredibly unhappy and that tugged at Quinn's heart a little more, yanking at that innate part of her that felt compelled to help anyone in need, but as she smiled down at her, the woman looked away, and Quinn felt as if she were intruding by just being in her presence, so she got on with the job in hand and continued on with her run.

About halfway through, Quinn switched off the audiobook she was listening to, she wasn't paying any attention to it anyway as her thoughts were awash with why the woman was there and why she was so sad. So, it was no surprise when she pulled up and decided to cut her run short again. Turning back around, she let her legs move faster, getting into a rhythm that had her returning a half-hour earlier than usual. Hopeful that the woman might still be there, though she had no clue what she was going to do if she were.

As Quinn rounded the small bend, she was pleased to see she was still there. It didn't look like she had moved at all. Focused solely on her thoughts and whatever they were, they took her line of sight to the ocean. More clouds had moved in, and another storm was coming. A never-ending vista of greyness. Her sight set on the vast greyness of the ocean and the horizon blurring into one.

Quinn could understand the lure of the ocean. Often, she let the water take her mind away somewhere her thoughts could swim and dive until they sorted themselves out into ideas that she could get down into words. The ocean was magical like that.

As Quinn slowed her pace, not wanting to rush past the woman at speed, she noticed how much the wind was whipping up. Sandblasting her face, her skin tingling from the abrasiveness of the gritty particles that hit her skin before the ocean spray literally rubbed salt into the wound.

The woman didn't look up this time. And Quinn found herself frowning as she took the final steps into her home. Her mind was filled with an ever-growing list of questions.

The writer in her came up with so many different explanations of why it might be that she had decided to come here, most of which she didn't want to think too hard about because none of them had a happy ending.

She quickly stripped out of her wet work-out clothes, the mix of sweat and sea spray making sure that she came home cold and damp. The kind of cold that seeped into the very marrow of your bones and took an age to warm you back up.

Standing in the shower, under the hot water, she resolved to do something if the woman was still there. Suitably warmed up, she got out, dried off and got dressed as quickly as she could, before heading downstairs. As she passed the lounge, she craned her neck to see out of the window that the figure was indeed still there. Then she raced down the hallway and into the kitchen.

Grabbing two mugs from the cupboard, she poured two cups of coffee. Thinking for a moment, she was unsure how the woman would drink it. With cream? Sugar? Or just black?

"Whatever," she said to herself, taking the two mugs of black coffee with her to the door where she placed them down and dragged on her coat. She carried them outside.

She was a little nervous, not really being the kind of person who made first moves or initiated conversations, but this felt like it was something that needed to be done. What was the worst that could happen? Rejection? Nothing she couldn't deal with; you didn't work in Hollywood for long if the rejection was something that triggered too hard.

Gradually, Quinn closed the gap between them then, without a word, she sat down beside her. Not so close as to be invasive or creepy, that wasn't her intention. But close enough that the woman would notice.

For a few seconds, she didn't move at all except to tense up and become very still. Slowly, she turned to her left and looked at Quinn, her brow furrowed in confusion. Quinn said nothing, just smiled a little and leaned towards her to place the mug down on the sand beside her.

"It's just coffee," Quinn said after a beat, keeping her voice as gentle as she could, but the woman just turned back to stare out to sea again, so Quinn did the same. Both of them silently stared into the grey.

The woman still didn't speak, but from the periphery of Quinn's vision, she noticed her surreptitiously glance down at the now-steaming cup. For the first time, Quinn watched her move. Fidgeting in the sand as though her body had suddenly realised how uncomfortable she was. Quinn was itching to speak again, to ask how she was, what was her name? Something about her tugged at Quinn's questioning mind. She wanted to know everything.

But Quinn waited, patience was indeed a virtue she had been graced with, and, finally, with long, slender fingers, she reached out and picked up the mug. Tentatively, the woman wrapped both hands around it and raised it to her lips, her eyes now watching Quinn the entire time.

A strand of hair was itching Quinn's face as the wind caught it, moving her right hand up to push it back behind her ear. To her utter horror, the woman flinched away as though she were expecting Quinn to hit her.

The hot coffee in her mug spilled out over her hand as she trembled, and yet that caused barely any reaction. It must have been hot enough against her cold skin to scald, but she did nothing more than to glance at it, shake the liquid off and wipe it against the leg of her jeans.

Quinn's mind went into overdrive now, the scenarios aplenty. She figured she was being a little irrational and overdramatic with some of them, but that was her job, so it was hardly surprising. Writing dull tales of everyday life didn't pay the bills, there had to be more to it, but she didn't want there to be more to this woman, for her sake. She didn't want to imagine why she felt the need to flinch at a simple movement of a hand, and yet a burn didn't faze her at all.

"I think the weather is going to turn again soon, don't you?" Quinn probed, unable to hold her tongue any longer. Glancing at her sideways, Quinn barely moved in case she spooked her again. The woman didn't reply but Quinn noted the small furtive peek at her from the side of her eye; that was it, nothing more other than to continue to sip her coffee. Quinn was just hoping to engage her in any way that she could, she didn't expect a full-on conversation, but maybe a word or two would mean something. Instead, the woman looked the other way. So, they sat like that, for what felt like hours, to Quinn's now-cold-again bones, but in reality, it had been no more than fifteen or twenty minutes.

The woman continued to drink the coffee in small sips until it appeared as though her lips had become accustomed to the heat of it, her small delicate hands wrapped around the mug and linked together holding the heat in her palms.

When she was finished, she put the cup down in the exact same spot that Quinn had given it to her.

"Thank you," she whispered quietly before she stood up, wincing as she grabbed her flank. Quinn wanted to help, but she knew she couldn't. She had to make do with watching as she walked away towards the small alley that led between the houses and out onto the street.

The slow, methodical steps, as though each one needed to be concentrated on in order to keep her walking in that direction and not back, towards the sea. Her right arm wrapped around herself, holding her tightly. Quinn had seen that motion before on film sets when someone was playing an injured and in pain character. She hoped that wasn't the case here, but something tugged at Quinn telling her it was.

When she was no longer in sight, Quinn heaved herself up, shook the sand from her clothes, bent down, and retrieved the mugs, emptying the dregs onto the sand. Walking back to the house, she continued to keep staring in the direction the woman had gone, just in case she came back for any reason. She didn't, and all that was left to do was go back inside and wash up the mugs.

But Quinn's mind was now racing.

Chapter Four

Quinn was writing like there was no tomorrow. For some reason she had ideas spilling from her brain, and she couldn't get them down onto paper quickly enough. Nothing tangible as yet, but she was sure she was on to something if she could just keep this up, something would pop and she would soon be lost in a fantasy world of characters and scenes. And then who knew where that would take her? TV or film, she had no clue, but she was enjoying the process again.

Today was a sunny day, still no warmer, but the sun had visited and decided to hang around and for that she was grateful. There was nothing nicer than to enjoy every season for its own unique arc of beauty, and from her desk in the lounge, looking out through the windows, she could enjoy it all.

Her laptop was open, page ready and fingers poised to begin typing. The hot cup of coffee she had just poured sat chilling on the side table atop a pile of paperwork that had numerous scribbles of concepts, random thoughts, and anything else that had popped into her mind these past few days.

She was so engrossed in her ideas that she never noticed the woman arrive. One moment the beach was empty and, the next, Quinn looked up from her laptop to find her sat in what was now being called *her spot*.

To say Quinn was intrigued by now would be the understatement of the century. A beautiful woman, with a deep sadness, was choosing to sit outside of her house, and Quinn had no idea why. Was it just a random coincidence, or not?

The beach stretched for miles, and yet, the woman continued to come to this place. To just sit and stare out at sea, and think? Quinn wondered if she ever found any answers but feared not if she felt the need to keep returning. Maybe soon she would be able to ask her.

From her vantage point, Quinn once again studied her. As before, she wore nothing warmer than a thin cardigan that clung to her small frame. Her arms wrapped around her, knees tucked up to her chin that rested on them, her usual pose. Her hair hung loose this time, however, fluttering around her face when the breeze picked up. Now and then she would raise a hand unsteadily, and gently pushed the escaping lock back behind her ear.

For a few minutes, Quinn just sat and watched her. Compelled to keep watch, to keep an eye on her. An innate need to be a safe harbor for her if she wanted it. At some point, a plan formed in Quinn's mind. Just like before, she figured it would help, or she'd be ignored.

She virtually ransacked the kitchen looking for a flask. When she found it, she filled it with coffee. Then she grabbed a clean mug from the drainer, and as she passed back through the hallway and into the lounge, she pulled the woollen blanket from the back of the settee and headed outside. Taking a wider circle so that she didn't come up behind her, Quinn eventually stood in front of the woman, blocking her view of the ocean, and forcing her to adjust her line of sight upwards.

Her eyes fixed with Quinn's, instantly filling with distress. Wide and staring. So much so, that Quinn almost turned and walked away, but something stopped her from doing that, a higher power maybe. Instead, she crouched down in front of the woman and held out the flask.

"I'm sorry for scaring you, you just looked like you could do with another of these," Quinn said, the hint of a smile on her lips trying to make clear that she was still nobody to fear. She poured some coffee into a mug and held it out to her.

The woman watched Quinn intently before tentatively reaching out for it. Quinn took the chance to notice more this time. Her fingernails, bitten down to the quick, tipped the ends of bony long fingers. The forefinger of the left hand was bent slightly, as though at some point it had been broken. The thought hit Quinn like a spear through her heart.

"It's quite cold," Quinn continued, very slowly opening the blanket as the woman continued to just watch. "I'm just going to place this around you, it will keep you warm while you sit," she explained. Carefully, Quinn reached around her. Once again, the woman flinched at the movement, her entire body tensing until she let the blanket drop around her shoulders and moved away a little bit.

"I don't want to hurt you," Quinn said gently. "I can see that maybe something is troubling you and you're wanting some space, so I won't stay. But if it gets too cold to be sat here, my house is just behind you, you are welcome to come inside if you want to. We don't have to talk, but it's warm and safe and you can still see the ocean through the window." Quinn offered up another smile and hoped that she'd conveyed things in a way that didn't freak her out. She was no therapist, but Quinn could see the need to be gentle and kind. In some ways, it kind of freaked Quinn out to have to explain to someone that she was safe, that her home was safe. She'd kind of just taken it for granted that those who knew her would never doubt that, but she reminded herself that this woman didn't know her, did she? Quinn was just a stranger on a beach who was offering to be kind, maybe her experience told her people were not always what they seemed.

"Okay, so I'll leave you in peace." Quinn placed the flask down beside her. "There's more in there, should keep you warm for a little bit," Quinn rambled. She didn't want to leave her, and she was looking for excuses to stay, she knew that. The woman just stared at her, silently, and so she took that as her cue to go.

As Quinn walked away, she felt tears begin to fill her eyes as she thought about the sadness in hers. This woman was beautiful, but her eyes were something else. And they moved Quinn in a way she'd never felt before. She wanted to throw her arms around her and promise her the world, which was so unlike Quinn. She didn't fall for anyone, friend or lover, quickly. She was a slow burner, she liked to ease into relationships and explore people before she made a real conscious decision to open up and let them in. But with this woman, it felt like Quinn wasn't going to get a choice like the universe had already decided for her and that was that.

She was still thinking about her as she pottered around the kitchen. She'd made a fresh pot of coffee and was considering some lunch when there was a light rapping of what sounded like knuckles on wood. Glancing out of the window, Quinn noticed that it was raining again, and the woman, the blanket, was all gone. Moving quickly through the house, she steadied herself to open the door. Although every part of her wanted to wrench it open and pull her in as quickly as she could, she refrained.

With the door open, their eyes met again before she quickly looked away. She had her hands full with the mug and flask, the blanket slung over her shoulder. Quinn took them all from her and then, without a word, she stepped aside, turned, and left her to decide if she wanted to come in. While Quinn waited at the end of the hall, hoping. And a few seconds later, Quinn heard the soft sound of the door closing, the click of the lock, and then soft footsteps nervously walking towards where Quinn was waiting.

When she entered the lounge, Quinn smiled, and held her hand up, pointing towards the windows. "Would you like to join me?" Quinn asked, leading the way. She looked around and realised that maybe it was time for a tidy up. There were piles of books and scripts all over the place and she quickly moved them from the couch and smiled nervously. "Sorry, I've been working," Quinn said as though that explained everything. When the couch was clear, she indicated that she should sit. At first, she hesitated, but then slowly, she all but glided into the room and sat down. Sitting perfectly still, perched on the edge closest to the door. Her hands resting in her lap, she watched every move Quinn made as she continued to move things out of the way.

"I really should be tidier, but I get going with an idea and then everything else gets forgotten about," Quinn blathered on, feeling the need to talk and fill the silence. Quinn stopped and looked at her. "Would you like some more coffee? Tea? Something else? I think I have some hot chocolate or lemonade? I have other stuff, you know...I mean, is it too early for wine?" She knew that she was rambling as she checked her watch and decided that it probably was too early, but still, who was she to judge?

She looked at Quinn with those big wide eyes, as though sizing her up through a veil of fear. Quinn hated that anything about her would create that feeling within anyone.

"Coffee then?" she asked, but she was still met with no reply. One more glance to check she was okay, and Quinn backed out of the room and walked the short hallway to the kitchen.

It didn't take her long to get the pot brewing again, and while she waited, she quickly made some sandwiches and heated a bowl of tinned chicken soup**.** She then had a sudden thought that maybe she was a vegetarian, or worse, a vegan. Everyone seemed to be vegan nowadays. She shrugged. If she was, then she wouldn't eat it, and that was fine with Quinn.

She carried everything on a tray, and just as she reached the door to the lounge, she stopped. "It's just me," she said gently, not wanting to scare her further by just appearing. Gently, Quinn toed the door with her foot to push it open.

"I made something to eat too," Quinn continued but was met with silence. A different silence because she was curled up and sleeping.

Finally, she looked peaceful. The sadness was not quite so evident now that her red-rimmed eyes were closed. Her facial muscles relaxed a little more.

Quinn placed the tray down on the coffee table and grabbed the blanket she'd given her earlier, and as gently as she could, she placed it over her.

The fire was now just embers, so Quinn added some more wood and got it burning brightly again. It was warm and toasty as she sat back in her chair, drinking her coffee, and nibbling on a sandwich. For a moment she just watched the dozing woman, but then, when it was clear that she was sleeping soundly, Quinn turned to her laptop and continued to work.

She had been working for a good two hours when she heard the woman begin to stir. Her face creased with pain and distress. She began to murmur and cry out quietly, pleading with an unknown force that was seemingly terrorizing her in her dreams.

Unsure what she should do, Quinn moved closer and continued to just watch to make sure she didn't hurt herself, and then thanked the gods above when she seemed to settle again.

Quinn studied her some more. Her clothes were expensive, and she wore a ring, a wedding ring, and Quinn felt the first hints of disappointment. Firstly, that some lucky person had already found her, and secondly, that said person hadn't noticed how sad she was. Unless they were the cause of her suffering, Quinn mused to herself.

She was clearly somebody that was used to the best in life: her nails, though bitten now, showed signs of glue. The kind they used to hold fancy nails in place, and her skin blemish-free from what she could see hidden by the hair that had fallen across her face. She was a little shorter than Quinn, but not by much, at a guess five feet six inches, and she was skinny. She had curves, but she looked like she needed a few hot meals inside her and some anxiety-free weeks in order to get her appetite back.

Quinn was so invested in her thoughts that she hadn't even noticed she was awake and staring at her. It was darker now; the sun was going down and the evening was well on its way.

"Hey," Quinn said, her smile feeling shy on her cheeks. "You seemed comfortable so..." Still, she didn't speak, and Quinn was beginning to feel a little foolish. "I made some sandwiches, please help yourself while I get some hot coffee for you." She stuttered and stumbled with her words, feeling as though she were being completely analyzed. Quinn picked up the empty tray, placed her own dirty plate, bowl and cup on it, and moved towards the door. As she glanced back, she smiled to herself when the woman picked up the smallest triangle of a sandwich.

Returning to the room, Quinn placed a fresh cup of hot coffee on the table in front of her and noticed that two more triangles had gone, and she found herself inwardly smiling at that. It was a small breakthrough. But her self-congratulatory thoughts were shattered as the woman reached forward to pick up the cup. Wincing, she grabbed her side.

Quinn reacted and moved too quickly. Wanting to check she was okay. The movement scared her, and as she jumped away, her foot caught the small table. It rocked and the mug of coffee spilled all over the wooden surface, dripping down onto the hardwood flooring.

"I'm sorry," she cried out loudly and cowered, raising her arms above her head in preparation for what? That Quinn would hit her? Now Quinn was understanding, it was all falling into place.

"Hey, it's okay," she said calmly. Ignoring her natural instinct to reach out and touch her, pull her close, and just hold her through this terror. Quinn knew that would be the wrong move, so she repeated again that it was okay.

She had no idea if the woman was even hearing her. Her eyes darted around the room one moment, then suddenly coming to stop on nothing in particular. It was like she had zoned out. She was there, but she wasn't.

"Are you alright?" Quinn tried once more, but nothing.

And then just like that, she blinked, took in her surroundings, and said, "I'm sorry. I'm so clumsy."

"It's okay, it's just a cup of coffee," Quinn reassured. "I can get another one, and there's no damage done. It's just an accident." She smiled at the woman as she grabbed a box of tissues and began to mop up the dark liquid that had spread across the table and all over her scribbled notes.

Quinn moved as unhurriedly as she could, not wanting to spook her any more than she already was. She was trembling, as though all the heat had been sucked from the room. Her eyes continued to dart around, searching the corners and the door.

"Hey? Hey?" Quinn repeated until finally, she looked at her, her body twisted and pushed back as far as she could into the cushions of the sofa. "It's okay, it's just an accident."

Her hair had fallen down over her face, and carefully, Quinn moved a hand to gently sweep it back behind her ear. But the woman panicked. She screamed and scrabbled backward, but there was nowhere to go and Quinn was lost, with no idea what to do now. She did the only thing she knew and pulled her into her arms. Wrapping them around her and shushing gently against her ear.

Expecting the woman to try to wriggle free, she was prepared to let go instantly, but she didn't. Instead, she froze and became still as a statue, but at least she was calm and no longer screaming. It frightened Quinn, but not in the way she first thought. She was frightened for her. What had happened to this woman to make her so terrified like this?

Just as Quinn was about to release her hold, the woman surprised her when she clung on and burrowed her face into the crook of her neck. Quinn could feel the hot wetness of her tears against her skin as they dripped like lava, pooling in the hollows of Quinn's collarbone.

They stayed like this for what felt like a long time. The night sky had moved in, and the fire had long since stopped burning. It was getting cooler and the woman was still sobbing and clinging to Quinn like a scolded child.

Loosening her grip slightly with her left hand, Quinn reached out for the blanket. It was a little difficult in this position to get it, but she fingered the fraying edge and pulled it gradually towards them. Somehow, she managed to drag the blanket over them both.

Eventually, the sobbing subsided to occasional jolts, like sad hiccups. Her grip loosening on Quinn's shirt.

"Okay?" Quinn asked her softly. The woman's breathing was returning to normal, and Quinn didn't want to set her off again. She felt her nod against her chest, and as Quinn dared to look down, she found the most beautiful eyes staring up at her.

And at that moment, Quinn needed her to understand that she was safe. "I don't know what has happened to you, but I won't hurt you. Okay?"

Another small nod and Quinn smiled.

"My name is Quinn."

"Natasha," she replied.

Quinn released the breath she had been holding. At last, a breakthrough. Her smile widened as she said, "Well, it's nice to meet you, Natasha."

"I-I'm so sorry, gosh you… what on Earth must you think of me?" Natasha said, "I should go." She checked her watch and climbed off the couch. "I need to leave," she continued as she checked her watch again. The fear and terror back in an instant.

"Really? Are you sure you're, okay? It's quite late, you're welcome to stay," Quinn explained, adding, "I have a spare room."

"No," she said abruptly. "No, thank you, but I have to go." She started to fold the blanket neatly. As she placed it on the couch, she winced once more, and this time Quinn didn't hesitate.

"Natasha, are you injured?" she asked looking intently at her as she shook her head, "I want to see," Quinn said, though she had no idea where her nerve to make such demands came from, but it was there. Maybe it was because for whatever reason this woman had become important to her. She felt compelled to help her.

"I am fine, honestly, it's nothing," Natasha insisted, but Quinn wasn't convinced.

"Please, let me see," Quinn repeated softly. Standing her ground and blocked the exit.

"Please, Quinn just… please I need to go," she pleaded, and Quinn moved aside.

"I need to know that you're…" Quinn said, following her down the hall. "I just want to know, you're alright," she repeated, trying to convince herself that whatever the problem was, it would be nothing too horrible. That it would all be alright, but she knew that she was lying to herself.

They stood there like they were in some kind of unarmed Mexican standoff and stared at one another before Natasha sighed and gave in, unbuttoning her blouse without a word.

Quinn watched her fingers as they expertly plucked at the white plastic buttons that held the green silk blouse together. Once completely undone she let her hands fall to her side and Quinn assumed that she was being given permission to move the material out of the way and look. So, she did just that, gently using the back of her hand to push the garment to one side revealing a large bluey-black mark the size of a fist. That had spread outwards and turned maroon as it snaked up under her armpit and back around under the breast.

"Fuck." She staggered back and couldn't help the expletive that left her lips. "Who did this?" Quinn asked but the idea was already forming in her head.

"Does it matter?" Natasha said quickly as she began to button up again.

Quinn reached out and touched her hand, aware that Natasha didn't pull away from her.

"It matters," Quinn insisted as tears formed in her eyes and threatened to fall. "Really, it matters." She waited, wanting her to see that she meant it. "Who? Who did this?" But Natasha looked away, continuing to button her shirt, and then pull her cardigan tightly around her again. "Natasha! Who did this to you?" Quinn asked one last time, but there wouldn't be an answer. Not tonight.

"I have to go, thank you for everything," Natasha said, turning to open the door, and leaving before Quinn could say anything else. As the door closed, Quinn felt her legs buckle, and her back hit the wall, she slid down until her backside hit the floor, sobs racking her chest.

How could anyone do that to someone?

Chapter Five

Days turned into weeks, and before Quinn knew it three months had passed with no sign of Natasha.

In those first days, Quinn had worried about something awful, getting up and spending hours just sitting by the window and watching, but nothing ever happened. And she had to start hoping that that meant Natasha was okay.

Finally, Quinn's agent gave up trying to lure her into other projects. Quinn was content to continue on with *Jackson & Jones.* It was a lot of fun, and the cast were an ensemble of well-known names and faces, as well as a lot of new ones.

Originally, the offer had come out of the blue the previous year and at first, Quinn did turn it down, but with excellent rates of pay and time off to work on other things if she wanted to. It also had a 9 p.m. time slot and that meant scripts and storylines could be edgier, explore the darker side of humanity.

The producers wanted something intense, but with a sprinkling of humor. So, she grabbed at the chance. Now, having scripts to concentrate on, meant she could at least try to keep her mind off of Natasha for several hours of the day.

The show runner was a guy called Nick Miles and he came with a huge reputation that everyone respected. He had won every accolade there was in TV, some twice over. And he was a nice guy; easy going, with a laid-back work concept that Quinn hadn't seen on any other show.

At the end of the week, after the last scene was wrapped, the entire cast and crew would be invited to attend a club for drinks and a chance to let their hair down. It was Nick's idea that those that worked best together, played best together. And hadn't Quinn been talking about venturing out again? She just wasn't sure that it would be a weekly adventure for her, but it was certainly a better option than sitting indoors by herself every weekend. So, most weekends, she had gone along and had a few drinks with friends. It was fun, she had to admit that.

The other thing Nick insisted on doing regularly was engaging with viewers via social media. He insisted that all cast and crew get on board with tweet sessions after each episode aired. Some of the younger ones were already masters of it, for the likes of Quinn and some of the older cast members it was a new construct altogether and it took a lot of persuading, patience and effort for some of them to bother.

Quinn found it quite unnerving really, the way so many 'fans' became obsessed with the characters, and the actors that played them. Some would attach themselves to anyone that had any contact with them. Meaning she herself had suddenly gained thousands of followers overnight after her first live tweets.

Admittedly most of the attention was fine, the fans were nice and just wanted to feel a part of it all, but there were a few that concerned her straight off the bat, and a few of them they placed on a watch list. Security would be given names and pictures to keep an eye out for any of them who might decide to get a little too close to the studio and the cast.

Quinn wasn't quite so sure that it was worth all the bother, but hey, she wasn't paying the bills, Nick was, so she got on board. But right now, she just couldn't concentrate on that. Being entertaining to the masses while her own life was so complex just wouldn't work.

So, this Friday was the first that Quinn planned to skip. It was almost seven when they'd wrapped up for the day, and she had plans to enjoy a bottle of wine and a movie on the TV with her feet up.

She'd even pre-ordered a take-out meal from her favorite local Chinese that she picked up on the way through.

Getting home, Quinn kicked off her shoes, unbuttoned her shirt to mid-chest, and walked down the hall with her dinner. The bottle of wine clinked next to the other she had bought with it just in case she felt like another glass or two tomorrow. The weather reporters were expecting an unusually hot and humid weekend, and if that was the case, then Quinn planned to nix her usual wander around the flea markets and just sit out on the veranda and enjoy the sun.

Quinn opened the bag and lifted out several containers of food. Way too much for just herself, but there were so many things that she liked, so a little of everything would be just perfect. The rest she could put in the refrigerator for another day. Just as she was about to pull the lid from the first, a container of seasonal vegetables with fried rice, there was a knock at the door.

Glancing at the clock, it was just gone 8 p.m. Who would that be, she mused thoughtfully.

She didn't get visitors often unless one of her neighbors needed something. Maybe it was Cam or Michelle. She put everything down on the table and then almost jogged down the hall, pulling the door open with a grin for her favorite neighbor

"Hi," she said brightly before realizing that it wasn't Cam or Michelle, it was Natasha.

"Hello, I..." She paused, her eyes darting around as though already scoping out an escape route. But eventually, the eyes that had haunted Quinn's dreams these past few weeks settled on her and she said, "May I come in?"

Quinn felt her heart rate quicken and the delicate tumble of butterflies flapped wings in her tummy as she stepped aside and made room for Natasha to pass. "Sure, go on through." Quietly, she closed the door and took a moment to calm herself before she followed up the hall and into the lounge where Natasha would be waiting. The first thing she noticed, was that Natasha looked well, at least physically better than before anyway. The bags under her eyes were gone and she didn't look quite so thin.

When Natasha looked up and found Quinn in the room staring at her, she said, "I...," and then she stopped and took a breath.

Using the pause to her own advantage, Quinn jumped in. "How have you been?" She hoped the simple question would be enough to lead Natasha into speaking and then into being able to say what she wanted to say.

"Oh, I'm...well, I am well, yes. Thank you for asking. You?"

Quinn spent a lot of time putting words into characters' mouths, and she was pretty good at being able to use words to read between lines. And right now, she wasn't so sure Natasha was as convinced about how well she was as she was making out. But for now, Quinn let it slide, it made no difference to their conversation.

So, instead, she answered. "I am good, yeah, new job, so that's been keeping me busy."

"That's good," Natasha smiled quickly as she fidgeted a little on her feet.

Quinn shook herself. "Sorry, how rude of me, please, take a seat. Can I offer you a drink? I just opened a bottle of Merlot. Are you hungry? I have enough food for an army?"

"Oh, I didn't want to interrupt your evening," Natasha said, looking worried.

"You're not, I just got home and was about to eat Chinese? Do you like Chinese? Come with me," Quinn urged and summoned her with her fingers. "We can sit at the table and eat while you tell me how you've been."

At first, Natasha seemed hesitant, but then gradually, she raised herself up from the couch and did as she was asked, following behind as Quinn led the way to the kitchen.

"Take a seat, I'll get some plates." Quinn busied herself finding plates, spoons, and two wine glasses. She laid it all out on the table and placed the bag of food in the middle of them. Thankfully everything was still hot. "Dig in." She smiled, pouring two generous quantities of Merlot into each glass.

"Thank you," Natasha said, but she waited for Quinn to sit and begin to spoon helpings of rice and noodles onto her own plate before she reached out and took some for herself.

Through small mouthfuls of food and sips of wine, both women remained silent, content to just enjoy what was on offer. For Quinn, it was the chance to study Natasha a little more. She wasn't sure what Natasha was thinking, but the cogs looked as though they were turning over something.

"I wanted to thank you," she finally got out. Quinn said nothing, there was nothing to thank her for as far as she was concerned, but she placed her fork down and listened. "I wanted to...I've thought about you a lot these past weeks, and I realize that what I did, well...it wasn't very fair of me to lay that all on you and then disappear like that."

"I have to admit that I've been a little worried about you since."

"Yes, and that wasn't fair. I'm sorry." Her head bowed and the look of fear appeared on her face again. It hadn't been there right up till that point and Quinn wondered what it was that had caused it.

"Natasha, there's nothing to be sorry for, I am just glad that I could help and that you're okay," Quinn said gently.

Those green eyes looked up at her and stared intently as if trying to read something in Quinn's face. When she was satisfied, Natasha took a small sip of her wine, placed the glass back down on the table and adjusting it until it was perfectly lined up with the table mat. She stared at it, as she chewed her top lip and considered something.

"Is there something else you want to ask, or say?" Quinn probed.

Slowly, Natasha nodded. "Yes."

"Then just say it, you're safe here. Nothing you say is going to change that."

Natasha nodded again "Alright, well, the thing is...that night, that was the first time that...it was the first time, you...you're the first person..." She paused and closed her eyes, blinking away tears. Quinn sat quietly, but she reached tentatively for her hand. At first Natasha flinched, but then she relaxed and let Quinn put her hand on top of her own. "I've never told anyone before. I don't have anyone to tell really, and I just, I wondered maybe...it was nice." She smiled with an edge of embarrassment. "I just, maybe right now, what I need is a friend," she finished quickly and looked down at the table as she waited for her response.

"Okay," Quinn answered, picking up her fork and beginning to eat again. She smiled as Natasha looked up and gradually understood what Quinn had said.

"Really?" Natasha sat back and looked at her, she seemed honestly surprised that Quinn would agree to such a thing.

"Sure, why not?" Quinn chuckled, and for the first time, Natasha smiled.

"I don't know," she said thoughtfully, and then she did something that Quinn would never forget, she laughed. And it was the most beautiful and infectious sound that Quinn had ever heard. But just as suddenly, she stopped. "I'm sorry."

Quinn's eyes narrowed. "Why are you apologising?"

"Because-," Her eyes were back to darting around the room. "I forgot myself, I'm sorry. I should have asked first."

"Asked?" Quinn questioned, "If you could laugh?" She wasn't sure she had actually heard her correctly. Had she really just apologised because she didn't have permission to laugh?

Natasha looked away from Quinn, seemingly filled with shame, and something else: fear. "I should..."

"I-, sorry what?" Quinn was just astonished. "Who do you need to ask for permission to laugh? Not in my house." It was then that Quinn realised she was still holding her hand. "Listen to me, I don't know what is going on for you at home, you can tell me or not tell me, but when you're here, you do not need permission to do that. Or anything, alright?"

She spoke as gently as she could, anger was already building for this monster who made Natasha's life so miserable. The control and power that they had over her was just too unbearable to think about.

"I am sorry, I shouldn't have said anything. This was a stupid idea; I shouldn't have come," Natasha said, jumping to her feet, readying to leave. "Thank you for dinner."

"Wait, please. Don't run off again," Quinn said quietly. "Please, I'm sorry, I didn't mean to tell you what you should do."

Natasha stood in the doorway and stopped. When she turned around and looked at Quinn, it was with terrified eyes. Her features pinched and hard as though she was considering what she wanted to say next

"I just - I just wanted somewhere I could feel safe and not have to talk about it, or think about it, but I see now that's not possible."

"It is possible, and if that's what you need, then that's okay," Quinn assured. "My home is safe, and it's yours when you need it. I won't ask questions, and when you're ready to talk, then I can listen. But I need you to understand something." Quinn stood up and walked slowly towards her. "My door is open, anytime. Whatever is going on for you, if you feel you need to get out, you come here." She had no idea why it was that she felt so compelled to want to help her, but she did.

"I'm not sure it's that simple but thank you, Quinn."

It was getting late, almost 10.30 p.m. "Look, why don't we take our drinks through to the lounge, and if you want to talk, I'm all ears."

"Alright," Natasha agreed. "Then I'll tell you my story."

Quinn picked up the glasses and the half-empty bottle and followed her into the lounge.

Chapter Six

Natasha sat on the edge of her seat, sipping her wine while Quinn got a small fire going. Hot days in the summer often led to chilly evenings as the cloud cover dispersed and all the heat of the day rose up and away.

"I was just 17 when I met my husband," she said with a shaky voice. "He was 25 and exciting, debonair and charming. He was at the start of his career, but already climbing the ladder, and drove a sports car." She smiled as Quinn took a seat and listened. "He took me to places that my teenage heart could only dream about. Restaurants and parties that the rich and famous frequented, and I was completely besotted with him." She turned away and glanced out of the window into the darkness.

"In all that time, he never laid a finger on me," she explained, turning back to face Quinn. "I went off to college, and then onto medical school. I was still in the state, so we continued to see one another at weekends mainly. He continued to impress in his career and in time, he got to the top. Respected and powerful." She said all of this with no emotion at all. It was as though she were reading from a book about someone else's life. "When I finally finished my schooling, I became a doctor." She smiled again then, a real smile. Proud of herself, as she should be. "I worked long hours and one night, I was finishing up a double shift, when a small child was brought in with a head wound. So, diligently, I stayed and dealt with him before heading home. I was 45 minutes later than he expected, and he punched me in the face."

Quinn sat in silence, mainly because she had no fucking clue what to say. What did you say to that? It was shocking but at the same time, she kind of expected it. She said nothing and continued to listen.

"The following morning, he was apologetic and couldn't do enough for me, and I guess I was in shock, this was the man I had been involved with for almost 10 years. The man I was in love with and planned to have a family with, a man who had never once laid a finger on me out of anger. I forgave him after he promised it would never happen again and it didn't. For several more years, we were happy and making plans, we wanted to have children, but as it turned out we can't. He blamed me of course, but in actuality, it was him that was virtually sterile. He became angry and withdrawn, as though it were a personal affront to his masculinity. I tried to tell him it was okay, that it didn't matter.

We could adopt, but all that did was make him angrier and before I knew what was happening, he was beating me." She choked up, her throat refusing to speak as the tears burst forth and she sobbed. Without thinking, Quinn moved to sit beside her and pulled her in close.

"It's okay, you're safe," she whispered over and over until the sobs began to ease, and Natasha took a shuddering breath to calm herself.

"I had a broken rib and a fractured wrist. I couldn't even dress myself without his help. He didn't apologise this time. I had to take time off from work and none of that was as terrifying to me as when he held my wrist, the broken one, and looked me dead in the eye and said, "Tell anyone and I will kill you." She wiped her face on her sleeve, but Quinn reached for some tissues and passed them to her. "Thank you." She blew her nose. "I'd been with him for 13 years at that point, and I'd never seen him like that, I never knew it was in him to be like that, but I believed him. I knew that he would kill me."

Quinn's face said all it needed to. She wanted to ask his name, track him down and do to him what he did to her, make him ask for permission to beg for his life. And Natasha could see it all play out on her features in those few moments.

"Don't - please don't, just don't," she said quickly and backed away. "Don't let him do that to you, don't become him because you're angry on my behalf."

"Sorry, I just - he has no right to do this to you."

"Thank you for caring." She looked at the time and smiled sadly. "I have to go, he's out tonight for business, and if I'm not at home when he returns then I..." she didn't need to continue to explain, Quinn got it.

"Stay," she said without thinking. "Don't go back, just stay here."

"You're very sweet, but I have to go."

"Why?"

"Because I'm not ready to do anything else, and because I owe him everything," she said honestly, for once keeping her eyes on Quinn and not looking to the floor.

"My door is open, anytime. Anytime." She reasserted. "I don't care what time it is, if you need me, or some space...I'm here."

"Thank you, Quinn," She smiled, "Maybe we can do this again next week." For a moment she lingered, their eyes held each other's gaze until eventually, Natasha looked away. Then she turned and walked away.

Chapter Seven

It was well known that Nick Miles was a player. As Quinn waited outside of his office on Monday morning, it was pretty obvious that the blonde assistant had been assisting in more than just appointments and paperwork as she left the room adjusting her dress. Quinn raised an eyebrow but said nothing, she didn't care. It was his business, and his wife's. No doubt it would be doing the rounds in office gossip in the next thirty minutes. It was the typical boys will be boys bullshit that happened in all corners of Hollywood. Less so since the whole *Me Too* campaign took off, but that didn't seem to faze Nick Miles, or the bevy of beautiful women who arrived at all hours. There were several rumours that many of them were hookers, safer to pay for it than risk a lawsuit from a young actress or intern. It was pathetic really how the male ego needed to be continuously massaged, but whatever. So long as nobody was hurt or coerced, Quinn could look past it.

When he walked out of his office, still tucking his shirt into his smart chinos, Quinn almost laughed out loud. Could he be anymore blatant? "Hey Nick, can I get a word?" she asked, sidling up beside him and falling into step.

"Sure, Quinn, what's up?" he asked, giving her his undivided attention. She could see why the women lined up for him. He was a good-looking guy, still in shape. His chiselled jawline and piercing blue eyes were a natural draw. And he was charming to a fault, always a ready smile for a pretty face. Quinn considered that must be the case for her too as he grinned at her.

"So, I wanted to have a chat about these live tweet sessions every week and the after-work drinks."

"Uh huh, go on," he said, touching her elbow and encouraging Quinn to keep walking with him.

"Yeah, well to be honest, I am not too comfortable with them, I'm - well I am kind of a private person, and I just don't feel comfortable with all of these people having access to me." She didn't mention Natasha, and how much she wanted to spend time getting to know this new woman in her life.

He stopped walking and gave her his full attention as he interrupted her. "I get that Quinn, I really do, but ya know the networks love this kind of thing and keeping the fans on board by chatting to them this way tends to help keep the ratings up. We all know they are only really interested in Riley and Jane, but that's show business," he said, before throwing a smile at her that she supposed was meant to leave her weak at the knees and agreeing with anything he said. He then started walking again.

Unfortunately for him that wasn't going to work. She wasn't sure just how much this was a networks thing either, it hadn't happened on any other show she had worked on, and she didn't see it happening much on other shows as yet either. Although she could concede that there were a few actors and crew doing it elsewhere but that was more of a personal choice than a studio instruction.

She tossed a disarming smile back. "I understand. The thing is, my weekends are...well, I've got things to do at the weekends, and I can't give up every Friday and Saturday evening like this."

"Oh." He stopped in his tracks and regarded Quinn for a moment. Frowning at her as though he didn't really understand what the big deal was. "But we're all one big family here Quinn and hanging out together is something I really like my staff to do. It bonds us all." There was the smile again.

"Right," she dragged the word out as she tried to comprehend why this guy had such a hard time letting this go. What was the big deal? She'd never been expected to socialise before, there had been events and invitations, but not this level of expectation to attend regular events. "So, what I am thinking is maybe I go to one a month? I've got a lot of projects on at the moment, and some personal things going on that I want to give my time to." She was a little annoyed that she needed to justify this stuff, but whatever, if that was what had to happen then so be it. "And I'll take part in the tweets when I am free to do so."

He studied her. Deciding whether he was going to push this or back off. In the end, he went with the latter. "That's the spirit! Okay, once a month Quinn, but I'll hold you to it." He grinned behind an icy stare as he walked away to a beckoning cast member waving a script at him.

~***~

The following Friday Quinn had spent most of the day hoping that tonight Natasha would arrive as planned. She left the office at five and headed straight to the store to stock up on ingredients for dinner, picking up a decent bottle of wine to accompany it and some flowers to brighten up the room.

Getting home, she parked the car and carried it all inside, dumping the bags down on to the kitchen counters. As she put it all away in the cupboards and the refrigerator, she wondered what the evening would bring. Her mind couldn't help but think about Natasha and whether her week had been happy, or safe. The sight of the bruise that first time they had talked still haunted Quinn. She just couldn't understand what kind of man, would do something so heinous, to someone they supposedly loved. It didn't make any sense at all.

When the knock on the door came, just before 7 p.m., Quinn found herself smoothing out her clothes and checking herself in the mirror before she headed down the hallway and swung the door open with a wide grin on her face. Her short dark hair was tidy, though it needed a trim. Her dark eyes looked tired, but she didn't care. She was happy to see Natasha again.

"Hey," she said stepping aside for Natasha to come in.

Natasha smiled a tight smile that didn't reach her eyes and continued down the hall to the lounge. As she passed, Quinn felt her heart sink as she watched the slight limp in her stride. She took a deep breath, closed the door, and followed her. Determined not to try and be her fixer. The last thing Quinn needed was a human project. But at the same time, wasn't that already the case the moment she stepped outside, and offered coffee and a warm place to sit?

"You look nice," Quinn complimented. The dark slacks fitting perfectly and resting on her hips complemented the cream-colored woolen jumper that fit equally well, showing off her curves. "Good week?" she asked quickly to avoid the blush from gawping just a little longer than was necessarily acceptable.

As she turned to speak, Quinn noticed Natasha was fidgeting with her fingers and avoiding eye contact.

"You don't have to answer," Quinn said. Desperately wanting to ask why she was limping and what had caused it, and yet, dreading the answer that might come.

"No, sorry, I just...I was considering whether it was a good week," Natasha answered, smiling weakly as she finally looked up from the floor. "Yes, it's been...my week was better," she finally concluded a little cryptically, but Quinn didn't push further.

"Good, that's good." Quinn pointed to the couch. "Take a seat, are you hungry? I have some chicken and vegetables cooking. I thought maybe we could eat while we talked? I mean...if you want to talk, no pressure."

"That would be lovely." She took a seat, gingerly bending to sit. It was obvious to Quinn that she was trying not to show how much pain she was in. A feeling of anger rose up in her as it went through her head what she would do to this guy if she ever found out who he was and got her hands on him. She wasn't a violent person at all, but every time she looked at Natasha, an innate wanting to protect her rose to the surface. She needed to get a grip on that. Offering solace and safety was the aim, not developing a crush that could never go anywhere.

"I'll be right back," Quinn said, snapping out of it. "Wine?"

"Thank you, yes," Natasha replied, fiddling nervously with the rings on her left hand.

When Quinn returned with two glasses, she noticed Natasha was still twisting the jewelry, and she wondered if she ever longed to take them off, or had they become something of a comfort to her now? "Here," she smiled, holding the glass for Natasha to take. When she did, their fingers brushed against each other, and Quinn was very aware of the blush that hit her cheeks at the feeling of something electric passing between them. Had Natasha felt it too? If she did, she did a good job of hiding it as she sipped from the glass.

Quinn took a seat and silently they sipped and stole glances at one another until eventually, Quinn said, "Dinner shouldn't be long."

It was a strange situation to be in. She barely knew this woman and yet, there was an air of comfortability between them already. Usually, she would feel nervous around someone new for a while, but with Natasha, it had just seemed so easy. And clearly, Natasha must have felt the same because why would she keep coming back otherwise?

Sitting down together at the small table in the kitchen, Quinn dished up some chicken and vegetables for them both. She was famished, it had been a long day and she'd barely had time for lunch, so she dug straight in. After a couple of mouthfuls, however, she realized that Natasha wasn't quite so enthusiastic. Quinn watched as she chewed slowly and pushed the food around her plate with her fork.

"Everything okay?" Quinn asked, pointing to the plate in front of Natasha with her knife.

Natasha smiled nervously before saying. "Yes. Sorry it's lovely I-, I realized that I'm not that hungry," she said as she placed her fork down on the plate gently and then placed her hands in her lap, bowing her head silently.

"Oh, of course." Quinn's own appetite dropped away as she studied Natasha. She placed her own cutlery down and elbows on the table, she steepled her fingers. "I just thought dinner would be a nice thing to do."

"No. It's a lovely thought and it really is delicious." She stopped talking and widened her eyes trying to curb the tears that had suddenly appeared there. "Sorry," she reiterated. Blinking hard.

"Natasha?"

Quinn moved quickly, too quickly. The scraping sound of the chair legs against the tiled floor made Natasha cry out, and all but jump out of her skin as she raised her arms around her head, curling into a tight ball in an effort to protect herself from the impending violence she expected.

The sight almost broke Quinn, and she stopped her movements, cursing herself for being so unthinking. Deftly, she reached out a hand and gently, very gently, touched Natasha's arm. The slight flinch was obvious, but she didn't pull away, and Quinn let her fingertips rest there. "It's okay," she said quietly. "I am going to move closer to you, okay?" she continued, having learned a very quick lesson. She waited for permission, then when it came, she stood up, and moved in front of her, kneeling at once to put them at eye level. "Do you want to talk about anything?" she asked quietly, barely a whisper.

There was a part of Quinn that prayed Natasha said no. Because she wasn't sure if she could bear to hear any more details of the abuse this woman was suffering. And yet, she wanted to know everything, so she could be of more help.

But as they sat like that, it became clear that tonight, Natasha just wanted company. The need to talk wasn't there. Not tonight. And for that, Quinn felt selfish, and grateful all at once.

Chapter Eight

The following Friday it was Natasha who brought dinner. A huge pizza from Donatello's. She also waved a bottle of wine as she smiled thinly at Quinn on the doorstep and waited to be invited in.

They ate in relative silence after sharing pleasantries about how they were, which Quinn didn't mind too much, her week had been exhausting with constant re-writes after one of the actors came down with a nasty bug that took them out of filming for three days.

But eventually, Quinn relaxed and after a glass of wine, she found her voice again.

"Did you always live in LA?" she asked, offering a top-up.

Natasha nodded. "Thank you." She wiped her mouth with a serviette, "No, my family moved around a lot until my teens, and then we settled here."

"Oh, sounds interesting."

"Not really." Natasha chuckled and for the first time, Quinn saw her visibly relax. "My parents were old hippies, we moved around a lot selling pictures they'd painted on our travels. But when I reached my teens, they suddenly got serious about the whole parenting thing, and we settled in LA. You?"

"I was actually born in Germany, on a US airbase where my father was stationed, but then we came home to Boston when I was two, and when I was eight, we moved to Virginia."

"So, you've moved around a lot too?" Natasha stated, understanding a potentially shared experience with their upbringings.

"Yeah, I came here for work once I'd finished college," she explained before asking her next question. "Do you see your parents often?"

Natasha's eyes closed as she held back her emotion. "No. my dad... had a heart attack when I was 15. He's the reason that I decided to become a doctor." She smiled sadly. "My mom passed away not long after I was married. I don't really have any other family."

"Your husband became everything?"

"I suppose so, yes," she acknowledged. "There was a small insurance payout when my dad died, that paid for my initial college, but then I was in med school and my husband, he picked up the bills. Made sure that I had somewhere to live, with him obviously. Now, when I look back, I can see that it meant I was totally beholden to him. But I owe him everything because without him, I don't know what would have happened to me."

"I think you'd have been just fine." Quinn smiled. "You're a capable, intelligent woman."

"Who had no money, no support system and a desperate need to be wanted by the charming man she'd fallen in love with," Natasha replied, "He wasn't always the way he is now."

Quinn nodded, accepting her need to defend and excuse him. Even if she herself still wanted to track him down and have him arrested, it wasn't her life and she needed to remember that.

The wine was almost finished, and it was nearing midnight. Knowing that Natasha would need to leave soon, Quinn had to finally tell her what she hadn't wanted to say. She'd spent all week trying to get out of it, but Nick was insistent, and she couldn't really argue.

"So, next week...I have a work thing I can't get out of."

Initially, Natasha tensed, but then she relaxed and nodded. "Of course. Don't worry about me, I'll be fine."

"Will you? I worry...If I could get out of it I would."

"Quinn, it's fine. Honestly. I'll be alright, can we meet the following week?"

"Definitely, I mean, you're welcome to come here at any time."

"Thank you, but Fridays work well for me. He stays out on Fridays, I've no idea where he goes," she admitted sadly.

"Do you care?"

For a moment she considered it. And then she nodded sadly. "I do, yes."

"Why?" Quinn just couldn't get her head around why this woman would continue to put herself through this life when she could just walk away.

"I know that you don't understand." She smiled, reading Quinn like a book. "I owe him everything, and I'll always be grateful for the life he has given me, the opportunities...and I know that logically it doesn't make sense, but it's where I am right now. And things are okay, he's busy with his career, and I have mine and we don't see each other very often, that makes it more bearable."

"Until..." Quinn left it unsaid but they both understood what she meant.

"I take each day as it comes, and deal with each mood as it arrives." Natasha checked her watch. "I need to get going."

Chapter Nine

The room was full and buzzing with chatter. Cast and crew who were tweeting sat leisurely about on chairs or perched on the edge of tables. It was bright, fluorescent tube lights lit the space brighter than daylight, and a few people even wore sunglasses as they added messages to their social media accounts.

For Quinn, it felt a little odd to be talking about an episode they had written and filmed months ago. They were nearing the end of the season and yet, it was only the fifth episode that had aired. She added a couple of tweets saying how much fun they were having, replied to a few viewers who had responded, and then she did the ultimate and posted a behind-the-scenes image of Riley and Jane, the show's two big stars. It worried her just how quickly the fans latched on. Her follower's list went from under 100 to over 2000 in the last few weeks. With the photo being shared instantly, she could already see her numbers going up again. Were people really so obsessed with celebrities? It worried her.

Placing her phone down on the table, she got up and grabbed a cup of coffee from the machine, and found her mind wandering to Natasha. She felt bad about not being able to meet her and hoped to God it didn't mean she would have to suffer another evening with her husband. She'd found her mind wandering like that a lot lately, always reminding herself that she couldn't fall for her. Natasha was married, regardless of how much of an asshole he was. But it was difficult to not let herself think that way.

With the tweeting hour over, Quinn followed the crowd onto the club. She'd been before and wasn't that enamored with it, it was too pretentious for her taste. A place that encouraged celebrities to visit, which meant a lot of people hanging around outside.

Quinn had barely gotten through the door when she heard Nick shout across the room. "Hey Quinn, come over here and get a drink."

She changed direction, heading over to where he was standing with Riley Tyler and Jane Hanson at the bar. They played best friends that had known each other since childhood and both became New York Police detectives, they were partners on and off-screen, but the fans were unaware of that little titbit of gossip.

"Hey, Riley, Jane," Quinn said, acknowledging the two beautiful women in front of her being charmed by Nick into drinking shots of God knows what. He slid one along the bar towards Quinn, so she grabbed it and sniffed.

"It's tequila." Nick laughed, knocking back another shot of his own. Quinn followed suit, wondering where the lime and salt were. She guessed that he wasn't that bothered as he called out another round.

"Epic show tonight," Riley said, her voice sultry like melted chocolate as she complimented Quinn. She'd been the head writer on that particular episode, so she was definitely feeling a little proud about it. It was an epic show. However, this was Hollywood, and compliments flowed both ways, at all times.

"Thanks, but I think we all know you two are the reason it's such a hit." The truth was, they were lucky to have got them both for this show. They were both in demand, but the chance to work with Nick had won them over. Quinn couldn't deny that he was an excellent producer and director.

Riley could be a little temperamental at times, she liked getting things done her own way and mostly that was accepted by everyone else. Jane on the other hand was much quieter, preferring to take a back seat and let Riley have all the attention she wanted. They were both likable, and Quinn had a lot of time for them and would have happily spent the rest of the evening talking had it not been for Nick's insistence on getting drunk. At 11 p.m., Quinn made her excuses and left.

Chapter Ten

Arriving back to work on Monday, Quinn was immediately aware of a buzz going around the place. Everybody was excited and jumping around as she wandered towards the writers' room. It was only when she arrived at her desk and found a huge bouquet of flowers and a bottle of very expensive champagne waiting that someone explained the show had been nominated for the TVSAA awards. The Television Screen Actors Awards was one of the biggest awards ceremonies after the Oscars, Golden Globes, and the Baftas.

Everyone was summoned to the main stage to be thanked and congratulated by Nick and the network suits who had shown up to bask in the glory. They were being nominated for Outstanding Performance by an Ensemble Cast, and Outstanding Performance by a Female Actor.

"I just want to say what an awesome achievement this is. We have an amazing group of actors and to have one of them honored this way is a testament to this show. I got on board when I was approached because I could see the potential in a show like this. We hired the best. From Make-up and Costume, everyone behind the scenes working their asses off, and of course, the awesome writing team who constantly pushes the boundaries with edgy, fun scripts that bring out the best in all of our players. I thank you all, and of course, I know that some of you will be invited along to the show, but hell, we're all going to the afterparty, right?"

There was a huge cheer as everybody clapped and congratulated each other again. For a moment, Quinn felt filled with pride. This was after all the cherry on top of any television cake. But by the time the clapping had died down, she was already heading back to her desk.

By the time Friday came along, Quinn had forgotten all about it. Her mind was firmly on the fact that Natasha would be arriving that evening, and she was both excited and apprehensive about it. Excited because she missed her, it was that simple. She'd been gradually accepting that she was falling in love, even if it would be unrequited, she couldn't stop it.

But she was more apprehensive, what kind of week had she had? What state would she be in? Did she miss her too?

When the doorbell rang, she all but ran to answer it, but the smile she had on her face soon faltered when her gaze landed on the bruised face in front of her. A cut lip that was slowly healing. Remnants of a black eye, now just a sallow yellow. There was a band-aid across her left eyebrow where another small cut was healing. As Quinn looked lower, she saw the rest. A bandaged hand and wrist.

No words were spoken as she stepped aside and guided Natasha inside. When they got to the lounge and Natasha turned towards her, Quinn did the only thing she could think of and pulled her close. Natasha winced, and Quinn let go.

"Let me see," Quinn asked gently.

Natasha shook her head, her gaze on the floor.

"Natasha, I need to see." Quinn bent at the knee and ducked her head to look at Natasha's face, but she looked away again until Quinn lifted her chin with a soft finger. "Don't do that...you've nothing to be ashamed about, can I please see?"

"It doesn't - it won't make any difference," she said through silent tears.

"It makes a difference to me." Quinn smiled sadly. She couldn't understand what must have happened, Natasha said he never hit her face. Not since that first time years ago. "Why? Why did he do this?"

"I don't know, I mean I - he came home drunk..." That part didn't surprise Quinn at all, he seemed to always be drunk when these things happened. "He wanted to have sex, and I explained that it wasn't the right time of the month...and..." Her tears began to fall again. "He said I was too old to be having a period, that I should be dried up by now and then he -" Quinn could barely listen. It was just so abhorrent. "He hit me."

Quinn took her good hand and led her to the couch to sit down before she fell under the weight of everything that was going on. She fell into Quinn's arms and quietly sobbed, her face pressed to Quinn's shoulder.

"It's okay, it's going to be okay," Quinn whispered against her hair, but the truth was, she didn't know if it would be.

They sat together quietly while Natasha got it all out. Natasha leaned against her, wrapped safely in the arm that held her. She let her head rest against Quinn's shoulder, while her injured hand rested against Quinn's stomach. It felt peaceful, and Quinn felt her relax against her.

Quinn sat quietly, enjoying the closeness while her thoughts were lost in how little information she had. She knew Natasha well, they'd talked about anything and everything, but things like a phone number, an address? She knew none of that, she didn't even know Natasha's last name, or whether Natasha was her real name. it had all been unimportant at the beginning when Quinn's only concern was making sure that she had a safe place to be. But she thought back to the time when she hadn't seen Natasha for months, and how she had worried then without even really knowing each other, but now, things were different.

The sobbing had turned to whimpers, that in turn changed to sniffs. Quinn instinctively kissed her hair. She hadn't meant to, it was totally inappropriate, and yet, the most natural thing in the world. When Quinn opened her eyes, she realized that she was crying, and when she looked down, she found those haunted green eyes staring up at her. It was mesmerizing, she couldn't look away, and didn't want to. Neither it seemed, did Natasha. Her eyes searched Quinn's face, but they always came back to her eyes and the silent conversation between them. Reaching up, Natasha wiped away the tears from Quinn's cheek with the tip of her finger.

And then it happened. Eyes moved to mouths and back again, asking and answering the question all at once. The kiss was unexpected and yet, it wasn't. Quinn had been daydreaming about it for weeks, and now, as she felt the touch of lips against her own, she panicked.

Quinn's eyes flew open as she realized that this was really happening. "I am so sorry." She blushed as the sudden realization of how inappropriate it was, that she was maybe taking advantage when Natasha was clearly not in an emotional state to understand, and not to mention, married.

Natasha stared at her. "Why?"

"Because I -" she began, but Natasha held a hand up and stopped her from speaking.

"I want you to," she concluded, pressing her lips against Quinn's once more. "I want you," she whispered against her lips.

At that moment, Quinn could see her, all of her, the woman she was behind the fear and the unpredictable life she lived.

But all too quickly, both of them were reminded, as Natasha winced at Quinn's touch.

"You're in pain," Quinn stated, not asked. It was obvious and she stopped all movement in an instant.

"Yes, but..."

"No." Quinn's fingertip rested against her lip. Gently moving until she found the small cut that looked angry and sore still but thankfully hadn't split again with the movement of their kissing. "I'll be right back," she said, smiling as she slid out from under Natasha and got up.

When she returned, she carried a small box and a glass of water. Dropping to her knees in front of Natasha, she passed the glass and some pills. "Here, take these."

"Thank you." Natasha smiled, doing as she was told. Quinn took the glass from her and placed it down on the table. "I feel better already." She grinned.

"Uh-huh, kissing will do that. Something about dopamine?"

Natasha laughed. And it was the most beautiful sight Quinn had ever seen.

"So," Quinn began, "will you show me now?"

She expected a refusal, instead, there was a small nod of assent. "Not here," Natasha whispered, standing, and taking Quinn's hand. Quinn followed as Natasha led her to the stairs, and up.

When they reached the top, she waited for Quinn to show her which room and then continued to lead along the corridor as directed and into the room that Quinn called her own. Once inside, Quinn closed the door and waited. Slowly, Natasha began to fiddle with the top button, her bandaged hand making the job more difficult until Quinn stepped forward and took her hands in her own. She moved them aside and one by one, she undid the small buttons. Natasha's arms dropped to her side and she watched Quinn's face as her fingers deftly went about their task. She watched her eyes, her mouth. She smiled when Quinn did, Quinn's eyes now fixed with hers as the last button gave in and she released it.

Quinn's eyes closed, just for a moment, as she prepared herself. And then she opened them and gazed down, gently sweeping the blouse aside with the back of her hand. She hadn't known what to expect, bruising yes, but the sight of a clearly outlined boot print hadn't been on her radar. She glanced up to see Natasha's smile change, her lips thinning out, her face becoming passive as she waited for Quinn to finish her inspection.

Her breath shuddered as she moved the blouse completely off Natasha's shoulder, letting it fall from her grasp. She watched as the material fluttered down and slipped from Natasha's arms to the floor, and then noticed the finger marks. Small black circles that had gripped her skin. Around her neck, her biceps. Natasha was now crying soundlessly as she allowed Quinn to explore her darkest moments. Silently, Quinn moved around behind her. Quinn gasped, and Natasha stiffened at the sound. Bruising covered her back. A whole rainbow of color. Small scars, healed over time scattered their way across her flesh. It was overwhelming and for a moment, Quinn was unsure what to do. But then nature took over, and Quinn let her fingertips trace the scar on her shoulder, before she knew it, her lips were kissing the marks. Not for any other reason than to try and desperately make it better. Like her mother had done when she was a child and had hurt herself.

She felt Natasha sigh and melt against her as she took every painful moment in this woman's life and tried to kiss the pain away. When Natasha turned in her arms, their mouths met again, and Quinn put all she had into that one kiss. Trying to heal and soothe and convey all she could before the moment came to an end.

"I want to show you, but -" Quinn whispered as the kiss became a need to go further. Her heart beat fast in her chest, her breath coming quickly as her chest heaved.

"Show me what?" Natasha breathed against her mouth, nibbling Quinn's lower lip until Quinn kissed her once more.

When they pulled apart again, Quinn stammered, "How you should be - how I can..."

"Then show me," Natasha whimpered, leading Quinn to the edge of the bed, she climbed on and moved backward, pulling Quinn with her. "Even if it's just for tonight, will you...show me?"

Hovering above her, Quinn dipped her head, her eyes closing as she pressed her lips to the awful boot-shaped bruise. She didn't want to see it, she just wanted it gone. To kiss it away and make Natasha feel better. It was absurd, of course, but it didn't stop her from trying.

Over and over, she kissed the area. Her eyes opened when she realized that Natasha was trying, and failing, to unbutton her own jeans. Smiling, Quinn lifted up, moving her injured hand away gently, they gazed at one another while Quinn finished the job. Sliding down the zipper and then with both hands, she shrugged them loose and pulled until Natasha could kick them off with her feet.

"Stunning," Quinn finally said almost in a whisper. "You are so beautiful."

"I am broken." Natasha smiled sadly, sitting up and reaching out to cup Quinn's face. "Very broken."

"No, no you... you're perfect. Just...perfect," Quinn gushed, taking her hand, and moving back onto the bed, letting Natasha know to follow.

Which she did, climbing on top of Quinn, straddling her thighs. She grabbed at the hem of Quinn's t-shirt and lifted it up and off over her head. Minute by minute, clothes were removed, kisses shared until both were naked but for the scars and bruises that covered her. Marks that Quinn kissed and touched with reverence.

"Show me how it should be," she whispered against Quinn's lips.

Deftly, slowly and with every consideration, Quinn touched her. Kissing away every painful memory, if only for a moment. Replacing each image with something else. Something filled with love, and affection. Something to hold on to.

Chapter Eleven

Quinn Harper could officially declare that she was blissfully happy. She wandered around the studio with a stupid grin on her face, wishing away the hours until Friday would roll around again and Natasha might be back in her arms.

She'd tried talking herself down from the euphoria, but it was useless, she was falling, and falling fast, and there was nothing that she could do about it. Then there was the added excitement of the awards. The place was buzzing with energy now. It had really lifted the team. By the end of the week, Quinn had officially received her invitation to attend the event and the after-show party. A few weeks ago, she wouldn't have been that bothered, but now, with this new spring in her step, she was enjoying the moment too.

Arranging to finish early on Friday, Quinn rushed home. She cleaned the house from top to bottom. Placed some fresh-cut flowers into a large vase that took center stage on the sideboard in the lounge. They were beautiful, and she hoped they would brighten the room. If she couldn't send flowers to Natasha, she would at least have them here so that she could enjoy them.

She had a lasagne cooking in the oven, and a huge salad to accompany it in the refrigerator. And she had remembered to shower and change into something clean. When the knock on the door came, she was buzzing as she all but ran down the hallway to answer it.

"Hi," she said just in time before Natasha stepped forward and smiled into a kiss. Her arms wrapped naturally around Quinn's neck. Quinn pulled back and studied her, she seemed different, more hopeful maybe? Happiness? Whatever it was, it was good for her, and Quinn was determined to bring out more of it if she could.

"I missed you," Natasha admitted, staring into Quinn's dark eyes.

"Makes two of us then," Quinn responded, leading her inside properly and into the living room, where she spun her around, pulled her close, and kissed her so hard that she thought her own knees would weaken.

When they pulled apart, their foreheads rested against one another as each caught their breath. "I got you flowers," Quinn said, her head turning slightly towards the huge bouquet. "I cooked too," she said, "in case you were wondering what that amazing smell is." She laughed and watched as Natasha followed suit. She loved doing that, being able to bring some joy to this woman, even if it wasn't for long, it was long enough.

"They're beautiful, thank you." Natasha pulled away to go over and look at them properly. Leaning in, she sniffed the nearest flower and smiled. "I love them."

Pleased with herself, Quinn grinned. "So, hungry?"

"Yes, let's eat."

~***~

With their meal finished, glasses filled with a rather nice red wine that Quinn had picked up earlier in the week, they lay together on the couch. Quinn curled her frame around Natasha, arms wrapping, legs tangling, breathing each other in. It was intimate and cozy, the gentle waft of Natasha's perfume, it was perfect. And she could honestly say that if she died right there and now, she would be happy. But that didn't stop the cogs of her mind from turning. Or her fingertips from searching.

"I am okay, it was a good week this week," Natasha said quietly as though she were able to read Quinn's mind. She twisted around to face Quinn, kissing her tenderly. "I'm okay."

Quinn nodded, accepting the answer. "I just wish you'd leave..."

Natasha frowned. "I know you do." She placed a finger to Quinn's mouth and let it smooth over the lip. "I - I'm not ready."

"I could..."

"I know you think you can deal with all of this, that you can just love me and make everything better." She was right, that was exactly what Quinn thought. "But it isn't that simple Quinn."

"It could be," Quinn continued, kissing her fingers. Did she not see how easy it could be?

"Do you think I don't want to believe that?" she said sadly. "I do, I want so much to believe that I could just walk away, and everything would be happy and fun like it is when I am with you. It's not that simple, sweetheart."

"We could try," Quinn argued, placing a kiss against her forehead.

"Quinn, please." Her eyes were misted over, tears threatening to spill over. "Maybe one day I will be where you are, but right now...."

"You're not ready, yes I get it," Quinn said, frustrated and a little annoyed, her ego getting the better of her. She got it; she just didn't understand it. Because for her, it was simple. From that first moment on the beach, to right now, lying together on this couch, it was all so simple.

"Don't be angry with me, I couldn't bear it," Natasha implored; big eyes stared at Quinn, and she softened, she would never be the cause of fear in this woman, physical or otherwise.

"Never, I could never be angry with you. I just...I want you to be happy."

A small chiming sound came from her phone on the coffee table. Natasha smiled sadly. "Time to go."

Chapter Twelve

Quinn had Monday afternoon off. For some crazy reason, the Television Screen Actors Awards (TVSAA) awards were taking place that night. She couldn't understand why a weekend day hadn't been the first choice, but who was she to complain? This afternoon off to get ready, and tomorrow morning off to recuperate from what were expected to be celebration drinks.

Unlike many women in Hollywood, she wouldn't be spending the afternoon at the hairdressers or undergoing a transformation with a stylist. She would go through her wardrobe, find something suitable, get dressed, and go. So, right now, she had her running gear on and was striding down the beach trying to set a new personal best.

She waved at her neighbor, Cam, as she passed, and considered whether she would see her and her wife, Michelle, aka actress Shelly Hamlin, at the awards later. But stopping to ask would mean interrupting her run, and she'd already been slacking lately. She pushed on, pumping her legs until she felt that burn of lactic acid filling her muscles. Sweat dripped down her spine under the close-fitting running vest, and though it was still quite chilly this early in the year, on her return journey, she thought about veering off and running straight into the ocean to cool off. But those thoughts were interrupted when she looked up and noticed the familiar figure sitting on the beach, in her spot. Putting a spurt on, Quinn closed the distance and flopped down on to the sand next to her, panting and gasping for breath as she lay there on her back.

"Hey," Quinn said when her breathing finally evened out enough to allow for words to escape and make sense.

"Hello." Natasha smiled, looking down at her and captivating Quinn in an instant. "You look hot."

"Ah yes. Sorry, I get sweaty when I push it," she explained like an idiot stating the obvious.

"That wasn't what I meant," Natasha whispered, leaning closer as Quinn pushed herself upright. "I mean...you look hot."

"Oh, sexy hot, not sweaty hot, okay. Well, whatever floats your boat I guess." Quinn laughed. "So, are you coming in?"

She nodded and allowed Quinn to pull her to her feet.

Quinn rushed upstairs to shower quickly and change. By the time she came back down again, Natasha had rustled up a sandwich. Coffee was brewing, and she stood in the kitchen looking like she belonged there. One day, Quinn thought to herself, one day.

"What's this?"

"I made you some lunch." Natasha smiled, moving to join her at the table. She pushed the plate in front of Quinn. "You're going to need some energy." She winked.

"Oh?" Standing, Quinn moved closer to her and pushed their bodies together, trapping Natasha between herself and the table. A move that weeks ago would have caused her to flinch, a look of fear would smother her features and Quinn would hate herself for causing it, but not now. There was a trust between them now, Natasha knew one thing, and that was that Quinn would never hurt her. She was relaxed as she could be when Quinn lifted her onto the table. Their mouths devoured one another, as Quinn's fingertips moved her dress up and underwear aside. But even in the intensity and passionate need of this woman, Quinn kept her movements slow and tender.

"You don't have to treat me like I'm fragile," Natasha said, grasping Quinn's wrist and taking control of the movement. Speeding her up until Quinn nodded, getting the message, she finally allowed her passion for this woman to erupt. And it didn't take long before Natasha fell back against the table, lifting her hips to meet every thrust, crying out as her fingers clasped the edge of the table.

Quinn reached out with her free hand, holding her down and in place as she continued the onslaught and took her over the precipice and into the throes of orgasm. She flopped down on top of her and enjoyed the feeling of Natasha's fingers running through her hair while, for the second time today, she caught her breath.

"I need another shower." She giggled against Natasha's stomach.

"Mm, I think I should join you this time. And repay my debt."

Quinn stood back up, holding her hand out for Natasha to take. "I'm not going to argue with that."

Chapter Thirteen

Red carpet events were usually a star-studded affair, and this was no different, as actors and actresses from TV and film made their way down the path that had been laid out for them all to follow. Quinn waved at several faces as they passed by in a haze of camera flashes and shouts from photographers and journalists all hoping to grab a moment with them.

Quinn walked amongst a group of the crew from Jackson & Jones pretty much unhindered. She wore her favorite black dress and had even managed a little light make-up. She had scrubbed up okay and was enjoying the compliments that had come her way.

"Quinn, can we grab a word?" one of the reporters from a more highbrow magazine called out. She moved across to them and let her group know that she would catch up.

"Hey, sure, how are you?" Quinn asked, ignoring the camera that was shoved in her face the moment she replied.

"We're just great, but how are you? You must be so excited about tonight?" the reporter gushed. Her blonde hair perfect. Make-up flawless, and the dress was good enough for any A-list actress.

"Oh yeah, absolutely, you know you always try not to think about these kinds of things, you have a job to do and that's that, but it's something special when your hard work is recognized. The cast and crew of this show have worked so hard."

"That's awesome, but of course, it doesn't hurt to have an Oscar-winning writer and an award-winning producer on the show either, right?"

Quinn blushed at the comment but deflected from talking about herself. "You know, Nick brings so much experience with him. You're always going to get the best following him, and of course

Riley and Jane, wow, they're really just superb actors, it's a real pleasure to be writing for them."

Someone called Quinn's name and she turned, waving. "Well, we'd better let you get going," the reporter acknowledged. "Good luck, and we're all rooting for you."

"Thanks." Quinn smiled and turned back to the red carpet. Hurrying along to catch up with her colleagues. There had been a buzz going around the studio that Nick would be attending with his wife for tonight's event. Everyone was intrigued as to what kind of woman she was, and why she would put up with his philandering. Quinn didn't join in the gossip, what business was it of theirs? As long as they were happy, so what?

Quinn took her seat next to Jerry Baker, another writer, and got comfortable. Jerry looked good in his rented tux. Blonde hair cut close to his scalp revealing a bald crown. He looked a little like a young Bruce Willis as he grinned inanely at the celebrities walking past.

She could hear Nick's larger-than-life voice booming from somewhere behind them and cringed a little at his over-the-top exuberance. He was definitely on the narcissistic scale when it came to personality, Quinn was deciding.

"If he gets any louder, he won't need a microphone should we win," Jerry said, leaning into Quinn and laughing.

Quinn chuckled. "I guess he needs to let his ego loose."

"Yeah." Jerry turned in his seat to look back at them. "I wonder what she sees in him."

Quinn shrugged, turning to try and catch a glimpse of them. She could see Nick, standing in the aisle with several men in tuxedos hovering around him. His wife though was out of sight, other than the sleeve of her dress. "Who knows, maybe he's the gift to women that he thinks he is."

"I doubt it, but yeah, let's think positive." Jerry laughed, just as the music struck up and the lights began to dim. "Okay, here we go."

Quinn sat back and listened as each new host read out the names of those nominated in each category. There had been a lot of discussion about whether Riley could really beat the competition, and on the whole, most thought she could. Her performances had been exquisite at times, but as the host opened the envelope and read out the name of another actress, Quinn groaned inwardly as she clapped politely and felt a little deflated. It was at that moment that Quinn realized just how much she wanted the show to win. Not for herself, but for the rest of them. She looked across at Jane, quietly soothing Riley's disappointment.

So, when the nominations in their category were read out, the nervous excitement that collectively hummed around the room was palpable. Quinn couldn't help but get excited in her seat.

"And the winner is...." The host smiled and paused for an effect like they always did. "*Jackson & Jones*," she said animatedly. A roar went up around Quinn, and she rose to her feet along with Jerry and every other member of the J&J family. Clapping excitedly as Nick headed up onto the stage with Riley and Jane on either arm.

"I can't believe we did it," Jerry said, kissing Quinn's cheek in his excitement.

Nick took the statuette from the host, passing it to Riley, he held her other hand, and Jane's in the air. "Woo," he shouted, grinning like the cat who got the cream. Finally, as the audience noise died down, he stepped forwards toward the mic.

"You know, I've been here a few times now, and each one is just as exciting as the last." The audience laughed, and a few whooped with excitement. "I want to thank my awesome cast, the crew, who work their asses off to get this show made, and the writers, whose strong scripts and enthralling storylines have made this show so formidable. But mostly, I want to thank my beautiful wife, who somehow has managed to stick by my side for almost two decades," he said, smiling up at her before adding, "I love you, babe."

The music kicked in and once more, Riley and Jane took an arm and escorted him backstage where journalists and photographers would get their fill.

Quinn leaned into Jerry. "See, even assholes know how to woo their wives."

Chapter Fourteen

The after-show party was in full swing when Quinn entered the room and was handed a glass of champagne by a smiling waiter at the door. She sipped it slowly as she glanced around trying to decide who she wanted to head toward until it was a reasonable time to slip out and head home.

Spotting Jane, Quinn waved and when she received a big smile from the actress, she wandered over. "Where's Riley?"

"She's with Nick, they'll both be back in a minute, some last-minute photographs."

"And you're not in them?" Quinn quizzed, "You're both the stars of the show."

"Oh, I'm good, let her have the limelight. Want another drink?" Jane grinned as she waved the bartender over and ordered two more.

It wasn't long before Nick's voice bellowed out Quinn's name, and she turned to find herself wrapped in a bear hug. But that wasn't what caused her to tense up and almost faint on the spot. Behind him, wide-eyed and looking terrified, stood Natasha.

"We did it," Nick said, letting her go and grinning from ear to ear. "More tequila," he shouted across the bar before he realized that Quinn was staring over his shoulder. He turned to see what she was looking at. "Oh, hey. Quinn, this is my wife, Natasha. Honey, this is Quinn, Quinn Harper, my head writer."

Natasha stepped forward; a smile forced its way onto her face but the fear lingered in her eyes. "Hello, lovely to meet you." She held her hand out, and Quinn had to push the bile back down from her throat and force the urge to turn and punch him in the face from her thoughts.

His wife. Her boss, Nick Miles, was the man responsible for all of the hideous beatings. It was all him.

"Likewise," she said, taking the hand. Turning to Jane, she said, "If you'll excuse me." She turned and moved as quickly as she could, heading for the ladies' room. The need to get away rushed her nervous system. So many questions ran through her mind. Why hadn't Natasha said he was a big name in Hollywood? Not once did she mention anything about the kind of lifestyle they must lead; the parties, and famous names. Why had they never talked about Quinn's job? Why hadn't she ever mentioned working on *Jackson & Jones*, or any TV show? The answer was simple, it wasn't about her. She'd spent all these weeks getting to know Natasha, giving her a safe space to be in, it didn't matter what Quinn did for a living, what mattered was what Quinn did as a human being.

Nick barely noticed as he swigged down another shot and ordered more. He was drunk already, what would tonight be like for Natasha? She couldn't bear to think about it.

Quinn pushed her way past the gaggle of people standing in her way, shoving the door open, it banged against the wall, and a woman applying lipstick almost jumped out of her skin.

"Sorry," Quinn mumbled before all but throwing herself into a cubicle. She barely had time to lock the door before she vomited into the pan. Breathing hard, trying to stop the world from spinning.

"You alright?" the woman asked.

"Yeah, uh...too much tequila," she lied, hitting the flush. She waited and listened as the woman walked away and the door opened, noise from outside filtering in, before it gradually quieted down again as the door closed.

"Fuck," she said loudly, punching the wall. "Fuck."

She cleaned herself up and checked her face in the mirror before she headed back out to the party. Keeping herself on the opposite side of the room, but where she could see him. Her eyes followed them as he paraded Natasha around the room. Showing her off as though she were the prize he had won tonight. Several times, she noticed Natasha scanning the room for her. When their eyes did meet, Quinn had to fight off the need to run to her. To take her hand and lead her away from him. Only Quinn saw the deathlike grip on her elbow for what it was. Only she knew that in the morning there would be finger marks on her skin where it bruised. Bruises she knew, she would need to kiss better. If she ever saw her again. The idea of never seeing Natasha again brought another bout of nausea, and she rushed back into the bathroom.

This time when she came out, a waiter passed carrying a tray of champagne flutes. She took two, swallowing down one instantly just to remove the bitter taste in her mouth. Pressing herself against the wall, she searched every face, but couldn't see Natasha anywhere. There was a panic rising in her, as she imagined her being dragged out to a waiting limo by a man eager to get home, to privacy.

The only hope Quinn had was that the win tonight would keep him in a good mood. But then she worried about what a good mood would mean, how would he want to celebrate in private. She shuddered at the thought of him pawing at her lover.

She swallowed down another glug of champagne and closed her eyes. When she opened them again, Natasha was walking past her and into the bathroom, a sideways glance and subtle jut of her chin suggesting that Quinn should follow.

Inside, Quinn found the room empty, one stall with the door closed too, but not locked. She knocked gently, and when it opened, she was pulled inside by Natasha, who then flung herself around Quinn's neck and clung tightly to her.

"Why didn't you tell me?" Quinn asked, her arms wrapping tightly around her.

Natasha shook her head. "I didn't know. We never...we didn't talk about things like that, it didn't come up and I never would have assumed..."

"No, of course, it's just...I can't believe it." Quinn said as Natasha stared at her.

"What do we do?"

"I'll quit tomorrow," Quinn said seriously.

"What? No, you can't do that," Natasha said, stepping back. The movement putting space between them.

"I can't work with him, not now, not knowing what he does to you." She raised her hand slowly and gently she cupped Natasha's cheek.

"You can't ruin your career for me, Quinn."

"My career? Jesus, Tash." Quinn shook her head. "No, I won't work with him, not now. My career will be fine. My reputation isn't on the line, his is."

Natasha grabbed her arms, staring hard at Quinn as fear gripped her. "You can't say anything, please, promise me that you won't do that."

"What do you expect me to do? I can't walk into work and talk to him; I can't even look at him without wanting to kill him," Quinn confessed as her jaw clenched, holding in her own anger.

"No, that's not you." Natasha reached up to caress Quinn's face. "I didn't fall in love with someone who could think that way."

Her words hit Quinn hard. She knew that she had fallen for Natasha, but she had never thought that the feelings were returned. "You love me?"

Shyly, Natasha nodded. "I do. But I'm not ready for what you want from me. I know that it's selfish, and I know that I'm asking more from you than I deserve..."

They both froze as the door opened and a group of giggling women bounced in, talking rapidly about a guy they'd met at the party. Quinn pulled Natasha towards her after she all but jumped out of her skin when the door to the cubicle next to them banged open and then closed.

When the women finally left, and silence enveloped them once again, Quinn let go and Natasha smiled sadly. "Can you give me some time?"

They were both in a terrible position, and Quinn felt the guilt of all of it. Coveting someone else's wife, sleeping with her, and encouraging her to leave. Even if she did argue that the abusive nature of the marriage was unsafe, there was still a selfish motive behind it; She wanted her. And now, discovering her husband was her boss. But when push came to shove, Quinn knew that she didn't care. The universe had put this woman in her life for a reason, and she wasn't going to walk away.

Quinn nodded. "Okay."

Chapter Fifteen

Her years studying acting came to fruition finally as Quinn stepped into the studio office the next day. Having to see him was bad enough, but actually speaking to and interacting with him, Quinn wasn't sure she could pull it off, and yet, here she was staring into the face of the man responsible for every kick and punch Natasha endured.

A fake smile plastered her face as she looked around the room full of smiling faces all now staring at her. She gave a performance worthy of an Oscar itself.

"Hey Quinn," he grinned. "I hear you're lead this week. Any ideas yet for the storyline?" He sat at the head of the long rectangular table and stared right at her.

"Actually, yes. I have an idea that I think would be just perfect," she replied, looking him squarely in the eye, forcing back the bile that threatened to projectile vomit from her at any moment. She sat back in her chair and tried to relax.

"So, I was thinking we'd tackle domestic violence. One of those crimes where the wife is found dead because the husband beat the crap out of her?" Quinn watched him intensely for any kind of reaction, but none came. He just nodded at her to continue. "But what I didn't want to write was another female victim. So, I'm looking at a married couple, both professionals. To the outside world they are the perfect couple, but behind the scenes is a completely different situation. He's a scumbag." She paused, again her eyes landed back on him. "We open with a death scene. He's dead. Then we tell their story in flashbacks, slowly revealing the wife's lover." There's a chorus of "oohs" and a couple of "yes's" from the other writers. "The lover has been plotting and planning his death for months. They met the wife by accident, and they became friends, but one day the wife turns up on their doorstep, battered and bruised. From that moment, they become lovers..." She held her hands out. "That's the main plot. I'm thinking that it would work better as a three-ep arc, rather than the usual one. And the kicker? The lover gets away with it. In every episode we always concentrate on the bad guy getting caught and going to jail. Let's switch it up. Where in this case, the actual bad guy dies in the first scene, and the audience is left almost feeling empathy for the lover and the wife." She looked around the room and waited for her fellow writers to jump in and add their opinions. Jerry went first.

"I like it, the slow reveal," Jerry said, grinning, but Quinn was still watching Nick, who just sat there impassively listening as others threw out their opinion.

"I was also thinking that maybe the lover is a woman?" Quinn added much to Jerry's delight.

Nick sat forward, elbows on the desk, fingertips pressing together and for a moment, Quinn thought he was going to toss the idea, but he didn't. "Alright, this is the kind of thing I'm looking for. Dark, edgy." He pointed a finger at Quinn. "Get a draft done by the end of the week, then we can get casting. Great work," he said, standing to leave. "I feel another award coming our way with this one."

Quinn stayed in her seat. Fully aware now just how much of a psychopath he really was.

Which was why it was worrying when Natasha didn't arrive that Friday. She tried reminding herself that this was always a possibility, they had no way to connect with one another, and anything could have come up. Natasha was a doctor, she could be working, but the reality of what else could be the cause of the absence hung heavy in Quinn's heart.

So many thoughts went through her head. Had the pitch pushed him too far? Had he worked out that she was talking about him, and that she was Natasha's lover? She kicked herself for being so stupid. For allowing her own ego and hatred to get the best of her. She would never forgive herself if she was the cause of anything happening to Natasha. But then she reminded herself, that it was never her fault. It was always him. No matter what happened, or what Quinn did or said, it was his choice to use his wife as a punchbag.

Trying to keep her mind off of it, she headed down to Venice beach. Mooched amongst the eclectic crowd that gathered to enjoy the scene or sell their wares. It was sad to see how many more tents had been erected. The homeless doing their best to keep dry, safe, and fed. Several times, Quinn dropped a few dollars into collecting pots and wished them well. It was a great place to find inspiration. So many wonderful characters all collided down here. Chic restaurants and bars next door to tattooists and souvenir shops on one side, with musicians and entertainers interspersing with the homeless shanty towns on the other. It was eclectic and vibrant. Noisy. The whiff of marijuana mixed with spices and the salty air.

Quinn loved it and wandered in the sunshine taking mental notes, but still, her mind would always revert back to Natasha.

Chapter Sixteen

When Nick didn't turn up on Monday, Quinn really began to worry. What the hell was happening?

"Where is he?" she asked Jerry, trying to appear nonchalant, but inside her stomach was doing somersaults.

Jerry shrugged. "Apparently, he's sick."

"Sick?"

"Yeah, I overheard his assistant telling Callie in Casting that they'd have to delay the auditions as Nick was sick."

Quinn didn't like it. Natasha not turning up on Friday was one thing, but now Nick was absent too? But then she had a thought, maybe Natasha was ill on Friday, a bug or something she picked up at work, something she had passed on to Nick? Maybe that's all it was. She breathed deeply and felt herself settle a little at that idea.

"So, you get the first draft done?" Jerry asked, bringing her thoughts back to the job at hand.

"Yeah. I put copies on the table. I thought we could work on it today."

Jerry clapped his hands energetically. "Yes, I have been thinking this over for days. I really love the idea of the wife's lover slaying the evil husband. Did you work out how?"

"How?"

"Yeah, how she does it. Most women poison or stab, but I'm thinking maybe we could be a little more elaborate."

Quinn smiled; she'd probably thought about this way too often if she were honest. Killing *him* that is. "No, not really, I'm intrigued to hear what you come up with."

~***~

Towards the end of the week, Nick finally returned to work. All smiles and in a very happy mood. Quinn held her breath as she waited to find out if this meant that Natasha was okay, or not.

"So, did you hear?" Jerry said, sidling up to Quinn and speaking in hushed tones. He looked around as though what he was about to divulge was of the utmost secrecy.

"Hear what?" Quinn asked, perplexed. She'd been in her office all day re-writing the script and adding in and deleting relevant scenes. "What did you hear?"

"You know that assistant that Nick's been...you know?" He nudged her conspiratorially.

Quinn considered the bevy of women who had been, you know, with Nick these past months. "Which one?"

"The latest one, blonde, about so high..." He held a palm up to indicate her height. "Sounds like she's sucking helium for breakfast," he finally said when Quinn looked blank.

"Oh, yes, I know... what about her?"

Jerry looked around again to make sure that he couldn't be overheard. "Well, rumor has it that she burst out of the office in tears, and when asked what was wrong, she spilled the lot. How Nick promised to leave his wife, give her a promotion, etc, but..." He paused, he had Quinn's attention now that, unbeknown to him, Natasha was involved in the conversation, and he was going to play out this scene as though he had written it himself and was pitching it. "This morning he told her they were done. That he and his wife were fixing their relationship. After the awards, he realized just what he was losing, and..." Jerry's words drifted away as Quinn felt her heart beat faster, the urge to vomit overcoming her.

"How do you know all of this?" she asked.

"You find out everything in hair and make-up, Sandy was talking to...I forget her name, the assistant. Apparently, Sandy found her crying in the bathroom and she spilled her guts..."

"Excuse me, I just need..."

~***~

Getting home that evening, Quinn was feeling more than a little down. She couldn't believe, that after everything, Natasha and Nick were giving it another go. She pulled on her running gear and hit the sand, hoping her feet pounding the beach would detox the anxiety and heartache out of her, but it didn't.

As she was pulling up to a gentle jog, she noticed her neighbors on the patio outside of their home. Looking relaxed, smiling, and being playful with one another, Quinn felt a pang of jealousy run through her. That was what she wanted. Catching Michelle's eye, she waved, and Michelle waved back. When Cam turned, she waved her over.

"Hey, we're just having a few drinks." She ran a hand through her short-cropped hair and grinned. "Some friends are coming over in a bit, pop in if you're free?" Her British accent was still as strong as ever, though here and there a few words were starting to sound more Californian.

"Oh, that's nice of you to offer," Quinn replied, she had been about to politely turn down the offer, but then she reconsidered. The alternative was to sit at home alone, bored, anxious, and watching TV with one ear on the door in case Natasha came. But it was Wednesday, and the likelihood of that was minimal. "Okay, let me go wash up and change. Can I bring anything?"

Cam continued to grin, shaking her head. "Nah, we're all covered. Maria insisted on cooking enough food for the five thousand." She laughed, indicating who Quinn assumed was her housekeeper. She'd seen the diminutive woman around, but they'd never spoken.

"Alright, see you soon." Quinn smiled before turning on her heel and heading home.

Standing under the shower, she closed her eyes, reminding herself that there was nothing she could do regarding Natasha. She had no recourse to find her. Quinn was safe because she hadn't known anything about her, maybe that was what was wrong now, she thought. Maybe Natasha had reconsidered things and realized that it was no longer safe to visit Quinn, not when her husband was so familiar with her. She didn't want to think about the other option, and she pushed it from her mind, switching the water to freezing cold.

Shivering, she quickly dried off and pulled on something suitable for outside drinks. It was still cool in the evenings, though she knew Cam had a couple of those fancy heaters that would keep everyone warm.

She hadn't been over to Cam and Michelle's before. Since she'd moved here, her neighbors had come and gone, as had she. Trips abroad, or to their place up at the lakes, but they always talked over the fence when they saw each other, but they'd never been the kind to meet up often for drinks or dinner.

Quinn liked it like that, not too much in each other's pockets, but right now, she thought it would be good to do something that took her mind off of things.

"Hey," Michelle called out just as Quinn appeared. "Come on in."

Quinn did as she was told, noticing a small group of people happily milling around on the patio, chatting amiably. It looked cozy, and she suddenly felt a little out of place, until Michelle took her elbow and slid her arm through Quinn's.

"Let me introduce you to everyone." She smiled and Quinn couldn't help but relax. Michelle Thomas, or Shelly Hamlin, as her adoring fans knew her, was a Hollywood actress. Known for her TV work mainly, Quinn was very aware of who she was well before they'd moved in next to each other. It had come as a huge surprise to everyone when out of the blue, she had hooked up with Camryn. Fresh off the plane from London, Camryn had invested in a bar, called OUT. Quinn had been in a few times and had to admit, that even as a homebody, she had enjoyed the atmosphere there.

"Don't look so nervous," Michelle whispered as she leaned in. "You're among friends here."

Quinn chuckled. "That obvious, huh?"

"A little."

Michelle guided them, and soon enough, Quinn was standing in front of several people she didn't know.

"Okay, everyone, this is Quinn, our lovely neighbor," Michelle introduced before continuing. "This is Kate, Cam's best friend. And this is Gavin. As you can see, the pregnancy bug seems to be catching." Michelle laughed, having had twins herself. Quinn said a shy hello and listened as Michelle pointed at a blonde woman; tall and elegant, who looked a lot like Cam. "Cam's sister."

"You do know my name isn't "Cam's sister"? Don't you?" the blonde woman joked before adding, "Caroline."

"As you can see, I am surrounded by Brits." Michelle winked. "And I kinda like it."

Sitting in a chair overlooking it all sat a brooding dark-haired woman with piercing green eyes that burrowed into Quinn.

"Ignore the menacing stare, she's a pussy cat really," said another well-spoken woman to her left. Quinn turned towards her. Long dark hair, older, around Quinn's age. She looked a little familiar, but Quinn couldn't place where she knew her from. "Andrea Parker," she said holding her hand out. "And dark and moody over there is my lover, Ren Dyer."

Ren raised a hand and smiled. Her face changed from serious to relaxed in an instant. "Hi, nice to meet you all." Ren said in a slightly different English accent to the others.

"Quinn's a scriptwriter," Michelle gushed, as though everyone in the group would be impressed. They all smiled and at least pretended to be, which made Quinn feel more relaxed than she thought she would be. Hollywood could be so pretentious at times; it was nice to sit around with a group of people who didn't care which celebrity had dated who.

"Anything I'd have seen?" Caroline asked politely.

"Oh, maybe." Quinn blushed. "I co-wrote Euphoric if you saw that?"

"Saw it? my goodness, I think I've seen it at least six times, and that's probably an understatement. Wow, so you wrote that?"

"Co-wrote, there were four of us, but yeah,"

"Fantastic, come tell me all about it," Caroline said, grabbing Quinn's arm and pulling her towards some chairs. "Did you always intend for it to end that way?"

Cam sidled over next to Michelle. A dark-haired baby in her arms. "Darcy wants you," she said handing her over to her other mother, who grinned like the cat that got the cream. "Careful Quinn, she's an excellent interrogator."

Chapter Seventeen

Talking to Caroline, Quinn found herself relaxing into the evening. She'd been passed a drink at some point, a fancy gin cocktail that Cam had mixed behind the small bar she'd had built. A drink Cam insisted was going to be the best she'd ever had.

As Quinn sipped and listened to Caroline speak, she found herself opening up and talking about herself.

"I have to say, Quinn, you look quite sad," Caroline said, her head tilting sympathetically.

Quinn's lips thinned out and pressed together in an attempt to smile. "I guess that's how I would describe myself."

"If you want to talk about it, I'm known for my confidentiality." Caroline grinned and sipped her drink. "I don't know what Cam put in this, but it's delicious."

Nodding, Quinn agreed. "Yeah. Can't put my finger on the flavor."

"Rhubarb," Caroline offered, taking another sip. "So, tell me, Quinn, what's going on with you?"

Quinn sat back in her seat and sighed. "You ever fall for the wrong person?"

"Ah, that old chestnut? I think we all have at some point, haven't we, is that what's happened?"

Nodding slowly, Quinn said. "I met this woman, here on the beach. She was just sitting there." She pointed over to the spot and could almost see Natasha sitting there. "She looked so sad herself, you know? And so, I went out, sat with her. I figured just having someone there might be good...honestly, I didn't know what she was planning, just staring off to sea."

"Gosh, sounds very dramatic."

"Yeah, anyway, she would appear sporadically, just sitting there. Eventually, I went out and I left her a flask of coffee but said if she wanted to come inside, then it was a safe space to do so...a bit later, she knocked, and from then on, she's been coming over regularly on a Friday, we just talked. One night she showed up, and it was obvious that she was in pain, physical pain."

"Goodness."

"She admitted to me that her husband...likes to use her as his personal punchbag."

Caroline covered her mouth with her hand. "That's awful, and she must have really trusted you to divulge such information?"

"I guess so, I was a safe space for her. We didn't exchange personal information. No surnames, no numbers, or addresses, nothing about work. All I know of her is that she is a doctor."

"That must be difficult?"

"Yeah, when she doesn't turn up as expected, like last week, it's hard. My mind imagines the worst, you know?"

"Of course, it would, wouldn't it...and you like her?" Caroline stated a clear understanding of what *like* meant.

"Yes, I fell for her. Which was stupid, I know...I just couldn't help it. The more we talked, the more I realized what an amazing woman she is."

"And she doesn't feel the same way?"

"Oh, no. she feels it, we..." Quinn felt herself blush and ran a hand over her face as she considered whether to say anything more. But Caroline just seemed able to pull it out of her.

"It's okay, you don't have to say anymore."

"She did feel the same way, we...we started sleeping together." She held her hands up. "I know, I know it's wrong, she's married. We shouldn't have..."

"Oh, poppycock. She's married to a pig." Caroline smiled, "You've nothing to feel guilty about if you ask me."

Quinn looked away, "Maybe, but none of that matters now." When Caroline's eyes narrowed and she frowned, Quinn continued, "According to gossip, she's making another go of it with her husband."

"How do you know that? I thought you had no way to contact each other?"

A cool breeze blew across them and Quinn shivered, but she wasn't sure if it was the weather or the way she felt. "I went to an event last week, and..."

"She was there?" Caroline cut in, her eyes wide.

Quinn nodded. "With her husband...who is my boss." She finally said it aloud and felt a relief wash over her that someone else knew.

"Holy...what are the odds?" Caroline said. She took a large swig of her drink and then waved at Cam. "Two more, please."

Cam laughed and nodded. "They're good, right?"

"So, your boss is the pig? And you haven't seen her since, and now the rumors are that they are giving their marriage another go?" Caroline repeated the facts.

"Pretty much. And so, I was ready to walk...but she pleaded with me not to, said she needed some time, that she wasn't ready to leave him."

"Clearly not, if they're making a new go of it." Caroline pursed her lips and reached out a hand, she gripped Quinn's and squeezed. "I am so sorry; it must be a complete head fuck."

"Yeah..."

"Here you go," Cam said, sweeping in carrying two more gin bowls. "Enjoy." She placed them down on the table and then turned to leave just as quickly as she arrived.

"Hold on," Caroline said. "We need to know what is in this?" She held up the remnants of the first glass.

Cam laughed, and tapped her nose. "State secret, sis." Then she ran before Caroline could interrogate her any further.

"Don't worry, I'll get it out of her."

Quinn smiled; it was nice to see people happy. Interacting with each other so naturally. She made a mental note about using it for a future character or two.

"I wouldn't give up just yet," Caroline mused. "In my experience, those kinds of relationships never last, but they are difficult to extricate yourself from. It's often more about the mental abuse than the physical, and she will feel somewhat beholden to him, unable to just walk away, even though she knows that if she stays, he will eventually kill her."

Quinn shuddered at the thought.

"But..." Caroline held a finger up. "You have to also be aware, that this isn't going to be easy for you. First of all to sit back and wait it out, and the chances are that she may never leave and therefore you're waiting for something that will not happen, but if you do wait, and she does find the courage to walk away, it won't be easy. She's going to need a lot of therapy, and patience, and time. You've known her a few months, is she really worth all of that? Or are you living under a cloud of illusion?"

The words stung. Quinn felt a little attacked and bristled for a moment. Caroline must have noticed because she added, "I don't mean to sound so...black and white, but you get a say in this too Quinn, you've invested time, patience, and love," she emphasized. "But the reality could be a totally different world to that that you have imagined it might be."

"You're right, and I don't know the answers yet. She asked for time, and now she's trying to work things out with him, so I guess I have my answer for now."

"I'm a firm believer in what will be, will be, and what's for you won't pass you by. Now, shall we go join the party and see if we can't cheer you up. Have you met my niece and nephew yet? They're just so adorable."

Chapter Eighteen

The sun shining through the window onto Quinn's bed was warm and welcoming, and yet, she didn't feel it. Instead, she pulled the cover up over her head and groaned. Natasha hadn't turned up the previous evening either and she was having to accept that maybe the rumors were right. She and Nick were all loved up and back on track.

By eleven though, Quinn was beginning to ache. Lying in bed all day wasn't going to be the remedy she had hoped for. As she swung her legs out and placed her feet on the floor, she was reminded of Caroline's words.

"What's for you won't pass you by," she said out loud, nodding to herself. She was right and sulking in bed all day wouldn't make a jot of difference; it would just be her day off that was ruined.

While she showered, she made a plan for the day. She was going to get dressed, head into town, and pick up some groceries. Place an order for some Chinese take-out for later, and just get some air into her lungs.

Arriving back home with two bags stuffed with actual food, Quinn juggled and tried to dig her key out of her pocket as she meandered towards the door. She almost jumped out of her skin when a figure stumbled forwards from where they'd been hidden inside the porch.

"Natasha?" Quinn said, dropping the bags to the floor and moving quickly to grab hold of her before she fell. "What happened?" The question was redundant, she already knew the answer, and felt sick at the thought of it. "Can you walk?" Natasha nodded, gripping hold of Quinn's shirt with all the strength she could muster.

Pulling the key out of her pocket finally, Quinn wrestled it into the lock and twisted, once the door was open, she bent and scooped Natasha into her arms and carried her inside, kicking the door shut with her booted foot. All thoughts of food and groceries were gone from her mind.

She walked slowly down the hallway, desperately trying not to bounce her around too much, each step earning a groan as it was. Once she reached the living room, she lowered Natasha to the couch. Where she curled up into a ball and sobbed.

~***~

For the next hour, Quinn perched on the edge of the couch. She'd already noted the cuts and bruises that she could see. A thin purple line around Natasha's neck made Quinn feel nauseous. Her lower lip was split and looked angry and sore. The crust of blood was still evident in the corner of her mouth and her nostrils. Natasha's left cheek was cut and a nasty shade of purple. What looked like a handprint on her right cheek, as though she had been slapped and then backhanded and caught with a ring. It was all just horrific, and Quinn knew it would only be worse once Natasha woke up and Quinn could check her over completely.

When she was sure that Natasha was as soundly asleep as she could be, Quinn got up and quickly went to the kitchen to make some coffee. Though she was unsure if she would actually be able to drink it, nausea still gurgled away in her stomach.

Before she'd left Cam and Michelle's the other night, Caroline had given her her number, and she debated whether or not to call. Deciding for now that she would wait, but if Natasha got any worse, then maybe it was an option.

She placed the mug of coffee on the side table and sat back down gently. Natasha whimpered, and when Quinn tried to touch her, to reassure her, even in her sleep, she pulled away, terrified. It broke Quinn's heart to witness it.

When it was clear that Natasha was going to sleep a little longer, Quinn remembered her groceries. She got up, went out, and picked it all up. The eggs were pretty much scrambled in their box, and the frozen stuff had begun to defrost. So much for the Chinese later, she was going to have to cook all of the items she had planned to stock the freezer with.

She collected it all up and took it in and down to the kitchen, as quietly as she could, she sorted it all out. She'd been at it for about 30 mins when she heard the cry. Dropping everything, she ran to the lounge and found Natasha sitting up but doubled over.

"Honey, what is it?" she asked urgently, dropping to her knees right in front of her injured lover.

"Quinn?" she whispered, reaching out a hand to touch her lover.

"Yeah, it's me. Can you look at me?"

For a moment, she wasn't sure if Natasha had heard her, but slowly, she raised her head, and with one eye half-closed, she looked at Quinn. Tears formed instantly.

"I'm sorry," she croaked. "I'm sorry."

It was heart-breaking, and Quinn just wanted to wrap her arms around her and make it all better, but she couldn't. She had no idea what kind of injuries there were, and if she were honest, it scared the hell out of her. "Can I help you upstairs, we need to clean you up?" she said gently.

Natasha nodded, Quinn could see that there was no fight left in her. But the effort to stand up was too much and she cried out, grabbing hold of Quinn when her leg gave way beneath her, and she almost fell to the floor.

"It's okay, let me help," Quinn said, slipping her arm around her tenderly. "Just put your weight on me."

She eased her into a standing position, and then step by step, they made their way through the lounge, and out to the stairs. Every step she took, Natasha winced or grimaced and Quinn felt it all hitting her heart like a perpetual bee sting.

"Alright?" she checked half a dozen times as they climbed the steps and finally reached the landing. Turning her gently, Quinn led Natasha into her bedroom. "We need to take your clothes off, is that okay?"

"Yes," Natasha said almost robotically.

"Alright, well let's start with jeans, then you can sit down on the bed." She smiled up at her as she dropped to her knees and loosened the belt and buttons. Once open, she pulled them down and did her best to hold back the gasp as the first bruises appeared. Her thighs were black and blue. When her jeans were down by her knees, Quinn said, "Okay, you can sit down."

Natasha said nothing, staring straight ahead as she lowered to the bed. Not looking at Quinn at all.

Quinn recognized it immediately, all she could do was continue on, not judging, just loving. She pulled the laces on her boots and slid them from her feet, followed by her socks. Part of a boot print marked her left foot, her big toe purple and bloodied around the nail bed.

"Maybe a nice warm bath would help?" she said, trying to keep her voice steady, and some semblance of normality to what she was doing. But the look of fear that filled Natasha's eyes was enough to tell her how impossible that would be.

"No bath, please... don't put me in the bath."

Quinn stopped what she was doing and looked at her, holding her gaze. "I won't do anything you don't want to do, okay?"

When Natasha didn't move, she reiterated, "Okay."

"I'm sorry," Natasha said quietly. Staring at the wall.

"Nothing to be sorry about," Quinn assured, pulling her jeans the rest of the way off. "You have nothing to be sorry for," she repeated, tilting Natasha's chin until she brought her eyes back around to Quinn again. "Nothing."

"I...so stupid, I...everything was..." She was mumbling and not really making any sense, but Quinn let her carry on. When she moved in closer, wanting to lift Natasha's sweater, Natasha flinched and pulled away.

"It's okay." Quinn sat back on her heels, hands back down by her side. "I just want to take off your sweater, can I do that? Is that okay?" She waited patiently until Natasha nodded. "Okay, I'm going to lift my hands, alright, and then I'm going to take hold of the sweater and lift." Then she had a thought. "Can you lift your arms?"

Natasha tried and managed to lift the left one unhindered but cried out when she tried to lift her right arm. "I'm sorry," she said once more.

"It's all good, I just need to be careful, so let's get the good arm out and then we can..." She lifted the sweater as she spoke, and pulled it off over her head and arm, then she ever so gently slid it off from her other arm and this time, she couldn't keep the gasp silent. Natasha's wrist looked like someone had grabbed it and twisted, all the way up her arm were marks from fingers grabbing and pinching and punching. The white t-shirt that she wore beneath the sweater was covered in blood.

"Nosebleed," she said unemotionally before Quinn could ask.

"Well, I need to take it off. But I think it's going to be difficult with not being able to bend that arm." Quinn got up slowly and went to the bathroom, returning with a first aid box and a small bowl of warm water. Opening the box, she grabbed the scissors. But the moment she held them up, Natasha threw her arms in front of her and tried to wiggle backwards on the bed.

"No, I'm sorry, I'm sorry," she kept repeating, pulling her knees up and curling herself into a ball. That was when Quinn saw it, the marks on her side as the material from her t-shirt lifted.

"Jesus," she whispered, dropping the scissors instantly. "Natasha, baby. It's okay, it's me, Quinn. I'm not going to hurt you." She leaned back on her heels, when every fiber in her wanted to lurch forward and hold this woman, keep her safe from the hands of anyone that could be so cruel. "Tasha, listen to my voice. Can you hear my voice?"

She watched intently until Natasha nodded.

"Good, okay, keep listening, you hear my voice? It's Quinn, everything is okay, you're safe, do you understand me, you're safe here. Nothing and nobody is going to hurt you."

It took what felt like a long time before Natasha slowly uncurled and sat up, timidly moving, watching Quinn's hands the entire time. "No...no...nothing sharp," she finally got out.

Quinn nodded. "Okay,"

Natasha grabbed the bottom of the shirt with her good hand and tried to pull it upwards, but it was a struggle.

"Can I help?" Quinn asked without moving.

Between them, they managed to get it off without too much pain. And then Quinn saw just how bad it was. Her entire left side was almost black. Tiny cut marks like someone had used a knife and nicked her skin over and over, in two lines. Thought had gone into each one. He had considered, and deliberated, as he tortured her.

"I'm going to kill him," she muttered to herself, but Natasha heard.

"No."

"You're still defending him?" Quinn asked, tears finally falling, she couldn't hold it back any longer. The fear and pain that this woman, her lover, must have suffered were immeasurable.

Natasha shook her head slowly. "No, don't be like him. You're not him."

And then Quinn got it. She wiped her eyes, helped remove her underwear, and then she picked up the washcloth, dipped it into the warm water, and held it up. "I'm going to wash your face, alright?"

When Natasha didn't move, she took it as an acceptance and gently dabbed at the areas that needed cleaning the most. Reverently, she moved from each wound to the next, carefully applying iodine, and, in places, band-aids. When she was done, she sat back on her heels again.

"I think you should get checked out at the hospital," Quinn said, trying not to hurt her as she wiped over her ribcage, Natasha wincing at the barest touch.

"I can't, and I don't need to," she answered.

Quinn looked at a wound on her thigh that was bleeding through the band-aid. "I know that you're the doctor, okay, but this isn't closing up."

"Can you get my bag?"

"Sure, let's get you downstairs, and then I can drive..."

Natasha shook her head. "No, I have a better first aid kit in my bag...I can stitch it."

Staring in disbelief, Quinn stood up. "You're going to..."

"Nothing is broken, nothing that they can do anything about anyway. And it will just take a couple of minutes to stitch this."

Quinn didn't like the sound of that at all, but the stitches were minimal compared to what could be worse. "What's broken?" She asked, sitting down again.

"Me, in general." Natasha tried to joke but then grew serious when Quinn stiffened at the joke "Sorry, that was flippant, and you don't deserve that. I think a rib, and my toe, maybe two. They'll heal by themselves."

A barely-there nod came forth and Quinn slowly got to her feet again. "Okay. I'm going to get rid of this, then I'll get you your bag, and then find something for you to wear, alright?"

She carried everything back through to the bathroom, and as she poured the reddish-brown water down the sink, the dam broke, and she had to cover her mouth to stop the loud sob that emitted from her.

Getting herself together, Quinn quickly washed her face. She looked at herself in the mirror. Her skin looked ashen, glassy eyes stared back at her.

"You can do this," she told herself before opening the door again and stepping out, trying to look as calm as she could.

When she returned to the room, she found Natasha still sitting in the same place as she was when she left. Quinn sat down beside her, hating herself when Natasha flinched away instinctively when she passed the small bag to her.

"Sorry," Natasha mumbled. "I don't mean to...I know you won't hurt me."

"It's alright, it's understandable, but I am glad that you know I'm not going to hurt you. You're safe here, and you can stay here for as long as you want to."

"Thank you," Natasha said, rifling through the contents of her bag until she found a small leather-bound medical kit and some individually wrapped bandages. Quinn watched as she opened it. She didn't know what all of the instruments were, but she recognized a few. "This won't take long." Natasha looked up, she grimaced as she twisted and reached up to cup Quinn's cheek. "You don't need to watch or worry. I'll be fine, I promise."

Quinn nodded, turned her face, and kissed the palm there. "I'll get you something to wear."

She took her time. Giving Natasha some privacy to fix herself. When she returned, Natasha smiled up at her. "All done."

Looking at the clean bandage that wrapped her leg, and the other that wrapped around her ribcage. Quinn wondered how she had done it so quickly and without any painkillers. How used to this was she? "Shall we get you into these?" Quinn held up a pair of warm plaid pajamas.

"Yes, thank you."

Quinn unfolded everything and helped Natasha into the top, buttoning it up with just the top button left undone and once again had to catch her breath when she looked at the strangle marks around her neck. What kind of monster was he? How did he appear so charming at work, and then go home and do this?

Dropping to her knees, Quinn eased the bottoms up Natasha's legs. "Put your arms around my neck so I can lift you," she instructed, and Natasha did as she was asked. "There all done," Quinn said lowering her back to the bed once she had finished dressing her. Natasha's arms still linked around her neck, and as Quinn pulled back, they stared into each other's eyes. At any other moment, Quinn would kiss her. Push her back onto the bed and make love to her, but now, here in this moment, she risked reaching up, allowing her hand to gently stroke her cheek. Natasha still flinched, but not like before and Quinn was grateful for some progress.

"What can I do for you?" she asked Natasha.

"Just be you," she whispered. "Just be you, I need you to just...be you."

"Alright, in which case, I'm going to help you to bed..."

Natasha shook her head. "I don't want to...I don't want to be alone."

"I'll just be downstairs."

"But I won't...I won't hear you. I need to...to know that you're there," she explained.

"Okay then, we'll set you up on the couch, and you can watch me work. How does that sound for entertainment?" She smiled and helped Natasha to her feet. Unsteady, but able.

"Perfect," Natasha said, attempting a smile before wincing at the pain from her lip.

"And maybe we should try and eat something?" Quinn suggested. Her own stomach had been rumbling long before she got home.

"I'm not sure that I can, but I'll try."

"That's all I ask. Something light, you need your strength, right, Doctor?"

Natasha said nothing, but she squeezed her grip on Quinn's waist, and that was enough of an answer for her as she slowly helped her lover out of the room and down the stairs.

Chapter Nineteen

The couch looked like it had been victim to a cushion avalanche by the time Quinn had finished with it. And when Natasha sat down and tried to get comfortable, it seemed almost impossible.

Frowning, Quinn stared down at the situation.

"I think there are too many," Natasha said, trying to reach around and pull a cushion out from behind her. She quickly retracted her arm though and cried out.

Quinn jumped into action, moving the offending cushion instantly. "Yeah, I think I've gone a little overboard. Alright, sit tight and I'll fix this situation." She tried again, moving, and throwing pillows around.

Natasha actually giggled, and to Quinn's ears, it was the best sound. Something that a few hours earlier, she didn't think she would hear ever again.

"It's good to hear you laugh," she admitted, moving several cushions, and then rearranging the blanket. "Warm enough?"

Natasha nodded, holding her gaze.

"Alright, let's try something to eat then, shall we? I'll just be in the kitchen; do you want the TV on?"

Shaking her head, Natasha said, "No, thank you. But do you have some Ibuprofen or arnica?"

Quinn wasn't sure. "I'll check."

"Thank you. They just help with swelling and bruising," she explained and Quinn nodded, she was aware of that.

"Okay, be back in a minute."

In the kitchen, she paused. Took stock of the situation and how she was feeling about it all. A mix of anger, frustration, and empathy all collided together and churned until they made a kind of nausea that constantly threatened to erupt.

Opening the refrigerator, she found one of the meals that she had cooked earlier and placed it into the microwave. Then she sat down at the table and let her head fall into her arms as she lay there and quietly sobbed.

For a moment, she contemplated calling Caroline. But then she reconsidered that. They barely knew each other, and as much as she was a great shoulder to cry on the other night, they were hardly friends. Right now, she just needed to get herself, but mostly Natasha, through these next couple of days.

Getting up, she opened the cupboard door where she kept her pills and medications. Ointments and cough syrups, all the usual things that an adult human might need when they feel under the weather. She found the ibuprofen easily enough, the arnica was shoved right at the back and she needed to pull almost everything out in order to get it.

Next, she loaded up a tray. Three pain pills, the arnica, and a glass of water. Beside that were two bowls filled with some kind of pasta, little fat tubes, covered in a creamy sauce with broccoli and chicken. It had looked nice on the packet when she had picked it up, now her stomach wasn't quite so invested in the idea of eating it. She added a spoon and a fork, unsure which Natasha would prefer.

"Here we go," she announced quietly as she brought the tray into the lounge. She placed it down on the table and then handed Natasha the pills and the water to wash them down with.

"You're a very good nurse." She smiled up once she had swallowed them.

"Yeah? Was never on my vocational horizon, but good to know that I have options should the whole scriptwriting career come to a sudden halt." She smiled back before helping Natasha to sit up more comfortably. "Okay, comfy?"

"Yes, thank you."

"Good, let's see if you can get some of this down you." Quinn handed a bowl over, then held up the fork and spoon.

Looking at the food, and then back to Quinn, Natasha said, "Spoon, please."

They sat quietly, Natasha on the couch, Quinn opposite on an armchair she had dragged over. Each of them forced a spoonful of food into their mouths, swallowing it down as though it were something unwanted. It was Quinn who gave up first, placing the bowl down on the table a spoonful before Natasha did the same.

"He's going to kill you if you keep going back," Quinn spoke softly, unable to hold back her own fears any longer. She needed Natasha to hear her, to hear the impact of this, the reality of it.

"I know," she answered with no emotion.

The sun was setting, and it had gotten colder in the room. Quinn got up and started a fire, pushing her chair back to its original position. When she was done, and the flames were roaring, Natasha patted the couch beside her.

"Will you lie with me?" she asked.

There was no way that Quinn would deny that request. She moved away all of the extra cushions and pillows, lifted the blanket, and gently climbed in behind her. She kept her arm along her own side until Natasha reached back and pulled it around herself.

"I'm not letting you leave this time, you know that, right?" Quinn stated firmly.

"I know," she whispered back.

"Promise me that you won't leave and sneak off if I fall asleep," Quinn mumbled as she relaxed and let herself mold into the embrace. Just feeling her warmth was enough to make her feel sleepy. The day had been a lot more mentally exhausting than she had expected and her eyes were starting to close.

"I promise, I won't leave," she said quietly, tugging Quinn tighter to her. She hissed again in pain and Quinn tried to retract her arm, but she held firm. "I'm ready," she said, barely audible, but loud enough that Quinn heard. Her heart raced at the prospect of Natasha finally leaving the bastard. "I can't keep living like this."

They lay there quietly, no words needed. But as the darkness began to fill the room, and the fire warmed them, Quinn considered her own position. She couldn't go to work after this. She couldn't look him in the eye and not want to punch him.

"I'm going to resign," Quinn announced, kissing her shoulder.

Natasha turned, wincing a little until she was on her back and looking at Quinn. "What about your career? I don't want you to ruin..."

Quinn smiled down at her, slowly raised a finger, and placed it to her lips. "Hold that thought." Gently, she extricated herself and got up, moving quickly to the cupboard. Opening it, she pulled out her awards, one by one until she had an armful. "I might not be a Nick Miles, but I'm not a newbie."

She placed them down on the table so that Natasha could investigate for herself. Three SAGs, two Golden Globes, as well as several smaller awards.

"You won all of these?" Natasha asked, as Quinn went back to the cupboard. When Quinn turned around, Natasha gasped. "An Oscar?"

Quinn nodded, smiling a little smugly. "Hasn't got one of these, has he?"

Natasha shook her head as Quinn passed the golden statuette to her. "No, he doesn't, and he would do anything for one."

"My point is that my career is already a success, and my leaving this job won't change that. I will still be in demand." She sat down at the table and reached for Natasha's hands. "I know that we've only known each other a few months, and I know that this is not the easiest of situations, but I like you Natasha, a lot. And I would do anything to make it so that you are safe, and away from this man."

"I know you would, but you shouldn't have to."

Chapter Twenty

Waking up Quinn felt Natasha stiffen in her arms. She loosened her hold and waited. "You alright?"

It took a moment before Natasha responded. "Yes, sorry I just...I lost my bearings for a moment." She explained. Gradually she relaxed and melted into the embrace when Quinn kissed her head. "Shall we start again," she chuckled, hissing as her lip split a little. "Good morning, did you sleep well?"

Quinn chuckled. "Considering you didn't, and I spent most of the night watching you, I feel quite refreshed."

Natasha pushed herself up onto an elbow. "I'm sorry."

"Don't be." Quinn reached up and gently pushed the hair away from Natasha's face, smiling to herself with she didn't flinch away. When Natasha dropped back down into the crook of her arm, she smiled again. The smell of soap, sleep, and iodine floated up. "I'd take 100 nights like that if it meant waking up like this."

"You're such a romantic," Natasha teased.

"Yep, and I won't be insulted about it either." She laughed and kissed the top of Natasha's head. "So, breakfast?"

"Something light, toast maybe?"

"I can rustle that up. You want to eat in bed, or come downstairs?"

As Quinn climbed from the bed, Natasha rolled onto her back and brought a fingertip to rub at her lip. "Hm, maybe I'll come down. I don't want to be up here alone."

"Alright, up and at 'em then." Quinn grinned.

"Yes, Doctor."

Leaving Natasha to get up and about in her own time, Quinn pulled on a robe and headed downstairs. Her mood had brightened considerably since last night's confession that Natasha was finally ready to leave Nick. Whether that meant they would be together or not, it didn't matter to Quinn. She would give up any chance of a life with Natasha if it meant her lover would be safe and happy. But at the same time, she had a little hope of something more, in time.

She had just about loaded everything onto the tray when she heard the shuffling sounds of Natasha making her way down the stairs. It was nice, to have the sounds of someone else in her home again. They met in the hallway just as Natasha took the final step. She moved aside to allow Quinn to walk past with the tray.

"Toast, coffee, juice," she announced as she placed it down on the table and turned to find Natasha smiling at her. "What?"

"Nothing, I just...it's nice is all." She stepped into the room, toe to toe with Quinn, as she leaned up and kissed her. "It's nice to have breakfast made for me that isn't an apology," she admitted when Quinn continued to frown.

"Oh, well, there will be no more apology breakfasts for you from now on," Quinn adamantly stated.

They were halfway through their breakfast when the tinny sound of a phone ringing drifted down the stairs. Natasha froze. The piece of toast halfway to her mouth halted in the air as her eyes widened.

"It's him," she stuttered, placing the bread down on the plate before she dropped it. They both sat there, still, and unmoving as the call rang out. And then it rang again. And again.

"I'm going to go and answer it. He's not going to stop," Quinn insisted. "And if you're serious about not going back then he needs to know so that he can stop harassing you."

She waited for Natasha to agree. The phone stopped ringing, and then it started again. "Okay, okay," Natasha said, bringing her hands up to cover her ears. "Just make him stop."

Quinn got up and raced up the stairs before Natasha could change her mind. She found the bag and pulled the phone from it. Nick's smiling face appeared, and Quinn rubbed her thumb across it to answer the call and listened.

"Where the fuck are you?" he hissed into the phone the moment it connected. He wasn't just angry; this was a man who was well past angry. Quinn said nothing. "Don't ignore me, I said where the fuck are you?" he paused, and the silence became louder, but his voice became lower. More unnerving and terrifying. "You better answer me, bitch, or I will fucking end you. You know I will. I'll slice you up and hold you under till you're done."

Quinn's mind went to the cuts on Natasha's skin, the fear of a bath. She wanted to throw up. But not before she dealt with this, with him. Breathing deeply, she spoke clearly and quietly. "Natasha won't be coming home tonight, or any other night. Don't call again."

She could hear him screaming, "Who the fuck is that?" as she lowered the phone away from her ear and closed the call. She slid the phone into her pocket, and then ran to the bathroom and threw up.

When she came back downstairs, she found Natasha curled up on the couch. Her big green eyes, tear-stained and swollen, looked up at her. Natasha tried to speak but nothing came out.

"It's okay. He's gone." For now, Quinn thought. Someone like Nick Miles, with that amount of venom about him, wasn't going to just walk away. She sat down, and picking up the TV remote, she then slowly lowered herself behind Natasha like they had done the previous evening. "Wanna watch a film?"

Natasha shrugged but didn't move away. When Quinn had finished flicking through the channels and settled on an old black and white with Barbara Stanwyck and Henry Fonda, Natasha reached back for her hand and pulled it around herself.

Lying there together, it was almost easy to forget about everything. Only when she looked at Natasha's face was Quinn reminded of the bruises. Just lying there, with Natasha wrapped in her arms, she let herself imagine, for just a moment, how wonderful her life could be.

Chapter Twenty - One

Monday morning couldn't come quickly enough for Quinn.

"You sure you'll be alright here by yourself?" Quinn fussed around as Natasha got comfortable on the couch.

"Yes." She smiled. "I'll be fine. I've taken some meds; I've changed the dressings. I just need to rest."

"Alright, well I doubt that I'll be long."

Natasha looked away. "Are you sure you want to do this?"

Quinn stopped moving and stared down at her. "Yes. I'm going to march in there and tell him to go fuck himself,"

"You'll need to give him a reason, you have a contract," Natasha reminded her. When Quinn was silent, she added, "You can be honest. You can tell him about me."

"I don't know if..."

Natasha held up a hand, pushed herself up as she winced, and grimaced, and when she was upright, she held out a hand for Quinn to help her up. Face to face, she looked into Quinn's eyes. "Do what you think is right. I trust you." And then she leaned forwards and kissed her gently.

~***~

Crossing the parking lot, Quinn spotted him. Standing by his sports car, hair slicked back. He was looking smart and cool, like a man with no worries in his chinos and blue cotton shirt, talking to the blonde assistant who'd left his office in tears the last time Quinn had seen her on set. There was a part of her who just wanted to walk up to him and punch him square in the face, but she knew doing that would firstly, hurt her hand, and secondly, end up with a lawsuit.

"Nick," she called out, and when he looked her way, she demanded, "I need to speak to you, right now." Her voice was loud, and several others turned to see what was going on. She was glad of that, she wanted them all to know what kind of man he was, but that wouldn't help her, or Natasha.

"Sure Quinn, what's up?" He frowned.

Realizing that he hadn't recognized her voice as being that on Natasha's phone, she felt emboldened and stepped up as close as she needed to be. Not that she wanted to be breathing the same air as this monster. It irritated her that his attention drifted back towards the blonde who was walking away, glancing back over her shoulder at him.

"I wanted to tell you in person that I am resigning, with immediate effect," Quinn said, loudly enough for anyone listening to hear. His head whipped around, now she had his attention.

"What?" he laughed, "Sorry, I don't think I heard that right." He took a step closer. "Because it sounded like my head writer just resigned, right in the middle of a season when she's contracted to the end." Now when she watched him, she could see the rage that lurked in his eyes. Something deep within that was always on the edge of eruption but hidden behind a cloud of over-confidence.

"No, you heard right. I'll clear out my desk and office now," she insisted.

He huffed, and turned one way and then the next, before finally setting his sights back on Quinn. She understood his upset. There was the producer, director, and stars of the show, they were the public face, but behind the scenes, you needed good writers, and she was one of the best, and she came with a name that garnered admiration and respect within the industry. Someone like Quinn Harper walking off of your show mid-season, wouldn't go down well with the networks, or the entertainment press. The rumor mill would be running wild.

"Why?" he finally asked. "Why, Quinn?"

She leaned in closer and firmly stated, "I don't think my reasons are something you want to discuss in public."

"What is the hell is that supposed to mean?" he asked quizzically. "I really don't under..."

"Natasha."

It was just one word. But the blood drained from his face, and he looked as though he might faint. With that, Quinn pushed past, barging against his shoulder as she moved towards the building and into her office.

It wasn't that long before she heard the door open and close behind her. She ignored it, continuing to fill the empty box with her personal things.

"Where is she?" he asked.

Quinn stopped what she was doing, turned slowly, and leaned back on her desk, watching him as he mirrored her against the door. "She's somewhere safe, somewhere you can't hurt her anymore."

He didn't even have the decency to look ashamed. "I want to see her."

Quinn shook her head. "Not going to happen."

In an instant, he pushed off from the door and moved quickly towards her. "She is my wife, and I will see her when I want to," he hissed through gritted teeth, the real Nick coming out to play now. If he expected Quinn to flinch or back down, he was in for a surprise.

At his movement, she reacted, pushing up from the desk and striding to meet him halfway. "I will end you," she repeated his words back at him. "If you so much as look at her again, I will end you."

He glared incredulously at her with cold steely eyes that held no emotion other than rage and anger. Fists clenching and unclenching by his side, but he held it together. It was different when it wasn't your wife and when it was someone who could actually hurt you, but that didn't mean he didn't want to lash out.

"I am deadly serious, you so much as breathe near her, and I will end you. Your career?" She snapped her fingers at him. "Gone. You touch me?" She snapped her fingers again. "Gone." When he remained silent, she stepped back one step. "Now, if you don't mind, you can leave, I have things to pack." She turned her back on him and continued to pack her things, her heart racing as she listened, waiting for the sound of the door closing. When it did, she placed her hands on the desk and breathed deeply. She'd never been so scared in her life.

A few minutes later, there was a knock on the door. Soft and gentle.

"Come in," she called out, smiling as Jerry popped his head around the door.

"Hey, so, someone said there was this ridiculous rumor that you were..." He was speaking as he stepped inside, smiling until he noticed the box on the desk. "It's true? You're leaving?"

"Uh, yeah."

"What? Why? We have that script to finish and..."

"The script's all yours, Jerry, I know you'll make it a great episode."

His shoulders sagged, and he huffed despondently. "But why? What am I gonna do without you here? Who's going to listen to me gossiping?"

Quinn smiled at him, moved closer, and pulled him in for a hug. "It's a personal reason, something that just can't be worked out, but you've still got my number, gimme a call, we can gossip all you like."

"Ah, it's not the same, but...yeah."

She grabbed the box. "I'll see you around, Jerry."

Chapter Twenty-Two

Checking the time, Quinn threw the box into the trunk. She'd been gone for an hour. Grabbing her phone from her bag, she called the number Natasha had given her. It rang for several moments before a sleepy voice answered.

"Hello."

"Hey, it's me. It's done," Quinn said, climbing into the car and settling herself. She watched as Nick stormed out of the building and did the same, climbing into his car. Screeching out of the lot a moment later.

"What did he say?" Natasha asked nervously.

"He wasn't happy, but I made it clear that if he came near you, or me, again, I'd end his career."

She heard an intake of breath from Natasha. "He won't like that, Quinn."

"I know, but what can he do? He's not going to risk his career, not now when he's worked so hard to get where he is." She turned the key in the ignition. "Listen, you go back to sleep, I'm going to stop off at the store and pick a few things up for you, you need some clothes and stuff, anything in particular?"

"I can't think of anything," she said.

"Okay, then I'll be home soon?"

"Alright."

Quinn disconnected the call and headed off toward the mall. She'd bought clothing for women before, but usually, it was of the more intimate kind that you buy a lover, this felt very different. Yes, they'd slept together, and yes, she had feelings that had evolved way past friends or casual lovers, but this wasn't a relationship as such, not yet anyway. And it felt a little weird wandering the shops looking for things to buy for Natasha to wear. She tried to think about what she had usually been wearing during the times they had met and tried to find things that matched those. Always blue jeans, she thought. So, she grabbed a couple of pairs. She found some plain t-shirts and added those to the cart. A couple of sweaters and some underwear later, and she was ready to get going.

She smiled to herself as she placed the bags into the trunk and thought about Natasha at home, her home. It was a nice feeling. Something she hadn't felt in a long, long time.

Chapter Twenty-Three

Holding several bags in her hands as she locked the car and made her way towards her home, she had a feeling that something was off. Something was wrong, something looked different, but as the sun shone and blinded her eyes, she couldn't quite make out what it was. Adrenaline was already kicking through her system, her heart was racing, and she felt tense; muscles constricting and relaxing as they realized before her brain had, that something was happening.

As she got closer, she saw instantly what it was. Her front door was wide open. What should have been a grey block of color, was now a dark, gaping hole. The bags landed on the floor, forgotten in an instant as Quinn sped up and into the house. She didn't think about who or why, she already knew.

As she crept into the house and along the short hallway, she could hear Natasha sobbing and pleading.

"Please, don't do this." The words hit Quinn's heart and piercing like a spear. How dare he come here, to her home, and do this to a woman he was supposed to love? Quinn felt the anger erupting. The anger she had been pressing down and keeping in check for Natasha's sake now had nowhere else to go. But she wasn't a hot-headed idiot, she needed to know what the situation was that she was about to run head-on into.

There was a mirror on the wall in the living room, if she angled herself correctly at the door, she could see in and through it at the scene, but the room was empty. The voices coming from down the hall, from the kitchen.

Silently, she crept further until she was at the door to the kitchen. He had hold of Natasha by the hair. Pulling hard as she reached up and grabbed at his hand, trying to prise herself free of his grasp, but he just pulled harder.

"You come home with me, right now. Or..." Quinn watched him drag her towards the stove, flicking the dial and lighting the gas. "I'll make sure nobody ever looks twice at you again."

Natasha screamed. "No, don't..."

Quinn rushed in. "Get your hands off of her," she screamed as she launched herself at his back, giving him no time to react. The move meant he had to let go of Natasha, who fell to the floor, landing with a painful thwack.

"Quinn, no," she shrieked as she scrabbled away and tried to pull herself up with the aid of a chair.

The anger now in full flow, Quinn didn't see or hear anything else other than him. Her legs wrapped around him, and her fists rained down on him in a torrent of hits that had her fists bouncing off of his head, shoulders, and when he turned to look at her, his face.

"You fucking dyke," he hollered twisting and turning to try and throw her off, but she held on. Her core strength taking no prisoners now, as she thumped him over and over.

"Get out of my house," she hissed. "Don't you touch her?" Her right arm snaked around his neck, and she squeezed. He responded by backing her into the refrigerator, the corner of a wall, and the countertop. She didn't feel a thing but knew later that she would be black and blue. Eventually, though, he managed to fling her off and she landed in a heap on the opposite side of the room to Natasha. He strode over, and kicked Quinn hard in the thigh, before turning on his heel. His face filled with venom as he zeroed in on his wife. Natasha huddled frozen with fear on the floor.

"I told you you're coming home," he sneered, reaching down and grabbing her thin arm in his firm grip. Her eyes searched across the room and found Quinn's staring back at her.

"I'm sorry," she mouthed before she was hauled to her feet.

Everything ran through Quinn's mind in an instant. The promises to keep her safe, that this was a safe place, that he wouldn't, couldn't hurt her again. She knew, that if he left with her now, the probability was that he would kill her. His perfect image was now in tatters as his world of secrets had been revealed. She could see by the look on his face that he no longer cared about anything more than what he would do to her.

Quinn didn't remember picking it up or even standing up. She had no recollection of limping across the room roaring like a wounded animal, or of the moment that she brought the pan down on his head. Swinging it back up and aiming again for him, connecting with a crack. But she had. She had no memory of watching him fall to the floor, blood seeping from a wound in the back of his head. Or of the moment that Natasha pulled her away and into her arms. Shielding her from the sight of him dead or dying in her kitchen.

"Quinn? Quinn?" Natasha whispered, her tear-stained face coming into focus as Quinn finally heard her name being repeated.

"Are you alright?" she asked, reaching up a hand to move aside the hair that hung messily across Natasha's face. Her lip was bleeding again. "Did he hurt you?"

"I'm okay," she said, turning to look at him.

Quinn stared across at his motionless body. "Is he?"

Natasha shook her head, tears flowing down her cheeks. "I don't know about...I'm a doctor, I should...but I..."

"It's okay. I'll check, you call an ambulance, can you do that?" she asked, crawling across the floor she felt every bruise on her battered body.

She was breathing heavily, fear of what this man did, and could still do, ran a warning through her exhausted brain. Reaching him, she prodded gently. He didn't move. Nervously, she reached a shaking hand forward and felt for a pulse. It wasn't like in the movies, where they reach down, press instantly to the right spot, and announce that the killer is dead, or the victim is alive. It took a moment, to locate and feel for it. She could hear Natasha speaking quietly on the phone, asking for an ambulance to come as she paced the room, looking at Quinn the entire time. When Quinn looked up and their eyes met, she said, "He's alive."

Chapter Twenty-Four

She wasn't sure if it was a blessing or not that Nick Miles was alive and being treated in hospital for a concussion and a nasty head wound. On the one hand, she wasn't a murderer. That thought had played heavily on her, knowing that she might have taken someone else's life. Not that he didn't deserve to be dead for what he had been doing to Natasha all these years, her brain had argued.

If he had died, Natasha would be free of him, physically at least. He would haunt her forever whether he breathed another breath or not. That much was obvious when she whimpered in her sleep.

After the police had arrived, everything had seemed to speed up, and Quinn could barely put a thought together. "It's pretty obvious what happened here," he explained, "But I still have to investigate. Dot all of the I's and cross those T's."

"Sure." Quinn answered, wrapping her arms around herself.

"The last thing I want to see is some hotshot lawyer get him off on a technicality because I didn't do my job correctly," he continued. They both looked toward the ambulance where Natasha was being seen by the EMT.

His name was Detective Gomes, and Quinn liked him instantly. "So, let's go through the events of today, and what led us here, can you do that?"

Quinn nodded. "Sure." She ran a hand through her hair and grimaced as the movement hurt her back and shoulder. The medics had taken a look at her earlier and she was deemed to be fit enough, but the bruising would take some time to heal. "I met Natasha earlier in the year. I used to see her sitting outside." She indicated the beach. Telling their story felt a little cathartic, made it feel a little more real, and as he listened, nodding, and jotting down relevant information, she felt heard and confident that Nick Miles was now going to be nothing more than a memory for them both. As she was finishing up, there was a tap on the living room door. A blonde head poked around the frame looking concerned.

"Hey," Cam said before Caroline appeared at her shoulder. "We saw the cop cars and...oh, hey, Detective Gomes."

"Camryn how are you?" he said standing and holding out a hand.

"I'm good, thanks. Just checking on Quinn." She turned her attention back to her neighbor. "Detective Gomes was in charge of my case when Jessica..." She left the story unsaid, but Quinn knew what she meant. The ex-girlfriend who had stalked Michelle and then attacked Cam.

"We're okay, good to know I'm in good hands." Quinn tried to smile but it wasn't really how she felt.

"Alright, well look, we're next door. If you need anything, just shout, alright?" Caroline butted in. She nodded at Quinn, before taking Cam by the elbow and practically dragging her back out of the house.

"Good people you have next door," Gomes said once they were gone.

"Yes," Quinn agreed. "They are." She sucked in a breath and exhaled slowly, trying to settle herself. The adrenaline was wearing off and the events of the day were finally taking their toll. "What's going to happen to him now? Is she safe?"

Gomes sighed, closed his notebook, and slid it into his jacket's top pocket as he considered his reply. "Honestly, I don't know. He's been arrested, and for tonight at least will stay in hospital. There's a guard on his door, so he isn't going anywhere, but when he is well enough, he's going to the station for questioning. At that point, I hope to have enough evidence that we can hold him, but in most cases." He shrugged his broad shoulders. "These guys have good lawyers. Even if we take him to trial, he'll probably make bail."

"So, there's no guarantee that he won't be back?"

"If he's got half a brain cell in that head of his, he'll follow his lawyer's advice and stay the hell away. But..." Another shrug. "We're not dealing with a man who thinks logically."

"What do we do?"

Gomes thought about it, then smiled as he said, "Speak to your neighbor, she's got a few resources at her disposal." He stood up, just as Natasha came back into the room. "I'll leave you both now, but I'll drop by tomorrow with any follow-up questions and an update on the case if that's alright?"

Quinn nodded. "Sure, that would be helpful, thanks." She followed him out of the room, touching Natasha's shoulder lovingly as she passed. "I'll be right back," she whispered.

Watching Gomes leave, she noticed the door. In too much of a hurry to get inside before, she hadn't realized that it was virtually off its hinges. She sighed and rested against the wall for a moment before she attempted to close it. It pushed closed and filled the hole, but there was no way she could secure it as it was. As she opened it again, a man was walking towards her. Tall, broad, and with short blonde hair, she recognized him as one of Cam's friends, though she couldn't pull a name from her memory.

"Hey," he said, waving at her. "Cam sent me over. Said you might need some help. Gavin. We met at Cam's." He held his hand out to her and she noticed the toolbox he carried in the other. "I can get this door back on for you."

"Really? That would be a godsend," Quinn said, feeling the urge to break down and cry.

"Yeah, no problem. And when I'm done, we'll talk about security."

Chapter Twenty-Five

Gavin really was a godsend and Quinn made a mental note to make sure that she thanked Cam and Caroline for sending him over. The door was fixed and locked, although it would need replacing as quickly as possible, but it would do for now, especially as Gavin had organized security to sit outside all night, front and back, with the crews changing shifts in the morning. Meaning they could go to bed at least content in the knowledge that for tonight at least, they were safe from Nick Miles and his sadistic intentions.

Downstairs was still a mess. Neither of them was in any fit state to deal with cleaning it up, and in all honesty, Quinn could care less about it. All that was important was that they were no longer in danger.

Easing herself into bed next to Natasha, Quinn grimaced and frowned as she felt the effects of battling Nick and the walls, the refrigerator, and the countertop. She was going to ache for a while, that was for sure.

"Are you okay?" Natasha asked. She shifted in the bed, gasping in pain.

"Yeah, I'll live. Feel like I've been kicked by a horse," she said as the grimace turned into a thin-lipped smile. "What about you?"

"Physically, I feel okay. I'm just feeling..." She shrugged. "Guilty I suppose."

"Guilty? What for?" Quinn twisted, stiffening with the movement. "Shit."

"That for a start." Natasha jutted her chin. "Him being here at all, I should have..."

"No, don't you do that." Quinn's smile turned serious. "Don't you take the blame for him? You are not responsible for what he chooses to do," Quin continued, "He's a sadistic bastard, and if I hadn't arrived back, I dread to even think what he was planning with that gas ring alight." She shook her head. "So no, you don't take that as your shit to own." Her arms reached around Natasha, pulling her closer. "It's not yours to own."

Natasha sobbed against her chest, and when Quinn finally relaxed, she found her own tears. The following morning, they were in the same position. The tears had stopped, and the exhaustion had taken over, but now as Natasha tried to move away, and Quinn tried to stretch, both women yowled laughing.

"Hell, I don't know if it's the bruises or because I haven't moved all night, but I am stiff." Quinn laughed as she rubbed the sleep from her eyes.

Yawning, Natasha nodded. "I agree."

"Maybe a nice bath would help," Quinn mused before remembering the last time she had suggested it. "I mean, it would be helpful...loosen your muscles and..."

"I'm not sure." Natasha bit her lip and quickly stopped as the cut split open. "Damnit."

Quinn reached over and gently swiped away the tiny dot of blood that had appeared. "How about I run the bath, make it all nice and relaxing, while you decide if you want to get in it, and if you decide not to, then I'll jump in."

Natasha's brow knitted. "Why don't you just have a bath anyway, you're in pain too."

"I'm going to, I was just being polite and letting you go first." She leaned in and kissed her cheek. "I'm still trying to impress you, even if the situation isn't the most romantic."

"It's funny, I never considered myself being with a woman before," Natasha admitted. "And yet, it feels like the most natural thing I ever did."

"I'll take that as a compliment." Quinn grinned, climbing out of bed. "Now, I'm going to run the bath. Be right back."

When Quinn returned, Natasha wasn't in the bedroom. She headed downstairs and found her, on her knees in the kitchen, picking up pieces of smashed crockery and glass and delicately placing each bit into a cardboard box. The one that had been home to Quinn's awards.

She looked up at the sound of footsteps and came to a halt. Frozen to the spot until she saw that it was Quinn.

"Hey, I can do that," Quinn spoke softly as she came closer and bent down to help. "The bath is ready."

"I...I don't think I can...I'm sorry." She stuttered. "Just the sound of the water running, it...it terrifies me."

"It's fine," Quinn said reaching out and taking her hand, stilling the movement from continuing to clean up. "Do you want to talk about it?"

"I don't want to burden you with that," Natasha answered honestly.

"It's not a burden," Quinn was saying before Natasha had the chance to continue.

"Okay, let's go into the lounge."

Chapter Twenty-Six

The day was cold, not just in the sense of the weather, but in her life. And it had been that way for a long time now. There was no one thought that had set things in motion, no one slap or punch that had pushed too far, it was just an accumulation of events and timing.

When she had set out that morning, she had no idea that she would end up sitting by herself on the sand contemplating just walking in and letting the waves take her. But that was what she had done.

She hadn't felt the cold either. It was like she was in a trance, everything around her just disappeared until all that was left was her internal monologue fighting back and forth with itself.

Nobody would miss her. She had no friends; he had made sure of that. Systematically pushing and pulling until even those who had clung and clung to keep her in their world simply gave up. Her family were dead, she had her work, that was all. But even there, she couldn't say that she really knew anyone well enough to call them her friend. His constant wearing down of her not to talk to anyone had gradually won out. Of course, she knew logically why he didn't want her to have friends and to talk to anyone. She might slip up and reveal his secret, not that people around her didn't know, hadn't seen the bruises she hid, of course, they had, but they never skirted the issue. Those who had tried to speak to her about it had easily been placated with a story, and in some ways, for that, she was grateful, or worse, they would try and force her to leave, to get help, the shame was unbearable.

Nobody had ever just given her a safe space to just be.

Until she met Quinn.

"Finding you, saved my life," she continued. "I'd never had anyone reach out the way that you did. No judgment, no shame. And it was nice to just have something that was mine, something safe." She smiled. Quinn remained quiet, waiting patiently until she was actually asked for input. Right now, this was Natasha's story to tell. "After the awards party, I fully expected rage, he'd been so aggressive all evening that...anyway, we got into the car, and he turned to me and smiled. It was unnerving because I wasn't used to that, I wasn't prepared for that. He said, "I know I have not always treated you right, I want to do better. I want to try again." And I was so shocked, and so relieved, that I just nodded. Then he kissed me. Like he used to do when we were dating." She wiped her mouth subconsciously and looked away, unable to stand the hurt in Quinn's eyes, hurt that she couldn't hide. "I'm sorry, shall I stop?"

"No." Quinn smiled sadly, reaching out to take her hands. "I want to hear your story."

"I know that it sounds ridiculous, that I knew it wouldn't last, but I needed to try. I'd always sold myself the story, the illusion, that one day he would come to his senses, and we would be happy again, and here he was...doing that, I put aside all thoughts of everything else...of you." She paused for a moment until she felt the gentle squeeze of encouragement from Quinn holding her hand. "For over a week, he was loving, attentive. We hadn't slept together as a married couple for a long time. He preferred the beds of his young assistants. I know," she acknowledged. "I knew he was sleeping around, and that benefited me, but now here he was, wooing me again, and when we went to bed, he made love to me. For a fleeting moment, I thought that we had turned the corner, I didn't know why, or what it was that had caused the change, and I didn't care. I had my husband back." She sat back and stared out of the window. "I know it was ridiculous, and I knew it wouldn't last."

"What happened?"

Natasha turned to Quinn, her eyes wet with tears. "I asked if we could have a baby." One tear broke the dam, followed by another and another. "He couldn't understand why I would want a child, wasn't he enough?"

"Fuck's sake." Quinn shook her head.

"I'm almost at the age where having children will be impossible, and here I was with the man...I should be able to say I loved, but I can't...I know that it wasn't love. A manipulation, he has...had a psychological hold on me, but he was all I had, and I wanted a child. I do want a child, though it's improbable now."

"You have options," Quinn offered. Children were not something she had considered, and she wasn't going to now. It was way too early in their relationship, and there were way too many issues to overcome before she would feel comfortable with planning a child in her future. But Natasha needed to know that she had options.

"Maybe, but I don't think the reality is that I'd be a good mother, not right now anyway. I'm too broken...I can't even get into a nice bath to soothe myself." She wiped her eyes with her sleeve. "I'm barely capable of looking after myself."

"Maybe right now that's true, but it's good to just know that the options are there, and if at any time you feel ready, then you can look into it." Quinn encouraged, "and I'll help if I can."

Natasha seemed to zone out for a moment, and Quinn was about to speak again when she said, "You know what? Maybe I will try that bath."

"Yeah?" Quinn beamed.

It was hard not to return the smile. "Ow." Natasha rubbed her lip. "Keep forgetting about that."

"You go up, I'll make us some coffee and bring one up to you? If you like?" Quinn offered.

She nodded. "That would be lovely."

Quinn got up and headed towards the kitchen but stopped at the door as a sudden thought struck her. "Do you...need any help?"

"Actually, would you come with me...just until I'm in and settled?"

"Of course."

~***~

The bathroom was still steamed up when Natasha nervously opened the door and stared in. She stood on the threshold and Quinn could tell she was debating whether she could actually go through with this.

"It's not the same." She whispered to herself. Taking a step forward, Natasha saw the mirror and froze, ready to turn and run.

"You okay?" Quinn asked, coming into view behind her. She watched as Natasha's vision moved to look at her.

"Yes, I just...for a moment it felt like I could see him, I know it sounds crazy..."

"It doesn't," Quinn reassured. "Your mind will probably play those tricks on you, you're traumatised."

Natasha turned to face her, "You're so very sweet and reassuring."

"Always." Quinn promised as she moved out of the way so that Natasha could look at the bath.

Bending a little, Natasha tentatively tested the water with her hand, ready to pull her fingers away quickly. "I remember enjoying a bath, before...before it became a punishment." She pulled her hand away from the water. "Scalding hot, but not enough to really burn me."

"I'm so sorry." Quinn said, passing her a towel to dry her fingers.

It was only then that she really looked around. "Oh, Quinn..."

Candles were lit in small lanterns, and something relaxing wafted in the air from a diffuser. There were bubbles, and to one side folded neatly, a washcloth and a fresh bath towel.

"I just wanted to make it something that maybe you can learn to enjoy again."

Natasha smiled at her. "You are wonderful."

Quinn blushed, but it didn't stop her from watching as Natasha stripped off, ignoring the sight of herself in the mirror, she climbed into the water. It was a process,

one foot, then the other, before she bent at the knees and sank down into the water. Remaining upright as she looked around again, "I'm safe." She said more to herself than Quinn.

"You are," Quinn confirmed. "I won't let anything happen to you."

Natasha nodded, breathed deeply a few times and then, gripping the sides of the bath, she gradually lowered herself backward. The water covered her little by little as slowly she leaned back against the coldness of the bath. There was a sharp intake of breath and Quinn flung forward preparing herself to lift Natasha out and wrap a towel around her. Until Natasha noticed the pained look on her face. "Just cold against my skin." She assured, slowly leaning back again.

Quinn let go of the breath she'd been holding.

"Safe," Natasha repeated. "It's safe."

"Okay?" Quinn asked when it looked as though she was settled.

Wordlessly, Natasha nodded.

"I'll go and get that coffee then."

~***~

"Hey, I got..." Quinn stopped mid-sentence at the sight of her lover's battered body half in and half out of the bath as she tried to get out as quickly as she could. "Sorry, I should have...damn," she scolded herself. She had planned to take the stairs quietly, but then considered that that might be worse if she just appeared without warning. "I'm sorry, I..."

Natasha looked up at her. Two mugs of coffee in her hands, and a look like that of a child who had been told off. She lifted her leg back into the bath and lowered again. "I'm alright," she said to Quinn.

"I just didn't know what was for the best, creep up quietly and scare the hell out of you when I opened the door, or just walk up and hope you'd know that it was me."

"Quinn? It's okay, honestly sweetheart, it's me, I'm jumpy and this is...well, this isn't my usual experience of a bath."

Quinn edged forwards and placed the mugs down on the corner of the bath. It was out of reach. Opening a cupboard, she pulled a short wooden board out and placed it across the bath in front of Natasha. Then she put the mugs on top. "Always handy for when I just want to lay in here for a while." She tried a nervous grin.

"Very handy," Natasha said, returning the smile. "Thank you."

"Everything okay? Can I get anything?" Quinn felt the need to fuss. She'd been feeling useless for months, and unable to do anything about it, but now, there was a lot to be done and she could throw herself into it if Natasha allowed her to.

"No, I'm good," she said, but her eyes became watery. "I'm sorry, I just...it's all been so..."

"Overwhelming?" Quinn answered for her. She dropped down and knelt beside the bath. "I'm here, okay?"

Natasha nodded. "I just think, am I ever going to feel safe? Really safe where the slightest little thing causes me to jump out of my skin and leave me...leave the people who care about me terrified to speak or move in case they cause a reaction?"

"Honestly, I don't know. I would hope that in time..." Quinn's fingers dipped into the water, it needed some heat, but she wouldn't interfere. "Maybe once he's been prosecuted things will feel differently?"

"Do you think they will? That he won't get off? He'll come for me again." Adamant and firm, Natasha stared at Quinn like a terrified rabbit caught in the headlights.

"No, he's going to prison for what he did," Quinn assured her, but the look on her face didn't change.

"I'm scared, Quinn. More scared than I've ever been."

"He's not touching you again. I won't let him."

"I know that you believe that, but I'm not sure...Quinn, I don't...I can't stand up in court and face him," she admitted. "Once the press finds out, it's going to be headline news...everyone will know."

"You have nothing to be ashamed of, nothing."

"And yet, that's exactly how I feel. Ashamed, embarrassed. I just want it all to end...I feel so useless," she sobbed.

"Shift forward," Quinn instructed before standing, kicking off her slippers, and climbing in behind her.

She squeezed herself behind her lover, pushed her legs down alongside her, and wrapped her arms around her. "Tasha, you are one of the most enduring women I have ever met. Your strength to get up each day and carry on regardless of any obstacle put in your way proves that you are far from useless. You are bright, funny, and tough. You are kind and I am so thankful to have you in my life, for however long you want to stay. I will never force you to do anything you don't want to do. And I will never give you any reason to fear me. I will stand by your side with any decision you make and if you don't want to face him, then that's alright." Natasha didn't move or say a word, but Quinn knew that she was listening. And when the sobbing quieted down to sniffles, Quinn added, "You are not alone any longer, baby."

It took a moment for Natasha to turn herself around. Staring intently into Quinn's eyes, Quinn held her gaze, determined not to falter now. She meant what she had said, she was in this if Natasha wanted her to be.

"You're wearing your clothes."

Quinn laughed at the simplicity of it. "Yes, yes I am." And when she finally smiled back, Quinn said, "Do you wanna get out of here and maybe get something to eat? Because I really need to get out of these clothes."

Chapter Twenty-Seven

Dressed again, and ready to spend the rest of the day on the couch with some old films and maybe a pizza delivery, Quinn was surprised to hear a knock on the door. She knew that it wouldn't be anyone to worry about, not with Gavin's security crew stationed outside still, but she wasn't expecting anyone except Detective Gomes, however, he said he would be calling ahead of time to check it was convenient.

Opening the door, she heard it creak, reminding her that she needed a new one. "Caroline?"

"Hi, I'm not stopping," she smiled, "I just thought I'd pop these in. I think you must have dropped them yesterday, so I picked them up and took them home." She handed over the shopping bags that Quinn had forgotten all about.

"Oh, thanks. You're right." She looked over her shoulder and considered whether Natasha would be alright with a visitor. "Do you want to come in?"

Caroline waved her off. "Another time, I've actually got to dash, I'm on babysitting duty and I am already late. But another time?"

"Sure, that would be great." Quinn waved and watched as she made her way along towards Cam and Michelle's place. Popping her head out, she noticed a black car parked two cars away. Two people sat inside watching the house. The woman, blonde and wiry-looking, waved and gave a confident nod. And as Quinn closed the door, she finally relaxed again.

"Natasha?" she called up the stairs as she began to ascend them. Her hands full, she swung the bags up in front of her and climbed almost two steps at a time until she reached the landing.

"Babe, I have something for you." She called out before entering the bedroom and finding Natasha sitting in a robe on the edge of the bed. Quinn's phone beeped as she stepped further into the room. Sliding it out of her pocket she read the text. "Gomes is coming over."

"Okay," Natasha said, looking pensive, she stared at the floor before she quickly changed the subject. "What's that?" she asked, looking up at Quinn and then down at the bags.

"So, I forgot all about these, Caroline just dropped them off. I stopped at the store on my way home yesterday and picked up some things for you." She dropped the bags down on the bed. "If you don't like them, I can take them back." She realized then that she was nervous. And then she realized why. Choosing someone else's clothing could be construed as controlling, and that was not what she intended Natasha to think or feel. "I mean, it's just a few things, you know, to tide you over until we can get your clothes, or you can buy some, or..."

Natasha smiled and stood up, rounded the bed to where she stood. She placed a finger against Quinn's lips and stopped her rambling. "Thank you, that was very thoughtful." She picked up on the bags and tipped out the contents, "I was just sitting here thinking I don't have anything to wear."

As she went through the bags and each item, placing them all neatly on the bed, she began to cry again.

"I'm sorry, I..." Quinn began, but Natasha turned quickly.

"Don't you dare apologize for doing something nice. I'm crying because it makes me realize how little I actually got with Nick. Not once did he ever think to buy me anything I might like, and yet, I saw his credit card receipts. I saw the gifts he bought his floozies. The only time he gave me anything was if it showed the world what he owned."

"I would never want to own you," Quinn said, brushing her lips with her own.

"Oh, Quinn, you are so wonderful. I wish I could be the person you deserve."

"You already are."

"I'm damaged," Natasha said, touching her mouth once more to stop the interruption that was coming. "Let me finish, I'm damaged Quinn, you cannot deny that. It is going to take more than kisses to fix me." She smiled at Quinn sadly. "I want so much to be enough for you, to be the person you can rely on to be there for you. Because I do love you, but that's why I can't be with you, not right now. You deserve more, so much more than I am able to give." Quinn didn't want to hear it, she turned to try and walk away, but Natasha held her firmly. "You need to listen to me, Quinn. I need to know that you understand. I can't ask you to wait for me. I won't ask you to do that."

"You don't need to ask me because I'd do it willingly."

"I know you would. And I love you for that." She cupped Quinn's face and gently wiped away the tears with the pad of her thumb. "It could take years before I am ready to be loved the way I know you can and want to love me."

"What are you saying?" Quinn asked, unable to make sense of things. They were fine a moment ago, weren't they? Where was this coming from?

"I am so grateful for everything that you are and for every minute I have spent with you. You loved me when I couldn't see what there was to love. But don't you see? I still don't see that and that's why you deserve better, you deserve someone that understands the way you feel about them and can accept it and treasure it. Right now, I am barely functioning..."

They were interrupted by someone knocking at the door.

"That's probably Gomes," Quinn stated the obvious. "Let's hear what he has to say and then..." She left it unsaid, but this conversation was far from over.

~***~

Gomes looked serious as he stepped inside and walked through to the lounge. His large frame waited patiently to be offered a seat. When Quinn inclined a hand towards the nearest, he sat down.

"How are you both doing?" he asked just as Natasha joined them.

"We have a lot to process," Quinn replied trying to keep her emotions in check. Her mind still whirring with all that Natasha had said. "Coffee?"

"No, thank you, just had one." He smiled. "So, let me get straight to the point, Mr. Miles was arrested this morning as he attempted to leave the hospital. At which point, he collapsed and went back into hospital, so I am unable to question him as yet, but we're used to these kinds of games."

"You think he was faking?" Quinn asked.

"I'm not a doctor, so I'll wait for their report, but off the record, they've already given me the heads up that Mr. Miles is fine and shouldn't be having any more health issues that stop him from facing the consequences of his actions."

"Right, so he's going to jail?" Quinn continued to question, aware that Natasha was yet to speak. She glanced around at her and noticed the tight-lipped grimace on her face. Her eyes steely as she stared at the wall behind Gomes.

"If it was down to me? I'd throw away the key, but that's something we will just have to wait and see, he's a wealthy man of good standing, and unfortunately, there are no priors. There is no evidence that he has done anything like this before."

"He beat the shit out of her for years," Quinn raved, rising up out of her seat to stand. She paced the room, breathing heavily until she could get herself back under control. That was when she looked at Natasha and saw the fear across her face. Her feet pulled up; arms wrapped tightly around her knees. "Shit, Tash, I'm so sorry." She dropped to her own knees in front of Natasha and cursed herself when she flinched away. "I didn't mean to...I just..." When there was no movement from Natasha, Quinn turned back to Gomes. "Do you see this? He did this." She was angry, angry that Nick Miles had caused so much pain to Natasha, and now, by proxy, she was going to lose her, because Natasha was right, she wasn't in any fit state to be in another relationship, no matter how much Quinn would love her.

Chapter Twenty-Eight

When Quinn rolled over in the bed that morning, she found the space where Natasha was sleeping empty. She felt the sheet with her palm and noted how cold it was. Natasha hadn't just gotten up.

Quinn stretched out her limbs, groaning as she felt the ache once more. It was getting better, or she was getting more used to the pain. Either way, it felt more comfortable. She swung her legs out of bed and listened. The house was silent.

"Tash?" she called out as she pulled on a robe and looked out of the window, the beach was quiet. A few people strolled along the shoreline, mostly with dogs or small children, but she couldn't see Natasha. "Tash?" she called again, as she hit the top step and made her way down. She had a sinking feeling hit the pit of her stomach. "Natasha?" she said more quietly as she searched first the lounge and then the kitchen.

She wasn't there.

Quinn moved back to the lounge and found her phone, picking it up she noticed the voice message icon flashing and swiped the screen to listen.

You were called today at 6.46 a.m., the mechanical robotic voice announced. Quinn checked her watch, it was almost 9 a.m.

"Hi…it's me, I'm sure by now that you've realized that I'm not there…" There was a pause. "I wish that things could have been different, that I'd met you years ago when I wasn't this broken wreck that I've become." Quinn could hear the emotion in her voice, the tears that were streaking down her face, it was all there in those words. She sniffed. "I love you, Quinn, of that much I am sure, and that is the reason that I'm doing this because I know that you won't, even though you know it's for the best, the best for you." More sniffles and the sound of a car horn blasting past. She was on the highway. "I'm going to go away for a while, find myself again. My hope is that you will be happy, in time. That you find someone who will love you how you deserve to be loved, who can be everything that I am unable to be, and maybe one day our paths will cross again. But promise me, Quinn, you won't try to find me, don't wait for me. Live your life. I'm going to switch this number off once I hang up. Take care."

There weren't many times in the life of Quinn Harper where she felt like her world had ended, but this was one of them. She crumpled, like an unwanted piece of paper that had been screwed up into a ball and tossed towards the wastepaper basket, only to miss and end up on the floor. She clutched the phone to her chest and wept. When the sobs subsided, she listened to the message again. And then she tried calling the number anyway, she had to be sure. It was unavailable.

And then she did something she hadn't expected she would do, she texted Caroline.

~***~

When Caroline arrived, two hours or so later, Quinn was dressed at least. She looked like crap, her eyes were swollen from all the tears, her nose was starting to turn red from how often she'd needed to blow it and her emotions were all over the place as she tried to figure out what had happened, and why Natasha had made this decision for them.

"Okay, let's get the kettle on," Caroline said as she waltzed in and took charge. "Go and sit down, I'll have some tea brewed in a minute and then we can talk it all out."

Quinn didn't question her except to say, "I don't have any tea or a kettle."

Caroline grinned. "Of course, you don't, but that's why I'm the Brit." She held open her shopping bag and pulled out a white china teapot. She placed that down onto the counter and then delved again, pulling a box of loose-leaf English tea out of the bag, and dropping it down next to it. "Now, sit. Here or the lounge, whatever works best."

Despite her upset, and the fact that her mind was awash with what if's, maybe's, and why's, Quinn was intrigued with the tea-making process. She'd never actually had English tea before. She pulled out a chair at the table and sat down.

"Alright, well if you're staying here, we might as well talk while I work." Caroline smiled as she filled a pan with water to boil. "I really don't know why America is so averse to a kettle," she complained.

"She left," Quinn blurted out, staring up at Caroline as though she might have all the answers.

"Yes, I figured that much when you text. Did she say why?"

"She's doing what's best for me," Quinn sneered. "Like I don't know what's best for me?"

"Is she wrong?" Caroline asked, gently but to the point. She found two mugs and placed them down next to the pot.

Quinn looked away.

"It must be very upsetting," Caroline continued when Quinn wasn't forthcoming with an answer. "Sometimes, it's not the people involved, but the timing."

"Is timing ever perfect though? Sure, it would have been hard work at times, I'm not so delusional that I didn't recognize that, but I know what I am capable of, and I could have dealt with it..."

"But maybe she couldn't?" Caroline offered. "Maybe there is more to this story, things she hasn't shared yet, trauma at that level can be very tricky, and she's a doctor, isn't she?"

Quinn bobbed her head in acknowledgment. "Yeah."

"Right, so she is maybe quite aware of her own physical and mental limitations, she has an understanding of her situation, both as lived experience, but also as a professional. She clearly has strong feelings for you, and you absolutely had to have had a huge impact on her, for her to have kept coming back the way she did. You gave her that safe space to finally see things more clearly so that she could escape her prison." The water boiled and she poured a little into the pot, swished it around, and then poured it down the sink. Quinn's brows knitted together in confusion and Caroline laughed. "Warming the pot, I don't know that it makes any difference, but my gran did it, so does my mother, so I do it." Picking up the tea leaves, she added two heaped spoons, and then another. "One for you, one for me, and one for the pot." Again, Quinn's brow furrowed. "Don't ask, ours is not to question why..." she quoted, stirring the pot with the spoon.

"I just wish that she'd said goodbye, not just sneaked off in the middle of the night."

"Of course, you do, because you are not thinking with the logic of a battered woman. Logically, she knows that you are safe, that you'd never hurt her, but she probably thought that about her husband once upon a time and look how that turned out. She lives in constant fear. Every person she engages with emotionally is a potential danger, but also, don't forget that she has strong feelings for you, and seeing you hurting will hurt her." She poured the tea into both mugs. "And she knew that you'd have tried to talk her round, wouldn't you? I know I would have."

Quinn couldn't deny it, of course, she would have. She'd have done anything, agreed to anything, and that was why, in her heart, she knew that Natasha was right, it wouldn't be what was best for her, it would have been what was best for Natasha, at the expense of Quinn.

"Why don't you do the same as her?" Caroline suggested.

"What do you mean?"

Caroline took a seat opposite and sipped at her tea. "Take a break, go away for a while?"

"And do what?"

Shrugging, Caroline said, "I don't know. Have an adventure, and explore the world. Have you ever left the States?"

"Does Hawaii count?" she smiled.

"No, definitely not." Caroline grinned. "There's an entire world out there Quinn."

"I know, I was kidding, I've done a few film fests and I mooched around upstate last year."

"Well, that was work, why not just chuck it all in and get out there, leave the country," Caroline dared. "What do you have to lose? Could be inspiring for whatever you write next."

"I guess...where would I go though?"

"Well, I know that if I had a word with my little sister, she would probably offer up her foreign abodes." Caroline winked.

"Abodes? Plural?"

Caroline nodded. "Oh yes. She's been quite smart and invested a lot into property. With a couple of days' notice, I could organize a European tour. There's the villa in Greece, the apartment in Paris, an old farmhouse conversion in Italy, she owns an entire block of apartments in Ibiza, but they're mostly rented out to young, hip kids who just want to get drunk and dance." She laughed. "Plus, we both have flats in London, Cam's is probably the nicer of the two."

"Wait..." Quinn waved her hands at her friend. "So, you're suggesting that I just head off abroad and float around Europe like a bum?"

Caroline stared at her. "Yes?"

Quinn flopped back in her chair. The idea was appealing, though she had never done anything like it in her life. She'd taken off last year for a few weeks to explore the western states, but that wasn't nearly the same as heading off to Europe and lording it up in Camryn's homes.

"And you're sure Cam wouldn't mind?"

"She's got the twins giving her the run-around, her wife is totally focused on this new film she's in. She's got the gym and the bar to organize ready for when they all take off back up north again, I'd say she would love someone popping over and making use of it all. I know they plan to head to Greece in a couple of months, and she does allow her staff to use the properties, I'd have to check if any are occupied."

"I dunno, it's a big step."

"It's a vacation. You're not working at the moment, you have the funds, you can pack up and go...do it."

Part Two

Chapter Twenty-Nine

In the almost six months that Quinn had been away, things had changed at the beach. Late September in Malibu was still warm, and people moved about on the beach enjoying it, but Cam and Michelle's home was closed up, the family having gone up north as planned. They had a place on the lake in Tahoe and had been back and forth for a while, but it was still a little weird to not have them around.

Her own home looked a little battered and weather-worn as she stood on the street outside and looked up at it. The door was new. Caroline had organized having a new one installed for her, and she had kept an eye on the place too, which was kind. It was strange to Quinn just how quickly she had become friends with Caroline. They'd talked on the phone every week as she had traveled, and she was looking forward to catching up and getting all the news about Cam and Michelle's new adventure. In some ways, she envied them. Especially now, when she had just enjoyed her own escape, but that was what it was, an escape, not an adventure. Now that she was home, she needed to face facts and reality.

London had been her first stop. She had stayed at Caroline's flat and for the first three weeks, she had wandered the city in a daze. Still heartbroken and unable to do much more than get up, eat, and sleep. But gradually, the pain lifted enough that she gave herself a mental slap. This was the opportunity of a lifetime, and she needed to enjoy it as best she could.

After a month, she headed to Paris. A month later, she was in Sorento, then onto the Greek island of Crete. She'd spent almost two months in Greece, island hopping. It had been the best experience of her life and she had fallen in love with the place just like Cam warned her she would.

The rest of her vacation had been spent back in London, this time at Cam's place on the river. She didn't waste any time moping around on her second visit and had felt much more like her old self. Throwing herself into the hustle and bustle a city like London had to offer.

But now she was back and ready to kickstart her career again and rebuild her finances. The trip had used up a big chunk of her savings. Pulling her wallet from her pocket, she slid out some cash and handed it to the cab driver when he'd put the last of her bags down on the sidewalk.

"Thanks," she said with a grin as she fished in her pocket again for the key.

One by one, she pushed and pulled the cases and bags until she had them all inside. It smelled clean, fresh flowers sat in a vase, and a small note leaned up against them.

"Hope you got home safe, I had the place spruced up and cleaned for you, so put your feet up and have a cuppa.

Caroline."

Quinn grinned to herself and wandered through the lounge and into the kitchen where she found the china teapot, two matching mugs and some tea leaves. Next to it was another note.

I am sure by now you know how to use these.

Caroline.

She smiled at the thoughtfulness of her new friend and made a promise to herself to one day pay her back.

~***~

Staying at Cam's place in London had had more advantages than she first thought. The number one being, that she had all of her washing done before she got home. All she needed to do now was unpack and put it all away.

It had cost a fortune in excess baggage fees, having left with one case and a shoulder bag, she had returned with three cases and a bigger shoulder bag. There had been a lot of things she wanted. Fashion in Europe was something else, and she found herself buying new clothes almost weekly. A couple of things she had shipped for fear of breaking them. Two beautiful lights with stained glass reminded her of the Tiffany-style, but with an Italian rustic feel that was just gorgeous and she knew they would look awesome in her living room. There were no large boxes in among the pile of letters that had been stacked neatly on the table, so she assumed they were still in the mail, so to speak.

She picked up the letters, rifling through them as she headed back into the lounge to sit at her desk and methodically go through them, but as she sat down, she caught a glimpse out of the window and at the spot where Natasha used to sit.

Not a day had passed that she didn't still think about Natasha, where she might be, what she might be doing, and if she was getting better. The sadness about it had evaporated over time, she'd even had a couple of flings while she was away, which had been a welcome distraction, but nothing had ever made Natasha disappear from her thoughts entirely, she wasn't sure anything ever would. Natasha Miles would always be the "what if" in her life.

She dropped the mail down onto the desk and grabbed her car keys. She hadn't driven much abroad, the odd car hire adventure somewhere remote, but on the whole, she had made use of the public transport available. She'd seen a lot of places and had a lot of ideas and was looking forward to putting her name back out there and getting another job.

But right now, she needed to do something, see it for herself.

Over the months while she was away, Detective Gomes had kept her up to date with Nick's case. Gomes was right about his wealthy lawyers and the grandstanding they maintained. They'd used every trick in the book, and Nick Miles was walking around scot-free. A slap on the wrists after he accepted a plea. The only good thing was that at least Natasha hadn't had to go to court, and neither had Quinn. And he was at least a social and employment pariah in Hollywood. Through the grapevine, Quinn had heard he had moved back to his home state and was keeping his head down.

Right now though, as she drove the winding bends of Laurel Canyon Boulevard, past Mt Olympus, she thought about Greece and how much she wanted to be there with Natasha. Showing her all of the amazing islands, sharing food and wine while they talked into the small hours. Wishful thinking, she knew, but did it hurt to hold onto hope?

She knew the address now. And as she slowed down checking numbers on the curb, she spotted it up ahead. Nick and Natasha had certainly been doing well, to the outside world they would have looked like the perfect Hollywood couple. Quinn gave a low whistle as the top of the property, what she could see of it behind the big gates and walls, came into view.

She couldn't see inside from where she was parked. Huge, whitewashed walls imprisoned it. Big wrought iron gates loomed impressively. She got out of the car and walked over to the gates. Peeking through them she could see that the windows were covered with shutters, but it all looked spotless. Someone was keeping it in good condition. For when Natasha comes home? Her hope for that would never dwindle. But then she saw it. To her right, a small sign read, "This property is currently for sale. For more details, please call Rick or Jan on..." Quinn pulled out her phone and called the number.

"Hi, this is Rick."

"Oh, hi...I was just driving past and uh...happened to notice a property you're selling up on Laurel Canyon."

"Oh, yes, that is some property too, I can tell you. Do you want to have a look around?" He sounded eager, which she assumed all realtors did when the potential for a sale this big meant a huge bonus at the end of the month. She felt a little guilty about that, she had no intention of buying the house.

"Uh, is it vacant?"

"Yeah, nobody had lived there for months. The owners have taken an extended break from LA." He spoke quickly.

Very diplomatic, Quinn thought.

"Sorry, what did you say your name was?" he asked, ready to make his sales pitch no doubt.

"You know what, on second thought, it's a little big for what I'm looking for." She lied a little lie, a white lie. She could live with that. "Thanks for your time." She disconnected the call before he could say another word.

Natasha wasn't here. She climbed back in her car and drove home.

Chapter Thirty

A few days had passed since she had arrived home, and she had caught up with

most of her friends. She'd even manage to go to grocery shopping and fill up the refrigerator But now she was feeling a little antsy, and she needed a job.

She took the coast road and drove down to Manhattan Beach, where she found herself sitting quietly inside a coffee shop looking through some options her agent had sent by email.

Molly's was quaint. Not too big, not too small, just the perfect number of tables and chairs to cope with the incoming footfall of people passing by and needing a refreshment.

Quinn ordered an energizing smoothie and a muffin, which she'd eaten the moment she had taken a seat, but now, with her laptop out and her phone at the ready, she was about to start making the calls.

"Quinn? Quinn Harper? Is that really you?" a man's voice said to the side of her. She glanced at him quickly and then again properly.

"Jerry?" Quinn grinned, standing up to hug him. "How are you?"

"I'm good, wow, it's been a while, huh?"

Quinn offered him a seat at the table, and he sat down, placing his cup down. "Six, seven months?"

"Yeah, well that's a lifetime in this town, right?" he laughed. "Man, it's good to see you. We were only talking about you the other day."

"Yeah, not all bad I hope?" Quinn chuckled and picked up her drink.

Jerry waved her off. "God no," he snickered, "No, we had a couple of writers get a new gig, left us in the lurch."

Now Quinn really laughed. "Reminded you of me? That's funny."

"So, it has been a while huh?" he repeated, "How ya doing, Quinn?"

"I am doing pretty good thanks, you're still on the show then?" She hadn't really watched much TV while she was away. Most of it was with Greek or Italian dubbing, and more often than not, she was busy exploring or sleeping to recover.

"Yeah, just back after summer hiatus. We got a new producer after... well, you know all about Nick, right?" he said all knowingly. Of course, the story had hit the news and gossip had been rife about who knew what. "He lost his job, of course, the network refused to release him from his contract which technically means he is unable to work anywhere else for the next five years." Jerry chuckled, "Serves the asshole right, huh?"

"Yeah, I heard," Quinn said trying not to get drawn into a conversation about Nick Miles and his wife. The last thing she wanted to do right now was discuss Natasha and add fuel to the gossip.

"Anyway, Abi Marsh, you heard of her, right?"

"Sure." Abi Marsh was an up-and-coming producer and director, she'd worked on some great shows already and was definitely on every *next big name in Hollywood* list.

"So, when are you going to come back to work?" he asked her in all seriousness.

"I don't work there anymore Jerry; you know I resigned."

"Oh, that's just semantics, you know they would have you back if you wanted it." He roared loudly, completely unaware of exactly how loud he was, it was one of the things she loved about him. He had this way about him that was just infectious, if he laughed then you wanted to laugh too.

"Well, I am not so sure that I do want it," she replied taking a sip of her coffee now that it was at a temperature her mouth could tolerate. The idea of walking back into that studio, with the memories it would evoke. Might not be the best idea she ever had.

He stopped laughing, staring at her across the table with a serious expression on his face. "Quinn, you were the best we had. We only won that award because you wrote the scripts, they judged it on."

"That's sweet of you to say Jerry, it really is, and I appreciate it but..."

"But what? Come on Quinn you're a writer and a damn good one. Come down to the studio and have a chat with the new producer. She's pretty good and well if you're still single, she's a looker." He laughed so loudly that other people turned to see what was so funny.

Quinn grinned at his enthusiasm. Would it really work? Going back on the show? It was certainly an easy option if it could be arranged. But the ghost of Nick Miles was raw. "I'll think about it Jerry, okay?" she said more to end the conversation than to actually agree. "

"Yeah, do that. I'll see you around, Quinn, don't be a stranger."

She leaned back in the chair and stared out of the window for a moment, her thoughts as always going to Natasha and wondering what she was doing, where she was in the world.

"Can I get you another?" The bright chirpy voice brought her back to reality. The name badge read Molly; the owner Quinn assumed.

"Yeah, why not. Thanks." As the woman walked away, she thought again about *Jackson & Jones*, maybe it was an option.

~***~

For the rest of the week, all Quinn could think about was *Jackson & Jones*. She spent an entire afternoon watching re-runs and catching up on what she had missed while she was away. She'd loved working on the show, but she could see that there had been some changes since she had left, and not all of them worked for her. But the biggest thought she had was, that they removed Nick, and what really was stopping her? Not to mention that Jerry text almost every day. He'd even spoken with the new producer, and she had been more than interested in the possibility of Quinn Harper re-joining the writing staff and having a meeting with her.

So, that's what she did.

The following Monday, Jerry met her at the gate. She'd sold the idea to herself that she was just catching up with some old friends and that if nothing came of it then it wouldn't matter, but secretly, she was excited about the prospect of working again with this ensemble.

As they crossed the lot, she noticed Riley and Jane getting out of their car and heading towards Stage 4, where *J&J* was currently filming.

"Quinn? You back?" Riley shouted, instantly turning Jane to look in the same direction. Then the pair all but skipped across the tarmac until they were face to face. "It's good to see you. You look really well!"

"Hey, yeah, been away traveling, I guess it looks good on me, huh?" Quinn replied, genuinely happy to see these two again. Jane reached forward and pulled Quinn into a hug.

"It's so good to see you. We were worried about you," she said sadly. "You know we came round to yours, but you'd already left."

"You did? Well, I am sorry that I missed you, but yeah, I needed to get away for a bit. Best thing I ever did though, I recommend it."

"So, you back or what? Cos, no offense, Jerry," Riley said, her voice low and secretive, "but some of the lines I've been fed lately..." She raised a brow and rolled her eyes all at once, which was something Quinn didn't think was physically possible until she just witnessed it.

"I'm here to see old friends and have a chat with Abi...who knows."

Jane jumped up and down like a child, clapping excitedly. "She's coming back."

"I didn't say that." Quinn laughed. She checked her watch. "Listen, let's catch up soon, okay? But I gotta get going, Abi is expecting me."

"Go, go, go...we're going to tell her to sign you up though," Jane called after her.

"You do that."

~***~

Abi Marsh was persuasive, laid back, and resolute. Jerry was right, she was a looker. Not in the glamourous Hollywood style that one might expect. She was understated. Casually dressed in beige cotton slacks and a white blouse, her jacket hung on the back of her seat. She wore heels and just a smidge of make-up. Not that she needed it, her fresh-faced look only made better by the smattering of freckles that usually came with a natural redhead.

"I want you on the show, Quinn," she announced before they'd barely gone past the pleasantries.

Quinn fiddled with some fluff on her sweater before she looked up and smiled at Abi. "That's nice to hear."

"Good, because the fact is, the show is..." She leaned forward in her seat and looked Quinn directly in the eye. In any other circumstance, Quinn would have seen the move as a flirtatious come on. "Ratings are lower than we want. And if something doesn't change soon, then..."

"The networks are threatening to pull the plug?"

She nodded. "I was brought on board to make changes, and we've pulled in some better figures since then, but...I know we can do more. We can take this show back to the top and into the awards arena again, but only if we have the best writers on staff, and that's you as far as I am concerned. When you were here before, the writing was sharp, it was edgy and dynamic...that's what I want now."

Feeling her ego suitably massaged, Quinn smiled at the compliments. "My reticence isn't the show itself...I have a history..." She tailed off as Abi grinned.

"I know all about the Nick Miles issues, he's gone. This isn't the same show. If you came back, it would be as head of the department, and it would be double what you were earning before. I'm willing to put my money where my mouth is, Quinn. Forget Miles, he's done. History. Don't let his story become yours."

"Can I think about it?" Quinn asked.

Abi considered it. Then with a small tilt of her head, she leaned forwards again and smirked. There was something else there too, Quinn noticed, attraction. "I tell you what, give me your answer over dinner tonight."

Now it was Quinn's turn to consider things. "Is this a business thing, or are you asking me out on a date?"

Sitting back, totally relaxed, Abi rested her palms on the arms of her chair. "Both. It's a win-win."

A date? Did she really want a date? But as she looked at this woman and considered what other options she had on the romance front, would it hurt? It was just a date. She found herself smirking back as she casually said, "Alright."

"So, I'll see you at 7, Marcello's?" Abi stood up and reached out a hand. Which Quinn took, noticing the little spark of something between them ignite. Abi let her fingers slide slowly from Quinn's grip but kept her eyes on Quinn's. "I look forward to it."

Chapter Thirty-One

She hadn't been on a date in a while, a couple of hook-ups with tourists on her travels hadn't exactly been dating. Abi Marsh was classy, and Marcello's was somewhere you dressed up for. So, Quinn searched through her wardrobe looking for the perfect outfit. She wanted casually sophisticated. Something that she would feel comfortable in and yet still look stylish. By the fifth change, she was getting frazzled.

"Caroline, I need your help," she said the minute her friend answered the phone.

"With?" came back the quick response. Her voice sounded distant. On a hands-free in the car.

Quinn flopped down onto the bed. "I have a date."

"Hm maybe Cam is best for this conversation," Caroline joked.

"I don't need that kind of advice, thank you, I am quite adept in that department...I think," she said, suddenly doubting everything. "I need clothing advice."

"Oh, and you thought of me?"

"Strangely, yes. You always look so put together, and I need to look sophisticated but casual, you know?" Quinn explained, trying not to feel like a complete idiot and doing a bad job of it.

"Okay, well I'm on my way over to Camryn's with Andrea, we will stop in and give you the *queer eye*. Well, Andi will, I'll just nod."

Quinn couldn't help but smile. "Alright, hurry up." She looked at her watch again. Almost 4 p.m.

"What time is this date?"

"Seven," Quin stated urgently.

"Oh, for goodness' sake, sit tight, we will be there as soon as..." She disconnected the call and Quinn fell backward on the bed.

When Andi and Caroline arrived 30 minutes later, Quinn had calmed her nerves a little. Not a lot, but a little. She'd spent the last half an hour in her head, convincing herself that this was no big deal. She was entitled to go on dates, and she was definitely entitled to enjoy them.

"Right, what have we got to work with?" Andi said, taking charge as she led the way up the stairs. "I assume you do have clothes worth wearing." She winked.

"I mean, I have some nice stuff, I'm just not sure if it's suitable," Quinn replied, pushing past, and opening the door to her room and all of her good clothes that were currently on the bed, discarded.

"Okay, so this date. What's she like?" Caroline asked. "I work best with all of the information." She laughed.

"Well, she's gorgeous and accomplished, classy," Quinn blushed before continuing, "she's also potentially my new boss."

Andi and Caroline looked at one another and smirked.

"I see..." Andi broke the silence. "And so you need to impress on two fronts?"

Quinn nodded. "I guess, yes...but also, feel comfortable, it's the first date in a long time and I'm kind of nervous," she admitted.

"What are you nervous about? You're everything you just described your date as being," Caroline assured. "What about this?" she said, picking up a red blouse. "It's perfect with your skin tone, you can carry it off. Add it to a pair of pants that show off your arse, and boom, you're in business."

Andrea chuckled. "I have to agree, if Ren arrived like that, I'd devour her."

Quinn raised a brow. "Okay, ladies, can I remind you that this is a first date, and potentially my new boss."

Caroline shrugged. "So? Look, her being your new boss isn't the issue, otherwise, you wouldn't be going on a date with her...so, let's cut to the chase. You're attracted to her, right?"

She couldn't deny it. Caroline could read her like a book. "Yeah, of course, but..."

"No." Caroline held up a hand. "No buts, Quinn. You're heading out on a date with a hot woman, one you readily admit that you fancy the pants off of, whether you sleep with her or not, you want her to want to. That's the game. Now, get dressed, and then we will decide whether it works or not."

"You know, I kind of like this bossy attitude of yours," Quinn said.

Caroline didn't even blush. "Clearly." She winked.

When Quinn returned, Andi stood there holding out a pair of shoes. "Put these on."

"You too?" Quinn mused with a grin. "Is it a British thing that women are bossy?"

"No, it's a femme thing, gay or straight, we know what you want," Andi said seriously before breaking out into a smile. "Which is why we're here? Right?"

"I guess," Quinn agreed, pushing her feet into the shoes. When she stood up and straightened her shirt, Andi and Caroline both nodded.

"Perfect, don't you agree?" Andi said, turning to Caroline.

"Absolutely," Caroline said. "Do you feel comfortable?"

Quinn turned and studied herself in the mirror. She looked good, more than good. "Yeah, thanks."

"Okay, our work here is done. We must be off; we have cocktails around the pool."

"Wait, aren't Cam and Michelle away?" Quinn quizzed.

Caroline raised a perfectly plucked brow. "And? What's Cam's is mine... as they say... it's too nice a day not to enjoy a sunset on the beach with a margarita or two. I would say join us but..."

"Well, have fun then." Quinn grinned at her new friends.

"You too, Quinn." Andi winked before dragging Caroline by the arm and out of the room.

Now, as Quinn stood in the middle of the room by herself, she chanced another look in the mirror. She did look good, she had to agree.

"Well, I guess we will see what Abi thinks."

Chapter Thirty-Two

Marcello's was busy; it usually was. But being a Monday in October, it wasn't packed, and it wasn't filled with celebrities hoping to get pictured by a waiting paparazzi. When Quinn climbed out of the cab, there were no photographers in sight, which was pleasing. Not that they were ever bothering her, but Abi might be a different matter. Her face was a recognizable one within Hollywood circles.

Sitting at the table by herself, she sipped on her drink; a Gin Rickey was just perfect to start her evening off. A few minutes early, she hadn't minded waiting in the bar and taking a moment. She checked her watch for the fifteenth time and just as she looked up, she saw her. A vision in white. Sweeping into the restaurant like she was the movie star they all expected.

"Oh, boy," Quinn muttered to herself before she chugged down the rest of her drink for Dutch courage. Her eyes watched as Abi spotted her. Maintaining eye contact, she smiled and walked towards Quinn as she spoke quickly with the maître d' about their reservation.

"Quinn, you're early," she said, leaning forward to kiss her cheek.

"And you are simply stunning," Quinn replied, enjoying the light blush that appeared on Abi's face, her cheekbones highlighted even more.

"Thank you. You look very dashing," she winked. Quinn mused over the description, dashing? She could go along with that quite happily.

"So, shall we eat, or would you like a drink first?" Quinn offered, thumbing at the bar over her shoulder.

"We could do both?" Abi suggested with a smirk that Quinn found rather enticing. A little too enticing, maybe this shouldn't have been a business dinner at all.

"Lead the way."

~***~

They were seated in a cozy little corner that Abi had requested. The lighting was a little more subtle here, and they could speak freely without being overheard.

"This is my favorite spot," Abi announced once the waiter had taken their order for drinks and appetizers.

"The restaurant, or this table?" Quinn asked unable to take her eyes away from Abi for a moment.

"Both?" she said slowly, keeping their eyes locked. "So, I'm going to put it out there right now, so we're both clear and on the same page. I'm not the only one getting the vibe that this isn't just business, right?"

Quinn chuckled and was about to respond when the waiter reappeared with two glasses and the bottle of wine they'd ordered. She waited, watching Abi watch her, as he poured the drinks. When he left, she said, "I think I understand the vibe too."

"Good, because I was about to make a complete fool of myself otherwise," Abi admitted.

"How so?"

Abi took a sip of the deep red liquid. There was definitely something mulling over in her mind, Quinn thought. When the edges of Abi's mouth curled up, Quinn knew she had concluded something.

"Let's eat and then discuss it later," Abi teased rather than sharing her idea.

"Alright, work it is...for now."

"Good, let's get that out of the way." Abi continued to grin, confident and unashamed of who she was. "I want you on the team, running it, it's that simple. So, tell me what it's going to take?"

Sitting back in her chair, Quinn considered what it was she did want. She wasn't a greedy woman, but hell, she wanted what she was due, but it was more than the money and title, it was the show itself. "The thing is, it's not about the money. You can negotiate all of that with my agent."

Abi leaned her elbows on the table and sat her chin on top of her hands. "Alright, you've intrigued me, go on."

"When we first started with the show, the one thing Nick was hot on, was that he wanted an edgy, almost darker shadow around Riley's character. And it worked, the audience is always left not quite knowing how far she will go for justice. They love that she takes no shit, and that Jane's character, though the more logical and methodical, backs her up. The on-screen chemistry between the pair is obvious, but..." She paused and took a mouthful of her drink, making sure that Abi was still intently listening, which she was. "Recently, there's been this shift and minor characters have been pushed forward, with humor...why?"

"Well, we had some issues with Lisa and Tom. They felt that they weren't being used to their best ability and their agents pushed for more airtime. The network agreed."

"And they wanted them to be funny?" Quinn asked, incredulous that anyone would agree to it in the first place.

"That came from the writers, and the actors...there was a half a season where the network panicked. They'd lost Nick and getting a new producer in mid-season was going to be difficult, so they settled for guest directors. It was a mess. Every week a different direction.

The writers just did their best." Abi shrugged. "But I agree, it's not what we want for the show. Which is why I want you back."

"I have a lot of ideas about Riley's character, and if I had my way, I'd be making them a couple on-screen too."

Abi laughed. "Okay, I can get a lot past the networks, but I'm not sure they're ready for that yet."

"Well, let's find out. TV is so far behind. Look at the streaming platforms and the characters they're creating. They've got a handle on it. They just nonchalantly mention same sex coupling as though it's no big deal, because it's not," she insisted.

Abi threw her hands up. "Hey, you're preaching to the converted, really converted," she assured, eyes narrowing.

Laughing, Quinn sat back. "Okay, so you know where I am coming from? If we want this show to really make its mark, we have to start letting the characters out of their little boxes and into the real world."

"I'll speak to the guys in charge and pitch the idea, but I'm making no promises," Abi acquiesced. "Now, do we have a deal?"

"I guess we do." Quinn held up her glass to toast the agreement.

"Great. I'm looking forward to new endeavors."

~***~

Walking down Melrose towards the boulevard, Abi linked her arm through Quinn's. West Hollywood was alive and vibrant tonight as it was any night. Music blasted from clubs and bars, drag queens wandered past looking like goddesses. Abi's apartment was right in the heart of it, and Quinn wondered how anyone could actually live here. It was a fun place to visit, but the noise was just too much. Or maybe she had just gotten too used to the quiet of the beach.

"Quinn, I have had a really lovely evening and I'd like it to continue but..." Abi faltered. For the first time, Quinn witnessed that small chink in her confident armor. "The thing is...I am not looking for anything serious."

"What makes you think I want anything serious?" Quinn responded. In all honesty, she had no clue what it was she wanted. Not in the long term, her heart was still elsewhere, she knew that much. But right now, at the moment, she couldn't deny that she wanted Abi Marsh.

"I just want to be clear. We will be working together, and I don't play favorites. I find you very attractive, and I'd like to invite you back to mine so that we can..." She leaned in close and put her lips to Quinn's ear to whisper. "Fuck. But if that's going to create an issue at work, then I guess I'll be spending the rest of the night alone."

As Abi stepped back, Quinn threw out a hand and caught her arm, pulling her back towards her until they were almost touching. She took a moment to study Abi's face. Those green eyes, that's what it was, reminding her so much of Natasha. She couldn't help herself, when she glanced down at ruby red lips, parted and wet. Pressing her lips against them, she felt Abi melt into her and couldn't help the smirk that appeared on her lips as they kissed. "I think going back to yours to fuck sounds like a great idea."

Chapter Thirty-Three

The key turned in the door and as they entered the condo, Abi twisted around and seized Quinn around the neck, pulling her inside and into an embrace that was hot and languid. Quinn took the initiative, and pushed her new boss back against the wall, intensifying the kiss as hands joined the party. Tugging and lifting clothing out of the way as the chemistry between them both ignited.

A picture of something arty in black and white fell off the wall and landed with a clatter on the floor.

"Shit," Quinn said, jumping back, ready to clean up the mess of glass that scattered the floor.

"Leave it," Abi purred, pulling Quinn by the hand until they were inside the lounge and kissing again. She kicked off her shoes. "You're a good kisser," she said continuing to nip at Quinn's lips between her own.

"Never had any complaints," Quinn bragged with a quick smirk as Abi pulled back and turned around. She lifted her hair out of the way and glanced back over her shoulder, aware that Quinn knew what she was asking.

Wasting no time, but in no hurry, Quinn slid the small metallic zip down, revealing pale, freckled skin. She bit her lip, considering all the places she wanted to kiss and touch this woman.

Circling around again to face Quinn, Abi watched her as she let the dress fall away, leaving her in nothing but her panties. White silk, with a small red bow on the front, that made clear Abi was a gift worthy of unwrapping.

"You gonna just stand there gawping." Abi grinned.

Quinn looked up from where her gaze was wandering and caught the glint in Abi's eyes. "For a bit, yeah," she teased but meant every word of it, this wasn't a moment to rush. "I mean, you're..."

Abi stepped closer. "I'm?"

Their mouths were barely apart. "Yeah, you're..." Abi pressed their lips together and cut her off.

"Finished talking?" Abi asked, unbuckling Quinn's belt, and loosening her pants. "Because these need to go." They fell with gravity to the floor and Quinn kicked them and her shoes off. When she was done, Abi pressed a palm against her chest, and pushed until the back of the couch hit Quinn's calves and she dropped into the seat, with Abi following.

"So, are you shy, Quinn?" she asked with deft fingers plucking the buttons undone on Quinn's shirt. She tilted her head a little as she said it, eyes boring into Quinn's.

"No, not shy. Just in no rush."

"No rush? You mean I'm not getting you all hot?" She leaned into Quinn's ear as the last button gave way. "Wet?"

Quinn reached up, thread her fingers through her hair, and tugged her to where she wanted her. In front of her face, where she could stare into those eyes, and kiss that mouth. "I'm plenty hot, and wet," she boasted. "Why don't you find out?" She let go of the handful of hair and moved her hand away. "Unless you're too important to get on your knees?"

Abi pressed her tongue into the side of her cheek as she smirked at Quinn and slithered from her lap to the floor, and her knees. "I can do as I'm told, so long as you can." Her head dipped lower, her eyes remaining where they were, fixed with Quinn's until that moment when her tongue took its first taste. Swiping upwards, teasingly slowly. Quinn's eyes closed, her head fell back, and a small groan emitted from between her own lips as Abi's wrapped around her clit and sucked. "Like that, huh?" Abi stated, the question didn't need an answer.

When Quinn came, she noted the lack of inhibition she had felt. She didn't think about anything, it was all just a natural progression. Abi was a woman who knew what she wanted and took it. That was a huge turn-on for Quinn.

"Come back up here," she summoned Abi, who eagerly crawled her way back up to straddle Quinn's thighs, pressing herself down, her hips undulating against the strong muscle. They kissed, languidly until Abi pulled away, breathing heavily.

"I need you to fuck me," she purred, rising up, she looked down into Quinn's eyes as her hand reached for Quinn's and brought it between her thighs. Quinn could feel the heat of her instantly as she cupped and pressed against her with the heel of her palm.

Enjoying the sighs and groans, Quinn prolonged the teasing until warm breath hit the outer shell of her ear and the wanton voice pleased.

"Inside, I want you inside me."

Deftly, Quinn slid the flimsy material barrier aside, her fingertips tantalisingly close to following the instructions,

"Quinn, don't fucking tease..." She felt Abi's fingers grip her shoulders and dig in.

Holding off just a moment longer, Quinn could see the words begin to form in the shape of Abi's mouth, before she could utter them, Quinn thrust into her. Abi's breath caught in her throat, and she gasped when Quinn slowed her movements to perfectly pressured, timed strokes.

"Don't you dare stop." Abi warned as her back arched and she leaned backward a little, pressing her clit into Quinn's palm.

For the first time in her sexual life, Quinn felt free. She didn't stop, not until Abi fell against her, slick with perspiration. Before she could barely get her breath back, Quinn flipped her onto her back on the couch and buried her face between her legs. Hungry to take her. Abi Marsh, naked, wanton, and demanding, was just the someone that Quinn needed right now.

She hadn't even felt guilty when at 4 a.m., she had climbed out of bed and wandered out naked into the lounge to get dressed. She left Abi sleeping and flagged down a passing cab. Sitting in the back seat with the biggest smile on her face.

Chapter Thirty-Four

At work on Monday morning, Quinn walked into a room full of smiling faces. Half hadn't known she was returning; the other half had been prepared and a huge "welcome back" banner hung across the back wall.

"Good to have you back, Quinn," one person said, patting her on the shoulder. Quinn had no idea yet who he was, but that would soon be remedied.

"Thanks, looking forward to getting back into it," Quinn replied.

When Abi appeared a few minutes later, all business and the epitome of professionalism, Quinn couldn't have been happier. There was nothing worse than an atmosphere at work, whether it was a hostile or amicable environment. Any whiff of romantic interludes between staff was usually picked up on if things spilled over, and both parties would become the gossip for months.

"So, everyone, as you've all seen we are extremely lucky to have Quinn Harper back with us and that means I am expecting something from you guys that is going to blow my mind, so, enjoy this happy little reunion, but then back at it. Get into that groove and give me something I can work with." She smiled amiably at everyone before turning to Quinn. "Can I have a word when you get a moment?"

"Sure, gimme a few minutes with these guys and then I'll head over to your office," Quinn answered casually.

"Great, thanks." Abi didn't wait for a response, she turned on her expensive heels and left the room. And Quinn knew full well, that Abi was very aware she was watched the entire way.

Quinn spent the next few minutes happily and politely chatting to her colleagues. They bandied about some wild ideas for a story, laughed at some ridiculous ones, and then agreed on a middle ground. A few of the ideas were good, and definitely something Quinn could work with. Quietly, she excused herself and left the room.

It was a little surreal walking the corridors again. Now and then she would see or hear something, and it would remind her of Nick, and then her brain would switch automatically to Natasha. It had been almost nine months now, and still, her heart pined quietly in her chest. A deep longing that she assumed would never leave, always a *what-if* scenario. Knocking on Abi's door though, at least distracted her from her thoughts.

"What's up?" she asked once she'd heard the permission to enter.

"Nothing, I just wanted to have a little chat and make sure we're still on the same page." All business and professionalism, Quinn still liked it. She sat behind her desk, everything neat and tidy. Her hair was up with light make-up. She looked stunning as usual, and Quinn felt herself clench within her core.

"Alright." Quinn took a seat, got as comfortable as she could under the circumstances of her arousal, and sat back, relaxed, and listened. "Go ahead."

Abi sat back in her own chair and cocked her head as she considered what she wanted to say. "As much as I do enjoy this slightly arrogant attitude. I just want to make sure that you understand that at work, we're just colleagues. What we do outside of work is just fun."

"So far, the same page." Quinn nodded.

"Good, I didn't want any miscommunication."

"No, I agree." Quinn nodded again. "I do have a question though."

Abi leaned forward and rested her arms on her desk. "What's that?"

Quinn met her move for move and leaned forwards until she too was resting her arms on the desk. "Do breaks count as work or out of work in this scenario?" She watched as Abi's eyes darkened, the tip of her tongue poking through her lips as she considered that.

"As tempting as that is, I think it's best to keep a professional image at work, and maintain very clear boundaries, don't you?"

Quinn's eyes narrowed. "Definitely."

"Good. You may go," Abi said, now sitting back in her seat. Quinn stood, ready to leave. "Oh, Quinn?" Abi called just as Quinn reached the door. When her lover turned to face her, she added, "Tonight? My place?"

"Sure."

~***~

It was a rush, turning up at Abi's knowing full well that the only reason she was invited was for sex. She didn't need to be charming, or romantic, bring flowers or any other little gift of endearment, or even think about anything. Instead, she was greeted at the door by a half-dressed goddess, who just wanted to get off.

"Knees," Abi ordered the moment the door was closed behind Quinn.

She wasted no time in acquiescing to the demand. Looking up at Abi, Quinn hooked her fingers into lace and slid it down to mid-thigh. She watched for a moment as Abi squeezed and palmed her own breasts, mewling and writhing against the wall in anticipation of Quinn's tongue or fingers. It was an image Quinn loved the most.

Quinn slowly dragged the material further down till it lay on the floor, looped around both ankles. Her fingers wrapped around the left and lifted it enough to slide the underwear off, and then she nudged at Abi's knees until she widened her stance enough that Quinn was happy.

"I wanted you on my desk this morning," she admitted before groaning out loudly as Quinn made her move. The heat of her tongue wet against her flesh made her legs wobble momentarily.

"I know," Quinn replied between swipes.

"Maybe this was a bad idea," Abi said, her hand landed on the back of Quinn's head and tugged at her hair until she was pressing more firmly.

"True, we should stop," she said, gasping a breath between words.

"Yes," she cried out, "we should." Abi panted, gasping she gripped Quinn's head with two hands and held her in place as her hips moved involuntarily against Quinn's mouth.

Quinn could no longer speak; she had a choice of words or air between strokes and decided air was her best chance of continuing this in the long run, because she was really enjoying this distraction.

Abi came with a shudder, holding Quinn to her until every ripple of orgasm had ripped through her. When she released her grip, Quinn fell backwards onto her butt. Breathless and gasping for air.

"I knew this was a good idea." Abi laughed. "Meet me in the bedroom."

Chapter Thirty-Five

Lying in bed, sated, and as relaxed as she had been in months, Quinn rolled over and checked the clock. Eleven. She'd been here for four hours and missed dinner, and yet, she didn't feel hungry at all.

"I spoke to Riley and Jane about your idea," Abi said, rolling over and tucking herself into Quinn's side.

"Which one?"

"The one where we make them an on-screen couple," Abi answered, leaning up on an elbow, she let the fingers of her other hand play lazily with Quinn's nipple. Soft fingers pinching gently as she pondered the point.

"And what did they say?"

"They're up for it but have concerns." She hooked a leg over Quinn's and pressed herself tightly against her. "If it became known about their off-screen relationship, it could be damaging for their careers," she said, rolling up and over but keeping herself pressed against Quinn's thigh. Quinn watched with an amused look on her face.

"You're insatiable, you know that, right?"

"Mm, I am, which is why I don't get into relationships," she admitted, "Now, are you going to make me do all of the work?"

"I think I am." Quinn chuckled, pulling her arms up and tucking her hands under her head. "It's a great visual, and I am all about the visuals."

"You're an ass." Abi grinned, moving her hips back and forth with more speed against the firmness of Quinn's thigh. Her palms moved to Quinn's chest to rest upon her bare breasts.

"So, are we going to put them together?" Quinn asked, bringing the conversation back to work. Pulling her hands free, she gripped Abi's hips and took control of the tempo of her thrusts. "Not so fast, I'm enjoying this."

Abi groaned and tweaked Quinn's nipples in protest. "I want to come."

"You will," Quinn promised. "So, are we going to?" She watched and grinned as Abi's torso began to shake. Her muscles contracting, sweat slowly dripping between her breasts.

"Please," she begged as Quinn used her strength to hold her still. "Please."

"You haven't answered my question." Quinn found her eyes and held them. "Are we putting them together?"

"I need to run it past..." She clenched her thighs around Quinn. "Please, for fuck's sake, Quinn."

"The networks?" Quinn grinned.

"Yes. The fucking network, now..." Before she had a chance to finish making her demands, Quinn flipped her onto her back and thrust into her. Hard, fast thrusts that had Abi's back arching and her toes curling within minutes.

When she finally stopped writhing, panting, and cursing Quinn, Abi collapsed against the sheets. "Fuck you." She grinned, as Quinn kissed her neck and shoulders. "Fuck you."

"You will, in a minute." Quinn laughed. "And then you can get your own back."

"Hmm, maybe."

Quinn laughed again. "Pretty sure you will."

Rolling over and on top of Quinn, Abi grinned. "You're pretty good at that. How did you know I'd like it?"

"Well, without wanting to stereotype..." She smirked and leaned up to capture Abi's lips quickly. "A lot of women in high powered positions tend to need to...let go, give up control in bed sometimes. They spend their life having to make all the decisions, and mostly they will still be very...instructional in bed." She laughed; Abi wasn't shy at telling her exactly what she wanted. "But sometimes, intimately, they just want to enjoy it. It would have been obvious quite quickly if you weren't into it, but seeing as you were..."

Abi narrowed her eyes at her. "Pretty inciteful."

"Which is why I know..." She ran her hand up and through Abi's hair until her palm could press down. "That you don't need much more encouragement than a gentle push in the right direction."

Wiggling down the bed, Abi kept their eyes fixed. "A little less gentle maybe," she said, just as Quinn tightened her grip. "Better."

Chapter Thirty-Six

The biggest surprise to Quinn after returning to the set of *Jackson & Jones* was that the Friday tweet event and after-work drinks were still going. The difference being that you didn't have to take part unless you absolutely wanted to. The second biggest surprise to Quinn was, that she actually did want to. Plus, Abi was away at a friend's wedding, so the prospect of a booty call was off the table.

Various members of the cast and crew would meet in the writers' room and crowd around the desk, either in the seats provided, on the desk itself, or in chairs they'd dragged in from other parts of the offices.

When she walked in, she was immediately called across the room by Jerry. He patted an empty chair next to him and shouted, "Saved you a seat." Just in case she hadn't worked out his meaning already.

"Thanks, be over in a sec," she called back before heading for the coffee pot. It was pretty late in the day for a coffee usually, but she intended to go out for drinks and maybe not get home till late, the caffeine hit would be welcome. Looking around, she noticed that the atmosphere in the room was a lot lighter than it used to be. Everyone was smiling, joking around, or seriously involved in conversations, it felt a lot different from before.

She poured the coffee into her old mug that had somehow managed to survive all of these months and wandered back across the room to sit next to Jerry and make small talk about this week's episode with strangers on the net.

Her Twitter account had been dormant since leaving the show, she wasn't one for keeping up with people via social media much. She had all the obligatory platforms set up of course. Over the years there had been more use on some than others. Myspace had been great fun back in the day, but then Facebook had come along, and she'd moved to that. For a while it was alright but then life took over and she didn't have the time to really keep up with it much more than to answer tagged posts. By the time Twitter came about, she really wasn't interested but she set up an account out of curiosity, same with Instagram, but she rarely used them. So, re-joining the *J&J* tweet group was a little daunting, she wasn't sure she would be able to keep up.

"So, how's it working?" she asked Jerry as she logged into her account and stared at the blank screen.

"Simple, we use the hashtag JandJTV then just start making comments. You'll only make a couple and then they tweet will be jumped on by those who are obsessed with Riley and Jane." He chuckled, "You might want to set your settings to turn off notifications."

"Alright," she said, looking perplexed. "How do I do that?"

Jerry laughed and took the phone off of her, fiddled with a few things, and then handed it back. "Here you go. Now, I'll send a tweet out reminding people that you're back, and you'll soon have them replying to anything you tweet. Mostly, it won't get going until after the show airs, most of us don't hang around that long." He leaned in towards her and held the phone up, snapping a selfie of the two of them.

"Hey, hold up," Jane called out. She came running over, grinning as she stood behind and between them, bending over so that Jerry could take a selfie of all three. "Don't forget to tag me." She laughed as she dashed back across the room to where Riley sat, casually leaning back on the chair legs with her feet on the table.

"That will get them swarming," Jerry said gleefully as he added the picture. Quinn picked up her phone and looked at the app. She clicked on the tag and opened it; it was a nice shot.

"What on earth do I say?" she laughed at the absurdity of it all.

"Anything," Jerry said, not looking up, his fingers pressing away rapidly.

QuinnHarp01: So, all set for the live tweet tonight. Who's joining us? #jandjTV

Instantly the little bell icon began to flick as one tweet became two, and five and ten. Her timeline opened up and she could see the replies on her thread. Lots of *I am* or *Me.* It was a little overwhelming and she did her best to hit the little heart icon and like as many replies as she could, but then one stood out with an actual sentence, which Quinn found easier to connect with.

Hatless_Aim: Glad to see your back where you belong Quinn. The show has missed you.

"You're right about that," Quinn muttered to herself as she typed out a response, throwing in an emoji hoping it kept it all light-hearted.

QuinHarp01: Thanks for noticing @Hatless_Aim ;) It's great to be back!

A crate of beer and some pizzas appeared on the table and Jerry got up to grab one. He waved at Quinn. "Wanna beer?"

"No, thanks," she replied, toasting him with her coffee cup. "But I'll take a slice." She smiled, jutting her chin at the nearest pizza.

He grabbed a couple of paper napkins, tossed a slice on each, and then brought them over. "How's it going?"

"Alright so far. Mostly there isn't much to respond to, just hitting the like button to be polite."

"Exactly. Just keep an eye out for the weird ones though, alright?" he said, snapping another picture just as they were both taking a bite of their pizza. A minute later the image flashed up on Quinn's timeline. Followed by a whole new set of likes and comments.

Jez56JJ: @QuinnHarp01 hungry for some action? #jandjTV

QuinnHarp01: Hey @jez56jj that's so unfair! You know I am always hungry for action! #jandjTV

They laughed at each other and carried on with the replies and hitting the like button.

Hatless_Aim: @QuinnHarp01 & @Jez6jj What kind of action, Quinn? #jandjTV

"Oh, here we go, Quinn's got an admirer." Jerry laughed loudly and read out the tweet from @Hatless_Aim. "Are we taking bets, lunatic or admirer?"

Some of the other people around them laughed. It was the hazard of being high profile in any environment, but especially Hollywood where some people would go to many extremes to get closer to the stars they coveted. Of course, just as many were genuinely nice people who just loved the show and wanted to be a part of it.

jez56jj: Oh, she does @Hatless_Aim ;) She's a looker is @QuinnHarp01

"Jerry, will you pack it in!" She glared and blushed at the same time. "I do not need you creating a stalker for me." He pulled a sad, sorrowful face and she couldn't stay mad at him. "If they are weird, you better deal with it." She chuckled.

"Aww come on Quinn, it's nice that you got a fan," Jane shouted across the table and joined in with Jerry.

JHanson4real: @QuinnHarp01 is all action here, about to smack @jez56jj for being rude. @Hatless_Aim #JandjTV

Hatless_Aim: Oh no I know Quinn would never hurt anyone. She's far too nice. Surely? @JHanson4real @QuinnHarp01 @jez56jj

QuinnHarp01: Yes, correct @Hatless_Aim violence is never the answer. But I am going to take away his beer as punishment.

Jerry grabbed his bottle and held it close to his chest, before quickly drinking down what was left and handing Quinn the empty glass bottle with a smirk. She got up and got him another, grabbing one for herself.

The banter continued on effortlessly and Quinn had to admit, she was having fun. By the time she checked her watch next, the show was over, and it was time to hit the bar for a couple more drinks. She re-read some of the comments from **@Hatless_aim** and chuckled, whoever they were, they were quite entertaining, and she felt that buzz of interest that she wasn't expecting. Before she even thought about it, she hit the follow button and then logged off.

Chapter Thirty-Seven

There were times when Quinn's mind had played tricks on her. When all the work to move forward and forget about Natasha would come undone in a fleeting moment. Going for a run with the sun beating down on her, tired legs, and an exhausted mind, staggering her way back towards the house, she would lookup. And in the distance, she would swear she saw her. Just sitting there in her spot.

Of course, as she moved around the bends of the beach and got closer, she would realize that she was wrong. She wouldn't be there. It would have just been a shadow, or someone else walking a dog.

Today was one of those days. It was just a random day at the end of November. Nothing else about it stood out until she went for her run.

The run had been a lot longer. The late night previously and the lay-in this morning meant she had woken up feeling a little out of sorts. She'd gone out for a run to clear her mind, ready to get stuck into a new script idea later. But the reality was that she had pushed herself a little too far, and now she was virtually walking the last part. Shaky legs almost buckling in the shifting sand. The only thought in Quinn's mind was to get home and shower.

When her home came into view, it was her intention to focus on that, rather than the endless sand at her feet. And that's when she saw her. This time, she was certain, there was definitely someone sitting on the sand in Natasha's spot. She shielded her eyes from the sun and tried to focus on them, but she was too far away. They were just a figure in dark clothing sitting on the sand. Quinn tried to walk faster, and when the figure stood up and began to walk away, she tried to run, but her legs were gone. She just didn't have the energy.

"Natasha?" she called out. Almost stumbling over her own feet. "Tasha?" she shouted more loudly this time. But she was too far away. The ocean breaking on the shore and the distance muffled anything she said. And as she watched the figure disappear between the houses and out of sight, Quinn dropped to her knees and collapsed onto her back. Gazing up at the sky, blue and clear, not a cloud in sight, and yet she felt like a storm was brewing inside of her. "Tasha?" she mumbled quietly as she closed her eyes to the brightness up above.

~***~

Showered and dressed, she felt a little better. Under the water, she shook the images off. It wasn't Natasha, that's what she needed to remind herself. Natasha was gone, and whoever it had been, it was just a coincidence, nothing more.

She cursed Abi for being away. If ever there was a more apt moment for a *friend with benefits* relationship hook-up, this was it. Every step down the stairs was agony as her muscles complained and fought against every movement. And by the time she got to the bottom, she needed to sit down and rest. Grabbing her phone, she threw herself onto the couch and put her feet up. Audibly sighing as she finally relaxed.

Checking the screen, she frowned. 15 was the number of notifications she hadn't heard. But she ignored those and opened the three that lit up the little envelope. Instant messages.

The first two were just crew members welcoming her back, and she sent a brief reply back in thanks, but the third was intriguing. It had been sent an hour ago.

Hatless_Aim: Hi Quinn, thank you for the follow. I am sure you must get a lot of messages from fans, but I just wanted to say hello.

What was most intriguing to Quinn was that she had no idea whether Hat, as she was calling them now, was a man or a woman, old or young, gay, or straight, she knew literally nothing. Quinn clicked on their profile. They didn't use a photo of themselves, instead, it was a meme that read. *Life has just begun, and so is the journey to knowing your true self.* She wasn't quite sure how to broach the subject, not that it really mattered, but she'd hate to misgender someone simply by not knowing. It was just every way she thought of sounded a little too familiar, and she wasn't sure that was a sensible route.

QuinnHarp01: Hi. That's sweet of you to say. Thankfully I am not as popular as Jerry would make out! Q.

Hatless_Aim: I think you do yourself an injustice. I am sure Jerry knows his stuff!

QuinnHarp01: Lol, I am not sure he does. But we let him think so.

Hatless_Aim: Well, I am sure your girlfriend would agree?

Girlfriend? Did she have a girlfriend? But more importantly, how did this person know about any potential girlfriend? Quinn's red flag waved, instantly reminded of Jerry's warning about *obsessive weirdos,* was that the problem here? She sat back on the couch and considered it, maybe she should just end the communication now. Stay on the safe side. But for some reason, she felt intrigued, her gut instinct was that it wasn't an oddball. So, she replied.

QuinnHarp01: Girlfriend?

This time, there wasn't an instant response like before. Quinn stared at the screen for a full minute before she put the phone down and went to the kitchen for more coffee. When she got back, there was a message waiting.

Hatless_Aim: Sorry, that was rude of me. Too intrusive, I didn't mean to offend in any way.

Quinn sipped her coffee and thought about it, was she offended? No, not at all, she wasn't embarrassed about Abi, not at all. They were both consenting adults, she'd just thought they'd been more discreet about it. She wasn't aware of any news stories about them, not that she paid any attention to the gossip pages. She made a mental note to Google later and see.

QuinnHarp01: I am not offended.

Hatless_Aim: Maybe not, but I didn't intend to intrude on your privacy, it was just a frivolous comment. I read an article about you recently that mentioned you were part of the LGBT. I really do appreciate you taking time out of your day to speak to me.

Quinn recalled the article, she'd been approached by a few local LGBTQ groups over the years, and always gave them her time if she could. She saw it as her duty to be out and proud in Hollywood, leading the way for others.

QuinnHarp01: I see. It's fine. But I do appreciate my privacy.

Hatless_Aim: Of course, again, I am sorry for being out of line.

She checked out Hat's profile again. Most people added their real name alongside their Twitter handle, but this was now Aimless Hat. Location LA and the date they joined. Which was only a few months ago. Was that suspicious?

QuinnHarp01: Okay, well, it was nice talking to you Hatless! Are you okay with me calling you Hatless? And just so I don't get it wrong, which pronoun do you use?

Hatless_Aim: Sure, Hatless will do. And for clarity, I'm 39, single, and not looking. My heart is still somewhere else. Quite happy with how my life is right now.

QuinnHarp01: Alright, well thanks for the information. It certainly helps to clarify things. No miscommunications.

With her coffee finished, and no further response from Hat, Quinn made a decision. It had been a long while since she had mooched around some antique stores, and there was a new restaurant opened up on Melrose that she wanted to try out.

"Time to get out and about," she said, hauling herself up and grabbing her keys.

Chapter Thirty-Eight

Sunday evening was drawing in. It was a cold December night and Quinn was in her lounge, sitting cross-legged on the couch as she worked on some draft script ideas. The quiet was abruptly interrupted by a sharp rapping on the door. Visitors were not something Quinn had many of, not unless invited, so a surprise guest had her on edge. Her heart beat faster when the fleeting idea of Natasha being the one standing on her doorstep.

Opening the door, she was still surprised to find a woman standing there. Abi. Looking all hot and bothered in a short-sleeved, emerald green dress. She'd piled her hair up on top of her head, but wayward strays had worked their way loose and framed her face. Red lipstick worn away to a paler hue that still made her lips kissable, and Quinn was quite inclined to do so.

"Oh, thank God," she said as she invited herself inside and past Quinn. "I have had the weekend from hell and right about now I need a..." She turned and looked directly at Quinn. She looked as though she might devour her. Her voice dropped an octave as she finally said, "...release."

Moving closer, Quinn asked, "And what kind of release do you require?"

Abi smirked, wasting no time, she unzipped her dress. Never taking her eyes from Quinn, as she let it fall from her shoulders, slithering down her hips and pool like an emerald puddle at her feet.

"The kind where you make me come over and over," Her hands reached behind her. "Until I forget what a horrid time I have had to endure," she said unhooking the bra and letting that fall to the floor also.

"I think I know the kind you mean," Quinn responded, raising an eyebrow, and jutting her chin down and towards her panties. She watched intently as Abi hooked her thumbs on either side and then, still holding her gaze, slid them down her toned thighs to add to the pile of clothing already on the floor.

There was only so much Quinn could do to hold off from pushing her up against the wall the moment she had strode in. She liked the game, the chase. Making Abi wait for it, and in turn, herself. But now, her resolve had passed, and she moved quickly, two steps and she had her in her grasp. A gentle push and she was backed up against the coolness of the wall.

"On your knees, I want you on your knees." Abi pointed to the floor, and Quinn obliged. It wasn't a chore. And she enjoyed the switching up of their power play.

She felt Abi's long fingers thread into her hair when Quinn's tongue made it's first strike against her. Softly sliding between folds in random patterns that Abi couldn't focus on. When Quinn heard the gasp for air, she tapped against Abi's calf until her boss widened her stance, giving Quinn all the access, she needed to send those delicious sensations pulsating throughout Abi's core.

"Inside." Abi could barely speak. "In...inside me."

Quinn's fingers push into her and she hooked her leg up and over Quinn's shoulder. "More," She cried out as Quinn thrust into her faster until a plethora of obscenity intermixed with the cries of ecstasy burned their way from the heat of her, out of her throat and into existence. She slid down the wall, collapsing in a heap, pulling Quinn to her breast, and cradling her.

"Fuck. Thanks. I needed that," she said between heaving breaths.

"I can see that." Quinn smiled. Standing, she reached for Abi's hand and led her to the bedroom.

It was midnight when Abi climbed out of bed and walked naked back downstairs, she dressed in the hall while Quinn watched. For the first time in her life, Quinn felt no emotional attachment. What she had with Abi was exactly what both of them needed, nothing more. A give and take of sexual favors without the guilt, the responsibility, or any of the other aspects that a relationship brought with it.

"I'll see you in the morning?" Abi said, pulling the zipper up on her dress.

Quinn nodded. "Sure will."

"Great." Abi smiled, checking herself in the mirror one last time. Seemingly satisfied that she looked good enough, she stepped towards Quinn, kissed her cheek, and left.

With Abi gone, Quinn picked up her phone and checked for messages.

Hatless_Aim: Do you ever have the urge to do something completely crazy?

Quinn checked the time the message was sent, it was several hours ago, and she was probably too late to reply now, not that she really knew what to say to that. What kind of crazy? Jumping out of a plane crazy? Bungee jumping crazy? There were so many different options. And of course, there were other options that maybe this kind of conversation shouldn't lead into.

She put the phone down and left it unanswered.

Chapter Thirty-Nine

For several days nothing much happened that Quinn needed to concern herself with. She met with Abi one night and had dinner with Caroline twice, but mostly, she spent her downtime hanging around the beach. The weather was still warm enough to be able to enjoy being outside. It surprised her though, how often she found herself looking forward to a message from Hatless. They'd been sending messages randomly for a while, nothing too intrusive, but little by little the conversations were becoming deeper. Topics of conversations about pop culture, or the news that day. Quinn was enjoying it, a lot.

Which was why she had her phone in hand now, typing out a message during a lull at work. The office was quiet, and in all honesty, she was a little bored.

QuinnHarp01: Hey Hatless, how's it going?

She put the phone down and wandered across to the window, looking out over the lot. Nothing much was going on and her thoughts momentarily went to Natasha, but when the phone beeped, her mind returned to the illusive internet friend.

Hatless_Aim: Hello Quinn, all good here. Nothing very exciting happening today, how about you?

QuinnHarp01: I am working on some scripts. Just taking a break.

Hatless_Aim: Exciting, I can't wait to find out what Riley and Jane get up to next.

QuinnHarp01: Top secret. But it's going to be something awesome.

Hatless_Aim: I can't wait.

QuinnHarp01: So, tell me, what does Hatless aim mean? I can't work it out.

Hatless_Aim: Oh, it's just an anagram of my name, nothing too interesting I'm afraid.

QuinnHarp01: Ah, alright, I guess when I get bored, I can try and work it out □

Hatless_Aim: You can certainly try. But I highly doubt you're ever that bored, Quinn. What are you up to at the weekend?

QuinnHarp01: Not sure really, I tend to just go with the flow nowadays rather than make plans. Live in the present, know what I mean?

Hatless_Aim: Yes, sounds nice. I'm the opposite I suppose, I need to have everything planned out.

QuinnHarp01: You never just do something spontaneous? What was all that about doing something crazy?

Hatless_Aim: Oh, lol. I think about it. But my life right now is a little complicated, I can't just drop everything and do what I want for now. I hope that things change very soon though. It's all just taking time to organize.

QuinnHarp01: You'll get there one day Hat. Sorry, I seem to keep shortening your name. Is that alright?

Quinn grimaced at her tendency to shorten people's names. It was a habit, she noticed, whenever she felt comfortable with someone. Which said a lot about Hat already, didn't it? She'd once dated a woman called Victoria, who got rather annoyed anytime Quinn slipped and used Vic or Vicky. Ever since then, she had tried not to do it, but it seemed like she was doomed to failure as her brain disconnected and did what it did naturally.

Hatless_Aim: That's quite alright, I've never minded it.

Jerry's head popped around the door. "Hey, we've been summoned."

Quinn raised a brow. "For?"

"Dunno, something isn't working right on set, they want a quick change."

"Alright," she sighed. "I'll be there in two minutes."

QuinnHarp01: Great because I do it without thinking! I need to get going, I am needed on set to go through some script changes. Living the dream!!

As she gathered her things, ready to go and battle for her words and try not to make any changes that would create an issue going forward with future storylines, she considered something. Coming to a conclusion, she picked her phone up again and added.

QuinnHarp01: Just a thought, but maybe when you've got less going on, you could be a little spontaneous and do something crazy, grab a coffee?

She hovered around the desk nervously waiting for a reply. Maybe it was a stupid idea? She really knew nothing about this woman, she could be an axe murderer for all she really knew. Wouldn't that be just her luck?

Quinn put the phone down, giving up on waiting for an answer. It was ridiculous, wasn't it? but just as she was about to walk away, the screen lit up and her stomach flipped nervously.

Hatless_Aim: I would really like that, Quinn. I hope one day sooner rather than later.

A smile made its way slowly across Quinn's face. What was the worst that could happen?

The hours between scenes could sometimes feel twice as long while everyone sat around and waited for hair, make-up, and costuming to all take their turn in dressing the actors accordingly for the upcoming scene. This was a particularly difficult scene and Abi had requested that Quinn sit in to make sure that any changes could be made instantly. Sometimes an actor would struggle with a line, or how Abi wanted it said, or the line sounded great in Quinn's head but listening to it being spoken out loud was a different story. The problem was that it was pretty boring now Abi had gone off to speak to Riley, and Quinn could have been doing a lot of other things. She picked up her phone and was going to play a new word game she had discovered when she considered something else.

She hadn't heard from Hat for a few days, which was another thing she liked about her. The woman didn't bombard her with messages like some of the other fans did. She'd even had to mute a couple of them as they were so excessive. Maybe it was an age thing, most of the fans were younger and more eager and over-excitable. They literally commented on everything Riley and Jane posted. Often it would end in a petty argument and Riley would step in, Jane would always be upset by it.

Quinn wrote "Hatless aim" on a page of her notebook and tried to think what the name could be. Moving letters in her head and then scribbling them down, she finally came up with something.

QuinnHarp01: Hey Hatless, Sheila Taim?

Hatless_Aim: ???

QuinnHarp01: The anagram of your name? Oh, it could be Mait, Sheila Mait?

Hatless_Aim: Oh no, sorry that's not it.

QuinnHarp01: Damn! I thought I had it, okay is it, Sam?

Hatless_Aim: Are you really that bored?

QuinnHarp01: You thought Hollywood was all glitz and glamour? Yeah, I am a little bored, sitting around waiting for everyone else to do their thing.

Hatless_Aim: Oh dear, that isn't fun. So, did you want to talk about anything in particular?

QuinnHarp01: I dunno. Okay wanna play 20 questions?

Hatless_Aim: Any question?

QuinnHarp01: Yep, go for it. I'll start. So, what is your favorite memory?

Hatless_Aim: okay so starting off with the easy stuff? I would say waking up with the person I love. What is your favorite thing to do in your spare time?

QuinnHarp01: That sounds nice. I like to run. Along the beach until my legs won't run any further.

What is your favorite day of the week?

Hatless_Aim: Wow, running, I've never been very sporty.

My favorite day will always be Friday. Do you ever think about people no longer in your life?

Quinn liked that Hat was deeper than just the usual, does Riley have a boyfriend? What's Jane really like? Kind of questions that came on the regular.

QuinnHarp01: All the time. What is the most important thing to accomplish in your life right now?

Hatless_Aim: All the time? They must have left an impression. To be able to finally get my life back.

QuinnHarp01: is that your question?

Hatless_Aim: It wasn't but it is now.

Did she really want to answer this question? She'd been doing alright recently not thinking about Natasha, and did she want to share this part of her with someone she hadn't even met yet? Or was that the attraction, being able to talk about it with someone invisible. No, she wasn't ready to share Natasha with anyone else right now. So, she went with the happy medium instead.

QuinnHarp01: Not all the time, but a lot, yes. She was someone I love very much. But things don't always work out how we want them to, right?

When was the last time you went on a date?

There was a long pause and Quinn wondered what she was doing? Did she work? Had a friend come over? Maybe this was the time to ask all of these questions.

Hatless_Aim: I haven't been on a date in a very long time. Before I was married.

QuinnHarp01: You're married?

Hatless_Aim: No, not anymore. Have we stopped asking questions?

QuinnHarp01: Sorry, that was rude of me. Why wouldn't you have been married? I guess, I dunno why, but my gaydar spiked a little.

Hatless_Aim: Gay people can be married. I was married to a man though. And then I met a woman, who opened my eyes to other possibilities. And I'm still processing all of that.

QuinnHarp01: Sounds complicated, but she must be an amazing woman. I'm glad you found her.

Hatless_Aim: It's very complicated, but I am hoping that one day, things will work out for us.

Quinn felt a pang of regret. Any half-assed idea that anything might come from meeting Hat had just flown out of the window. But maybe a good friend, an understanding friend, would be more what she needed right now. She looked up and noticed Abi strolling across the set, looking gorgeous. Quinn reminded herself that things weren't all bad.

QuinnHarp01: If she feels the same way then I think you will make it work, love has no boundaries that cannot be crossed if both people are willing.

Hatless_Aim: Maybe, I like to think so. But I think I might be too late.

QuinnHarp01: What makes you think that?

Hatless_Aim: Women like her are always going to find someone who can love them.

Logically, Quinn knew that she was speaking to Hat, but her heart began to answer for her as though she were speaking with Natasha. She felt tears burn her eyes and wiped them away quickly as she punched out a reply single-handedly.

QuinnHarp01: Maybe she is waiting. You said you're dealing with some issues? Maybe she's just giving you space to work it all out.

Hatless_Aim: the crazy thing is that as much as I wish that was true, I also don't want to hold her back.

Are you happy Quinn?

QuinnHarp01: back to asking questions? okay, yes, I guess I am happy. Somebody brought donuts and coffee in this morning, what more do I need?

Hatless_Aim: Living the dream.

QuinnHarp01: Coffee and donuts, the way to this girl's heart.

You wanna grab that coffee on Saturday? I found a great little coffee shop in Manhattan Beach, Molly's, you heard of it?

Hatless_Aim: I would really love to do that, but I am not able to just yet Quinn. Would you allow me to take a rain check?

QuinnHarp01: Yes, of course, sorry that was kind of presumptuous of me.

Hatless_Aim: No, actually it was a lovely idea I just need to work through a few things and find some time.

"Quinn, can you take a look at this line here? I'm not sure that it's working." Abi's voice cut through the thoughts in Quinn's mind. She got up, pushed her phone back into her pocket, and wandered over to where Abi stood, one hand on her hip, a look of frustration on her face, and a guest actor staring at the floor.

"We've tried it several times and Gregory just can't get his tongue around it. Can we swap out something, to make it easier? She raised an eye that told Quinn she was not happy with it, but what else could she do? It was quicker to change the line than get another actor.

"Sure, let me take a look at the reel. See where the issue is."

Chapter Forty - One

"What are you doing for Christmas?" Caroline asked as they sipped tea and Quinn gazed out at the beach. The weather had turned a little chilly and they both had a jacket on, though Quinn's was much warmer than the one Caroline wore. The English woman insisting that this was not cold and that if Quinn wanted to know what cold was, she should visit the Afghan mountains, or somewhere called Yorkshire.

"Haven't really thought about it," Quinn replied, turning to face her. "My folks are trying to get me to fly home, but I really don't feel like doing that."

"You could come with me, up to the lake. Cam has got a houseful, but we can always find room for one more."

"That's really kind, but I think I'm just going to hang around here and do some work on a screenplay that I've been neglecting."

"Fair enough, but if you change your mind?" Caroline sipped her tea again, and Quinn could see she was mulling something over. "Are you still dating Abi?"

"We're not dating," Quinn reminded her. "We're having sex."

"Isn't that the same thing?" Caroline grinned.

Quinn placed the teacup down and smiled back. "No, because we don't go out. There are no dates. Just hot, sweaty, frantic sex." Anyone else would expect their friend to blush at such a candid explanation. Not Caroline, she took everything in her stride. Years of training not to respond to provocation made every conversation fun for Quinn.

"So, you have no feelings for each other at all? It's been a couple of months now."

"Almost three, and no. I mean, I like her. She's a lot of fun and I have a great deal of respect for her, but we both know that long term, we're not who each other wants. But for now? I'm going to take what's on offer."

Caroline pondered the reply. "Maybe I should find someone similar?"

Sitting up, Quinn fidgeted around until she was facing her properly. She'd never heard Caroline mention her love life before. "Right? Got your eye on someone?"

"No, no...but I do miss it, you know, the hot, sweaty, frantic sex." She laughed as Quinn blushed at her own words reflected back at her. "What? You think I have no idea what it's like to cavort naked with someone until we're both sated, and done for?"

"Of course not, I just...you've never mentioned anyone before."

"I guess I am guarding my heart. It was difficult, losing Andrew the way that I did, and having to hide us for so many years...I guess I don't really know how to have a *normal* relationship."

"Maybe it's time to spread those wings and open those closed doors?"

"Maybe...I certainly would like to share intimacy again with someone, I just don't think I want someone permanently hanging around. I like my life as it is, is that selfish?"

Quinn's head shook. "No, absolutely not. It's honest, and that's refreshing. And there are a lot of people out there who will feel the same way. Love can be in many forms. Society is changing."

"So, heard anything from..."

"Natasha?" Quinn butted in. She smiled sadly. "No, I..." She noticed how Caroline moved, just slightly, her interest piqued by something. "It's silly really," Quinn said, shaking her head at herself.

"Oh, come on. You might as well tell me anyway, at the very least, we can have a giggle about how silly it is," Caroline encouraged, and Quinn liked that about her. It was so easy to tell her things because half the time, Quinn felt that somehow, she already knew.

"I thought I saw her. Out there." She pointed to the beach. "On her spot, like always...by the time I got back here whoever it was had gone."

"And you think it might have been her?"

Quinn shrugged. "Maybe, or maybe I just want it to be so now I'm seeing things that aren't there, or it was just someone else who happened to stop at that precise spot."

"What do you think is most likely?" Caroline placed her cup down on the table and listened intently.

With her brows knitted, Quinn thought about it. "Logically it was just a random person,"

"But?"

"I don't know, there was just something that...call it a gut feeling, but it felt to me that it was her."

"And if it were?"

"Then I am kicking myself that I missed her. I just couldn't run; my legs were like jelly."

Caroline smiled, that all-knowing smile she had. "It would mean she came looking for you, and if she came once, maybe she will come again. Just be patient. Live your life, enjoy Abi," she finished with a wink.

"Actually, I am hoping to have coffee with someone else soon."

"Really? You are a dark horse, aren't you?" Caroline laughed. "Reminds me of Cam before she met Michelle."

"I've heard those stories." Quinn laughed. "I am not that bad."

"There are a lot of stories...so, who's the new one?" Quinn didn't respond right away. "Oh my god, you're blushing."

"I am not." But she was, she most definitely was feeling the heat on her cheeks. "Okay, fine, I am a little because it's...why is nothing simple with me?" She ran a hand through her hair, much to Caroline's amusement. "I met her online."

"Okay, and...everybody's doing it nowadays, apparently."

"This wasn't a dating site. It's work. We do this live-tweeting event every Friday during the show airing, and she kind of popped up and we've been talking."

"Well, that's good, isn't it?"

Quinn nodded. "Yeah, sure. It's just...I don't know, it's that gut feeling again. She's really easy to talk to, it's like she knows me. I don't even know her name."

Caroline stiffened. "You don't think..." She stopped to reconsider. Quinn stared at her expectantly. "I mean, as ridiculous as it sounds, do you think this new woman might be someone you know? Someone who maybe just showed up at your home after all these months?"

Now it was Quinn's turn to ponder. Could it be? She felt the rush of nerves or excitement, it was hard to tell, probably both. The idea that Hat and Natasha were the same person. It couldn't be, that was just crazy, like a soap opera plot. "No, I don't know her name, but

I do know that the handle she uses is an anagram of her real name and there isn't an N in it, so, it can't be her."

"People have been known to lie in my experience. Well, you'll find out if you're going to meet her for coffee."

Chapter Forty-Two

Lying back in the water, the scent of warm vanilla sugar filled the air as bubbles settled against her skin and covered her to her collarbone. Only her head and knees popped out from the warmth of the water. It was relaxing, and exactly what Quinn needed. She did the obligatory phone calls and messages wishing everybody she knew a Happy Holiday while she lay in bed drinking coffee.

When she was finished, and fully awake, she got up and went for her run as usual and then spent the day doing exactly what she wanted, which was laying on the beach all day. It was unseasonably warm the weatherman had said, predicting a mini-heatwave that was expected to hang around for a good while. The good weather and warm sunshine had brought many out to the beach for the day, and Quinn considered that she might drag on her wetsuit tomorrow and take her board out.

The bathroom was small compared to many, but she liked it that way. It meant that she could drop the lid of the toilet, throw a towel over it and create a reachable table. On which was a glass of whisky, on the rocks, with a splash of soda. A bowl of chips to nibble on, and her iPod that was playing the dulcet tones of Melissa Etheridge. The tiled walls created a perfect echo to complement the music.

Her thoughts drifted between Abi and Hat. Things with Abi were great. She had no complaints and would continue to enjoy that relationship when Abi got back from visiting her folks. She knew long term that Abi wasn't the answer. Yeah, they had great sexual chemistry but other than work, they had little in common. But the sex was out of this world and exactly what Quinn needed right now in her life. She felt in limbo. If Quinn were honest, arranging a visit to Abi would have been just the thing right now. She felt antsy. There was anxiety lurking within her since Caroline asked if Hat and Natasha were one and the same. She knew a lot about Hat, but the fundamentals of things like hair color, did she have a crooked nose, thin lips? Was she tall, short, thin, thick, she had no clue, and maybe that was why she kept thinking about Tasha, using her image to fill the void she had with Hat?

Hat had been very clear that she wasn't interested, that her heart lay elsewhere. She hadn't once flirted or tried to engage in any way other than as a friend. So why was Quinn always fighting the idea that they could be something more?

One thought continued to move around her mind intermittently. Who was Hat really? Was she crazy to be talking to this person who she knew barely anything about? What if she was....no, she shook her head. "You just want it to be her," she said to herself, and with that, her mind flooded with images of Natasha. Big green eyes staring up at her, closing slowly as they kissed.

She groaned loudly and slid beneath the surface of the water. But still, the image floated around her mind's eye. Rising up from the water, she shook herself, wiped her face, and then reached for her glass, downing the amber liquid in three quick gulps. She cursed as the heat of it seared her throat, flowing into her stomach to warm gently.

~***~

The following morning, she didn't bother with the run. Instead, she gathered her things and strolled outside to find a spot on the sand. She considered Natasha's space, but it was too far from the shore, so she kept walking. Slamming the end of the board into the sand and dropping her bag down, she pulled her towel out and lay it on the warm sand. It was already hitting the mid-seventies and expected to go a little higher as the day went on.

She stood back from it all and took a photo with her phone's camera and posted it to her Twitter account.

What else do you do in LA for the holidays? #J&J #Surf

She already had several likes before she even had a chance to put the phone away. Looking around, it was quiet. A few people strolled along enjoying the weather, but ultimately, this part of the beach would stay quiet for most of the day. Later on, the surfer dudes might turn up with some beers but until then, she had the waves and the ocean pretty much to herself.

Grabbing her board, she took off, running towards the incoming waves and into the water until it was safe to jump onto the board and paddle out further. The Pacific Ocean, despite the sunshine and heat, was still cold. She found it refreshing as it splashed her face.

Once she was far enough out, she swiveled up to sit astride the board, watching the water and waiting for the wave she would ride back into shore. Arriving in LA in her early twenties, she had quickly become part of the beach scene, her friends excited to show her how to surf. She'd picked it up quickly, and though she would never win any prizes for it, she found she enjoyed the rush it gave her. A battle of balance and nature.

Each time she rode in, she would paddle back out, and do it all again. On the fifth or maybe sixth return, Quinn sat up on the board and ran her hands through her hair, pushing the wet strands back off her face. It was then that she looked back towards her things on the beach, and the figure standing on the sand, watching.

It was Natasha. There was no doubt this time.

She didn't wait for the next wave, instead, she flattened down and began to paddle. Frantically trying to get back to shore and to Natasha. She tried to keep her eyes on her, but the spray from the water was stinging them, and then a wave snuck up from behind and flung her off the board, sucking her under the water and pushing and pulling until finally, she scrambled back to the surface. The board floated there as though nothing had happened. She pulled herself up and back on it, her eyes scanning the beach.

There was nobody there.

Reaching a depth that she could place her feet on the sand and run more quickly than she could paddle, she unhooked the Velcro strap around her ankle and flung the board to the sand. Bypassing her towel as she ran up to the house to search, but it was pointless, Natasha was gone.

She dropped to her haunches and rested her elbows on her knees and her face in her hand as the tears threatened to flow. Was she going mad? She had seen her, hadn't she? It was her; she was so sure of it.

Slowly, she forced herself back to her feet, eyes on the sand, she started walking back. Her shoulders slumped and a million questions whirling around her head. But as her mind began to clear, she noticed something else.

Footprints. One set, two directions. She looked back up the beach, following the line of steps. They led away from Quinn's house, towards Cam and Michelle's. She picked up the pace again, and followed in that direction, remembering the short alleyway that ran down the side of Cam's property, and led from the street to the beach.

Sand changed to concrete beneath her feet as she ran the short distance. Out on the street, there was nobody. She wasn't there. The only sign of life other than passing traffic was the small red sports car that pulled out from halfway down the street, joining the traffic and heading back towards Santa Monica.

She turned and trudged back. Unable to stop thinking about it. Was Natasha back? Looking for her? Why then didn't she wait for her to come out of the water?

"Fuck." She hopped from one foot to the other as something sharp cut into her foot. A stone, thankfully nothing serious, but it hurt, and she hobbled back. When she reached her towel again, she dragged off the upper part of her wetsuit and flopped down onto the towel. The sun warming her bikini-clad skin, drying her hair. It should have been relaxing, instead, she felt her insides tumble. The adrenaline rushing through her body caused her to shake until finally, with some deep breathing, she calmed down.

She had no concept of time. She might have been sitting there for a minute, it might have been an hour, she didn't know. Her mind was on repeat as she stared out at the ocean for answers that just wouldn't come.

Her phone beeped and brought her back to the reality of the day. There wasn't anything she could do, if it was Natasha, then she clearly didn't want to speak to her yet. Maybe in time that would change. She could only hope so. Even if they would never be together, she needed to know that Natasha was alright, that she had found a happiness somewhere, somehow. She deserved that.

The glare of the sun on the screen made it difficult to see who the notification was from. Holding the phone in one hand, she used the other to shield the screen, and then swipe across it to open and read the message.

Hatless_Aim: Enjoying the summer sunshine?

What could she say to that? *Yeah, loving it, the love of my life is stalking me, and honestly, I'm not even sure she's real.*

QuinnHarp01: Of course, What are you up to? Did you have a nice Christmas?

Hatless_Aim: Yes, we did, thank you. I went out for a quick walk, some amazing views. Quite overwhelming really.

QuinnHarp01: Where did you go?

Hatless_Aim: Just around. So, you're at the beach today? I saw the photo on my timeline.

QuinnHarp01: Yep, figured I'd take the board out for some waves.

Hatless_Aim: Oh, you went in the water? It must be freezing.

QuinnHarp01: That's why we wear wetsuits. But yes, it was cold. And then I almost had a heart attack.

She'd written and sent it before she even realized what she was saying and cursed herself for it. Hat didn't need to know about her crazy shit.

Hatless_Aim: A heart attack? Are you alright?

QuinnHarp01: I'm fine. Just my mind playing tricks on me. Must be the water, it's frozen my common sense.

Hatless_Aim: I am sorry.

QuinnHarp01: What are you sorry for? Seriously, I'm alright. Just gonna lie here and soak up some rays, and then spend the rest of the day watching more old movies. You?

There was no response, and after waiting a moment or two, she got up and stripped completely from her suit. Quinn picked up the sun lotion and poured some into her hands, rubbing them over every exposed inch of herself that she could reach. She had an all-year tan, but that didn't mean she was risking anything by not using sunscreen. When she was done, she lay back and looked up at the cloudless blue sky. Why wasn't her life simpler when it came to women she loved? Before her thoughts could runaway with themselves again, her phone buzzed. She rolled over, pulled it from her bag and read the message.

Hatless_Aim: So, I was thinking maybe its time to meet up, if you still want to?

QuinnHarp01: I'd love that. Let me know when, I'm free most weekends, and of course, we're on a break right now, so... plenty of free time.

A distraction from thinking about Natasha might do her good.

Hatless_Aim: Thank you Quinn. Your patience has been invaluable.

QuinnHarp01: No need to thank me, but you could tell me your name?

There was no further response, and Quinn shrugged, what did it matter? She'd find out eventually, and who didn't like a little mystery in life? She pushed the phone back into her bag, took a swig from the water bottle she had in there, and then lay back and gazed at the blue cloudless sky again.

Chapter Forty-Three

It had been a couple of days and Quinn still hadn't heard back from Hat. And it rankled a little. Really, what was the big deal with knowing her name? They were friends enough now surely to at least trust one another with such simple things, but then she considered how little she knew about Hat's life. Maybe she was just swamped with work, or a big family thing had come up, it was still the holidays after all for a lot of people.

The idea that Hat was a weirdo stalker had been something she was concerned with, maybe Hat thought the same thing. Just because Quinn was a writer on a big TV show, didn't mean she wasn't someone to be concerned about. The MTV show *Catfish* had shown over and over how easy it was to pretend to be someone you're not online. So, she sucked up her concern for now.

She needed something to take the edge off, to push all of these thoughts from her mind. Picking up her phone, she didn't have to scroll far to find the name.

"Abi? You home?"

"Hey you, how have you been?" she teased, and Quinn knew that home or not, this could be an interesting phone call.

"I'm good," she said with the intention of hiding her feelings. But then she remembered what they were and that she didn't have to explain anything, she could just ask for it. "You free tonight?"

"For sex?" she asked, her voice sultry and seductive.

"Yes," Quinn replied confidently.

"So, just to fuck?" she confirmed, even though they both knew that there were no other options. Work talk was at the office, sex was in a bed, or on the couch, or counter.

"Yes, to fuck," Quinn confirmed before adding just as seductively, "multiple times."

"Hm," she said as though she were really thinking about it. "I think I could go a few rounds. My place or yours?"

Quinn needed to get out of the house, away from the memories. It was going to be at Abi's that was for sure.

"I'll be there in 20 minutes. Get naked." She grabbed her keys and left the house.

It took less than 20 minutes to arrive at the condo. Parking in the lot, she got out and virtually ran up the steps that led to Abi's apartment. She raised a hand to knock on the door, but it opened seconds before her knuckles rapped. Abi stood there, one hand on the door, the other on the frame, naked in all her glory. She really was a sight for sore eyes.

There were no pleasantries. The urge to take control pushed Quinn forward and inside the house. Pushing Abi roughly against the wall as she kicked the door closed behind her.

"Somebody seems a little eager tonight," Abi purred as Quinn's mouth found her neck, kissing and sucking the flesh while her hands roamed the naked flesh on offer.

"You got a problem with that?" Quinn asked, nudging her thighs apart and pressing her own thigh between them, pressing upwards hard and fast.

Abi gasped, a low moan escaping her mouth before she said, "No, I want you like this. But I'm not an easy fuck." She began to rotate her hips, gaining traction against Quinn's thigh. "You know you're overdressed, don't you?" she said, yanking Quinn's shirt open, buttons flying as she pushed the material roughly from her shoulders, trapping Quinn's arms by her side. "And you know how much I like to be in charge, don't you?" she smiled, before quickly twisting and rotating their positions until it was Quinn who had her back firmly to the wall. "So, why don't you tell me what's got you all het up like a coiled spring while I make myself useful and remove all of this unwanted clothing." She was unbuckling the belt as she spoke and for a moment, Quinn lost all sense of what was up and what was down.

She considered the question, calming her breathing enough to make her brain work again, what was she so het up about? The buttons to her jeans popped one by one and took her thoughts away to more pleasurable things. She fought the brain fog, and the sensations, and finally came to a conclusion that matched her feelings.

"I'm...I...frustrated," she got out just as Abi slid her palm inside her underwear and touched her.

"Frustrated with who?" she asked. Her fingers pressed against Quinn with just the right amount of pressure to have her bucking her hips, her mind blank once more as she relaxed into the touch.

"Fuck. So good," she mumbled almost incoherently. The sensation taking away her frustrations instantly. "An ex."

Abi's fingers slid lower, a reward for honest communication. Abi was a big fan of that, and Quinn wasn't in any state to deny it. This was what she was here for. She could talk things through with Caroline, of course, but she couldn't get this. This innate need for sexual relief.

Abi pressed her entire body against Quinn, whispering in her ear, "Uh-huh, an ex? Did she fuck you like I do?" Her fingers entered Quinn in a slow, rhythmic motion that had her hips rocking in tandem with them. "Like this?"

"No, we only ever made love," Quinn admitted with a sharp intake of breath as Abi's thrusts inside of her became more forceful, more intense. Quinn finally freed her arms from the restriction of the shirt and pushed her trousers down from where they clung to her hips, to mid-thigh. Desperate to open her stance and allow Abi to bring her to the edge; she needed to come.

Abi smirked at her frustration. "You still love her?"

Quinn's hands gripped at the wall, her palms flattening against it. "Yes," she hissed out, her head twisting back and forth as the sensations became more intense until finally, with a shudder and a cry of a further, more insistent, "yes," she came.

Chapter Forty-Four

Lying in bed together, Quinn considered that this was the first time either of them had stayed longer than was necessary. Usually, they'd have sex and then go their separate ways. Neither had ever stayed over. And she wasn't sure that was the plan now, but with Abi in her arms, snuggled against her, it felt right.

"Just because I am your boss and we are only fucking for fun, doesn't mean I can't be your friend Quinn," she said looking up at Quinn. "If you need to talk, we can do that too."

Quinn thought about it, it made sense. They were intimately involved, but did that mean she needed to share her innermost thoughts with Abi too? Quinn rolled onto her side and shifted down the bed putting them face to face.

"Have you ever met your person? Someone, you just know you should be with," Quinn asked. She let her fingers along Abi's thigh.

"Hmm no, I don't think I have," Abi said, shifting herself into a more comfortable position. "I take it you have?"

Quinn smiled but couldn't disguise the sadness in her eyes. "I have. I fell in love, and then lost her."

"That's sad, where did she go?"

"I don't know, she had...." Quinn thought about the words she wanted to use. "Issues she needed to deal with."

"So, what happened?" Abi asked, reaching out and stroking Quinn's arm with a reassurance that Quinn hadn't realized she needed it until the gentle fingertips moved against her skin.

"Her husband was violent; he would take out his frustrations on her. I guess I was her escape; the person she could go to and know she was safe with."

"Why didn't she just stay with you then?"

"It's never that simple. I wanted her to. I asked her to, but she said she couldn't. She said that she was broken and needed to fix herself, and she couldn't do that without having to worry about me. I think that she knew it would be difficult and that my feelings would potentially be hurt. It was a really bad relationship she was in, not just a slap here and there, but real violence, torture really."

Abi remained silent, just listening as Quinn fought back the tears.

"And you're still waiting. Hoping she will come back to you?"

Quinn nodded. "Yeah, I guess I am. I didn't really think I was but look at me." She laughed sadly. "I'm deliberately not getting involved. I can't shake her from my mind."

"How long have you waited?" Abi probed gently.

"Too long, not long enough?" she whispered. "She left last April, so it's been almost a year."

"April? That's a long time, right about when I took over on *J&J*." Quinn nodded. Watching as her brilliant mind put two and two together and definitely came up with four. "Is that why you resigned? Because Nick Miles was her husband?"

Quinn sighed and fell backward onto the bed. "Yeah."

"Wow, I was not expecting that, but I guess I did hear the rumors at the time. Nobody understood why he attacked you the way that he did, everyone just assumed it was a work argument that got out of hand? So, why didn't you two get together?"

"She needed to get away, find herself. We made love and then the following morning I woke up and she was gone."

"That must have been hard?"

"Well, I wasn't expecting it, so yeah, was a bit of a shock, but I guess I understood. She called and left a voice message on my phone."

"Kind of harsh, for you at least. So, you haven't seen her since? In all these months?"

Quinn shook her head. "No...well, I mean..."

Abi rose up and stared into her eyes intently. "Tell me."

Feeling stupid, Quinn looked away, but her chin was tilted back to where Abi still stared. "Sometimes I think...I think I see her. At my house, on the beach. Always on the beach."

"You see her?" Abi sat up, clearly more intrigued now.

"I...yeah, from a distance you know? I'll be out on the beach and look up toward my house and she's, she's standing there, but then she leaves before I can reach her. I sound crazy right?" She raised an arm and covered her face as though that would protect her from any potential pitying looks.

"I don't think you are crazy," Abi said, her fingertips casually rolling and pinching Quinn's nipple as she thought about it. "I mean, if it's her then it's either really romantic and at some point, she is going to feel able to make contact. I can imagine she's nervous about it all."

"Or?"

Abi smiled devilishly and swung her leg over Quinn's to straddle her. Her hot wetness pressed down against Quinn's torso, automatically grinding against her hard stomach. "She's stalking you and you're about to end up on *Crimes of Passion, a Hollywood*

Lesbian Nightmare Story," she said in a deep voice like the actor who did the show. Quinn smiled at the joke, her hands moving to Abi's hips, helping to guide her movement. There was something sexy about the way this woman could move her thoughts away from one topic to another with such ease. "If it is meant to be, if she is really there on your beach, then she will come to you, but in the meantime, you have to let her go, and if someone else comes along..." She left the sentence unfinished, and Quinn's mind automatically went to Hatless.

"I guess that is another reason why maybe I am frustrated," Quinn admitted, watching her take her pleasure, her abdomen flexing and relaxing as she pressed harder against her and moaned, fingers gripping reflexively on Quinn's chest.

"Why?" she forced out quickly.

"There is this woman I have been talking to..."

"Go on," she said reaching for Quinn's right hand and placing it where she now wanted it. Between her legs, her slickness guiding Quinn inside of her. Now, her movement changed to rising and falling. Her orgasm building slowly. Quinn pushed herself upright, her left arm hooking around her waist, holding her close against her. Hot flesh against hot flesh, perspiration dripping between breasts. The softness of her, velvety and smooth, tightened around Quinn's fingers as she began to climax. "Have you met her?"

"No, she isn't ready to do that just yet."

"Why not? Do you want me to tell her how good you are in the sack?" She laughed and then whimpered as Quinn curled her fingers slightly to hit that one place guaranteed to make her come. "Yes, so good baby, keep fucking me like that," she drawled, as she leaned back, her hands squeezing and caressing her own breasts.

"I don't think she needs to know that just yet, we're going to meet for coffee soon," Quinn said, as she tightened her grip around her waist, forcing her to stop the movement. The loud whine of frustration made Quinn smile. She held Abi still as her own movement took over. Thrusting upwards, hard, fast. Her thumb pressed against Abi's clit as she begged Quinn not to stop.

Chapter Forty-Five

Hatless finally reappeared so to speak, as much as you can appear on a social media messaging system via the phone, on the following Thursday. Quinn had almost begun to think she was being ghosted until the surprise message came through.

Hatless_Aim: I am sorry I haven't replied before now. Your question made me realize that I still had some things I needed to work out with the therapist I am seeing and having to explain to you that I was seeing a therapist bothered me for some reason. So, I took the time to work that through. I am sorry if you felt like I was ignoring you. In hindsight, I should have messaged something. I am sorry.

Before Quinn had finished reading the DM, a second one beeped at her.

Hatless_Aim: Which is ridiculous because I know you well enough to know that you wouldn't judge me.

QuinnHarp01: I appreciate your honesty. I was surprised not to hear from you, and to still be in a space where I don't know your name. We've been talking for a while now. I'm not really an online tech-savvy being, it's all a little out of my comfort zone. I'm a simple being who just wants to have coffee with a friend.

Hatless_Aim: You're right, it's ridiculous and Illogically I do know that. I guess I'm just a little nervous about it.

QuinnHarp01: It's cool. I think this is more about me than it is about you. I seem to be spending my life always waiting for someone.

Once more, there was a long pause before Hat replied. Quinn wondered why? Was she just pondering her reply? Did she have something else to be doing? She wasn't expecting the question that followed, however.

Hatless_Aim: Who are you waiting for Quinn?

QuinnHarp01: A ghost, someone who doesn't need me.

It was only once she had placed the phone down, that she realized she was crying. Natasha, Hat, Abi...three women, maybe it was all too much for her right now. Natasha had left, Abi had never wanted her, and Hat was elusive when it came to meeting. Even though she understood that she couldn't help but feel a little hurt, a little rejected, she didn't like the feeling. She had always been so secure in herself but now look at her. Who had she become?

~***~

With five days left of her break, Quinn made a decision. Getting away earlier in the year had helped a lot, so why wouldn't it now? She was just going to drive until she found somewhere to stop.

Before leaving she made sure to send texts to everyone that mattered. Caroline and Abi being the main ones. She didn't want anyone worrying when she switched her phone off and wasn't reachable.

She debated whether to message Hat or not, in the end deciding she would.

QuinnHarp01: Hey, so last night I did some thinking and I have decided to take a few days away and get my head together. My phone will be off, and I didn't want you to think I was just ghosting you. When someone just leaves our life that way, it's hard. Take care.

She packed a bag and jumped into her car with no idea where she would end up. She didn't wait for a reply from anyone before turning off the phone and tossing it into the pocket between the front seats. The radio was on and playing a song she knew as she pulled onto the highway. She turned it up and sang along.

After almost four hours and three Starbuck drive-throughs later, she was on the outskirts of Vegas. The bright lights of the city weren't what she needed, so she took the turning that said "Grand Canyon" and kept on going.

She found a place called Lake Mead, and then from there, she got directions down to Temple Bar Marina where she rented a small self-contained lakeside lodge for less than $100 a night.

Throwing her bag on the bed, she followed it and flopped down on her back to rest. Her legs and hips ached from all the driving, but hunger was her number one point of action. Her stomach had been rumbling since passing Boulder City, and she should have stopped for something to eat, but stubbornness had kept her moving. Picking up the leaflet she had been handed when she registered the room, she noted that there were several cafés and restaurants in the area. Mostly within walking distance.

It felt good to be away from everything. She breathed deeply as she stepped outside and started to walk back up the track to where she thought the first café would be found. The lake was still. No boats were out on it just now, and it looked like a huge mirror reflecting back the world to itself. A huge universal message of *take a look at what you're doing*. She had every intention to do just that over these next few days.

Chapter Forty-Six

The one thing Quinn was sure of, as she sipped her coffee at the café she had been using while here, was her career. She loved her job and had no intentions of changing anything with regard to working on *J&J*. Unless the networks said otherwise, of course.

"Anything else I can get you?" the waitress asked while cleaning the table next to Quinn. She'd pretty much been the same server every time Quinn had come in.

"You know, I am thinking about a slice of that pie you keep taking to other tables, any left?"

"Sure is, let me get you a piece."

Quinn grinned up at her. "Thanks."

She had spent hours hiking trails and climbing canyons. The time that had given her plenty of opportunity to clear her head and think everything through had clearly made her hungry too. The sugar rush wouldn't hurt as she shifted through the thoughts and feelings that had been evoked these past few days.

She was surprised when the first person to infiltrate her head had been Abi, and not Natasha. Everything with Abi was easy, but that was the problem, it was too easy, and Quinn knew that if she didn't make changes now, there was a real risk that she would want more from Abi, and that wasn't the deal and hadn't ever been on offer. In the long term, she didn't think a relationship with Abi would work anyway, but she knew herself well enough to know that she could easily slip into one anyway and just go with the flow. But that had always been her problem, too easily drawn into things that she already knew it would never last. That's what had felt different with Natasha. The idea that what they had could be forever. It was that she was finding hard to let go of.

And, she considered, having access to hot sex with no strings meant that she was putting off meeting anyone else or allowing anyone else in. Because when it really came down to it, she knew that it wasn't just Hat who had been reluctant. Yeah, Quinn had been the one to offer coffee, but she had to admit that there had been a sense of relief when Hat had said no. And why was that? Because she felt guilty. Even though Hat had never shown anything but an interest in being friends, Quinn had found herself attracted to the words she wrote. And that meant she felt guilty. Disloyal to Natasha, a woman who had left her and until recently, wasn't making any attempt to reconnect. Was she even doing that now? Standing on the beach watching Quinn but walking away before they could speak. None of that made any sense to Quinn.

"Here you go. One slice of peach pie, made fresh this morning." The waitress placed the plate and a large slice of pie down in front of her before adding a fork and a napkin. "And if you can find a better piece of pie anywhere in the state, well, I'll eat this pad." She laughed. Holding her order pad and waving it.

"I'm pretty sure I won't," Quinn said, picking up the fork and digging into the pie. The waitress, whose nametag read "Carol", stood by and watched for her reaction. Sliding the fork into her mouth, Quinn was expecting something good, but the burst of flavors that hit her tongue was intense.

"Wow, this is really good," she said, already loading another forkful.

"Knew you'd think so. I'll leave you to enjoy, just give me a wave if you want anything else," Carol said before turning on her heel and crossing the floor to another customer.

While Quinn continued to eat, she listed in her head what she had concluded so far, other than this was the best piece of pie she'd ever eaten.

Firstly, she needed to stop her expectations of Hat. If all they ever were going to be was two people who talked online now and then, then so be it.

Secondly, and most importantly. She realized that she was ready for a relationship. Something real with someone who could be in her life on a regular basis, and that meant letting go of the illusion of Natasha. Because the likelihood was, that Natasha was a different person now too. They had both had time to grow and reflect and make changes. But Natasha was back, wasn't she? That was her third decision, she was sure that the person she was seeing at the beach was Natasha. And if that was the case then the assumption had to be that there was the potential that Natasha was trying to engage, but for some reason was holding back. That was the part that still stumped Quinn. What was the point of coming to the beach, and not speaking to her? There had to be something else going on, and she wanted to find out. She didn't want any if, buts or maybes in her life moving forwards. And thirdly, as much as she was enjoying it, she needed to stop sleeping with Abi.

Pushing the last forkful into her mouth, she sat back and gazed out of the window. For the first time in a long time, she actually felt like she knew what she was doing. Even if she had no clue how she was going to do it.

Chapter Forty-Seven

The following morning as she packed her things ready to leave and head back home, she remembered her phone. It would probably need charging, which was a good idea seeing as she would be on the road for hours. If there was a problem, she might need to call someone.

Retrieving it from the center console, she pressed the on button and waited for it to load up. The battery icon was at half. Which would probably be okay, but she preferred to be on the safe side and plugged it in. Just as she pushed the wire into it, it beeped several times as her messages came through.

Abi: When are you home, I was thinking we could hook up? Call me.

Quinn: Hey, I'm heading back now, so should be around this evening. I'll come over.

Caroline: Again?

Quinn: Lol. Yeah, what's wrong with that? Anyway, heading back today, coffee soon?

Her Twitter app had notifications. So, she opened it and looked. A message from Hat was waiting.

Hatless_Aim: Hi Quinn. I hope you're having a good time on your break. I've been doing a lot of thinking too and, well, if you still want to, I'm ready to meet and talk. Your last messages gave me pause for thought and I think it's only fair that I explain everything to you, face to face.

QuinnHarp01: That would be great. Will be cool to put a face to the name at last. I'm heading back now, and have plans for this evening, but maybe tomorrow?

She felt a little thrill of excitement. She hadn't expected this to be the outcome at all, but she really was looking forward to meeting Hat. They had a lot in common, and a new friend was always welcome as far as Quinn was concerned.

Tossing the phone on the bed, she continued folding and packing her things. Shirts she hadn't worn and shoes that hadn't moved from inside the wardrobe the entire time she had been here going in first. When her phone beeped again, she glanced at the screen. It was a reply from Hat.

Hatless_Aim: Great, it's still so warm, shall I meet you at the beach?

QuinnHarp01: Sure, why not? I'm in Malibu...or were you thinking somewhere busier?

Hatless_Aim: Malibu is fine. Shall we say 2 o'clock?

QuinnHArp01: I'll be there.

She blew out a breath. Abi tonight, Hat tomorrow...who knew, maybe Natasha would be by soon too. She chuckled to herself and zipped the bag up. Slung it over her shoulder, grabbed the phone and charger, and then took one last look around the room. She had everything she needed.

Stepping outside, she breathed in deep and slow, felt the sunshine on her face, and closed the door behind her. Everything felt finally as though the universe was settling around her.

After handing the key back to reception, she climbed into her car and headed back toward the highway. Music blaring, she sang along again and let the world drift by.

~***~

Knocking on Abi's door later that night, Quinn felt a little nervous. She'd been held up in traffic on the drive home. An accident had closed the highway for nearly two hours, and she had had to just sit it out. By the time she got home, tossed her things inside, and grabbed a shower, it was time to head over to Abi.

She'd been preparing a little speech all day. How it had been a lot of fun and she enjoyed every minute but now was the time to get serious about her love life. All of that went out of the window the moment Abi answered the door in a barely-there silk robe, the belt loosely tied around her waist. She was naked beneath it, and the moment Quinn had the door closed, she was pounced on.

"I have had a hell of a day," Abi whispered to Quinn. "I need you."

"Alright, but then we need to talk," Quinn answered just before she found herself pinned to the wall.

~***~

Quinn sat up, threw her legs over the edge of the bed, and ran her hands through her hair. Abi was asleep, face down on the pillow; spent from the exertion of the evening. Quinn stretched her back and arms, noticing that delicious ache that permeated her muscles, and pulled at her ligaments. Sex with Abi was better than any workout at the gym ever had been. She rubbed at her wrist, the red mark still evident from Abi's enthusiasm earlier. Reaching down, she found her clothes and began to get dressed. It was almost dawn; the sun still wouldn't be up for a while though. Checking over her shoulder that Abi was still asleep, she wandered out of the room to find the kitchen and make some coffee, or at the very least, grab some juice from the refrigerator.

The machine was something out of this world. She filled the coffee compartment, found where to put the water, and then pressed buttons until it finally began to whir into action.

"Maybe I should leave instructions," Abi said, standing in the doorway. She'd wrapped a robe around herself, but it had come undone a little and hung loosely on her.

"Might be a good idea." She smiled and searched cupboards for mugs.

"Second on the left," Abi instructed helpfully as she pulled a stool out from the breakfast bar and climbed on. "So, you said you wanted to talk?"

Quinn twisted around to glance at her quickly before continuing on with the task. "I did, yes."

"You want to stop doing this? Right?"

Quinn spun around again to find Abi smiling at her. Quinn's lips pressed together, and she nodded. A little sad to be having this conversation, especially after the night they just had. "Yeah."

Abi thought about it for a moment before she too nodded. "Alright."

"We're, okay?" Quinn asked, placing a mug of steaming black coffee down in front of Abi.

She twisted the mug around to take the handle. "Sure, it was what it was, Quinn. I've had fun." She looked at Quinn's wrists and grinned. "Did you?"

"Yeah, of course. It's just..."

Abi held a hand up. "You don't have to explain, I'm a big girl. I said at the start, that this can end whenever. I'm good with it."

Quinn let out a quick breath. "I'm glad."

"So, I'll see you at work." She stood up with her mug in her hand and came around to where Quinn stood. "It's been fun. Thank you." And then she kissed her cheek and headed back to bed.

Chapter Forty-Eight

She couldn't decide if the way she was feeling was excitement or nerves. In an hour Hat would be arriving and she would finally get to see the woman she had been speaking to all these weeks. She'd already been for a run to try and get rid of some of this energy flowing through her system. Showered and dressed, she now had nothing much to do but wait.

As she sat back and considered the last year or more, she marveled at how much things had changed. There had been two Christmases since she had met a stranger on the shore. Time seemed to fly by.

Her phone ringing interrupted her thoughts and she smiled when she saw the name "Caroline" flash up on the screen.

"Hey."

"Hello, just wondering if you're in. I'm popping by Cam's later and thought we could have some drinks by the pool?"

"Uh, sounds good. What time were you thinking?"

"Oh, I don't know, maybe five-ish? You're still on Christmas break, aren't you?"

Nervously, Quinn paced the room, taking quick glances outside to the beach in case Hat arrived early. "Yeah, I am."

"What's going on? Why are you pacing?"

Quinn stopped moving. "How do you know I was?"

"I can hear it. You forget I am trained to hear, see, and notice anything out of the ordinary, I can't help it, it's ingrained. So, why are you pacing?"

"I'm not sure, nerves? Excitement?"

"I see, this sounds intriguing."

Quinn chuckled before saying, "Well, I'm meeting someone I've been talking to online."

"And you didn't tell me you plan to meet them? Have you spoken on the phone yet? Facetimed? Had a full and thorough background check run?"

Now Quinn laughed loudly. "No, how would I do that?"

"Oh, I don't know, ask your new best friend who just happens to be ex-MI6 and has contacts who can find out anything. Quinn, this person could be anyone."

"I know but...hold on, did you run a background check on me?"

"Of course, I did," Caroline said without a hint of embarrassment. "Back to the point. Are you sure they're who they say they are?"

"As sure as I can be. Look, if you don't hear from me by three, call me and..."

"Do you know how long it takes to kill a lone woman?"

"I'm meeting her on the beach, in public."

"So, they know where you live?" As Caroline said it, Quinn realised just how stupid it had been to agree to meet here.

"Well, yes..."

"Oh. for the love of God. Quinn Harper, you're as bad as Camryn. You cannot just trust that people are who they say they are." She huffed, and Quinn could hear her moving around now. "I'm coming over."

"It will be fine...I'm sure," Quinn began but was cut off.

"Camryn thought it would be fine when Jessica turned up, look how that ended. I'll be at Cam's, quietly keeping an eye, and if she is who she says she is, then all good...but if not..."

"If not?" Quinn was pretty sure that meant there would be a S.E.A.L squad leaping up from their hiding spots under the sand, ready to take out whoever dared to try and hurt Caroline's friend.

"I have my ways," was her reply before adding, "I'm on my way."

Quinn disconnected the call. Now, she was pretty sure it wasn't excitement, it was definitely nerves that were flooding her body with unwanted adrenaline.

~***~

At 2 p.m. exactly, she stepped outside and looked out onto the beach. Her mouth went dry when her eyes fell on the only woman on the beach. Sitting in her spot. For a full minute, Quinn stood there. Blinking and rubbing her eyes, her throat constricting and stopping any sound from coming out. She felt her heartbeat as though it would pound its way out of her chest, her legs felt as though she had just run a marathon and her stomach was flipping and flopping, but there was no doubting it.

Natasha was sitting on the beach in front of her house.

Quinn could feel her feet moving, but she didn't seem to be getting anywhere fast, and then just like that, she was stood to the side of Natasha, looking down as she turned her head upwards. Smiling at Quinn, she lifted a coffee cup for her to take.

"It's just coffee," she said, watching as Quinn stood there in complete confusion.

The words resonated with Quinn. They were the first she had uttered to Natasha. When she had come outside with a blanket and a flask. "It's just coffee," she had said.

Quinn continued to stare. She looked, beautiful; 10 years younger. Fresh-faced and happy. The weight of everything finally lifted from her shoulders, her hair was still the same honey blonde shade, but it was longer, with maybe more blonde highlights and she wore it up in a ponytail. Not hiding herself from the world.

She appeared relaxed, but maybe a little nervous, why wouldn't she be? Quinn sat down gingerly on the sand next to her, still too afraid to move her eyes away from her in case she disappeared again.

Maybe she really was going crazy, and this was just an hallucination.

"I - I'm -" She didn't know what to say. She had spent months thinking about this very moment, all the things that she thought she would want to say to her if she ever got the chance, declarations of love and want, and need. The urge to throw her arms around her and hold tight was intense, but she couldn't move.

"I have a lot to tell you, a lot to explain," Natasha said quietly, as she sipped on the coffee and looked out to sea. She turned once more to look at Quinn, locking those beautiful green eyes that Quinn had missed so much on her. "Hi, my name is Tasha."

Quinn's brain worked overtime moving the letters in her mind, H-a-t-l-e-s-s-a-I-m, Tasha Miles. She had never considered that. She had counted the letters and realized right away that Natasha Miles wouldn't fit, no N and only one A. But Tasha, she was calling herself Tasha. It suited her.

"Hatless," Quinn finally whispered, still looking at her. Tasha smiled at her, that beautiful thoughtful smile that she had seen so little of in their time together. And then everything came crashing in on top of her. "Why? Why would you do that?" Quinn said, astonished as every conversation they had ever had over the last few months come flooding back to her, she felt deceived.

"I can see that you're angry, my therapist said as much but, I - " She looked to the sky taking in a deep calming breath before turning back to face Quinn. "I needed to be close to you, and yes, I know how selfish that was, but I wasn't ready Quinn. I wasn't ready to turn your world upside down if I couldn't be the person you deserve."

"That was never your choice." Quinn's voice was quiet as she tried to make sense of it all. Conflicted between happiness, confusion, and a feeling foolish.

"Yes, it was. For once in my life, I made decisions that were best for me." She sounded so confident as she spoke. And Quinn felt a pang of guilt and then hurt.

"And that wasn't me?" she asked.

"That isn't what I meant Quinn. When Nick was arrested, I lost everything. My marriage, as pathetic as it was, was all I was accustomed to, it was all I understood of how to live. Nick did everything, he had total power over everything. Finances, the house, cars. Even my wardrobe; he decided what I could or couldn't wear. I didn't know how to do anything for myself. I didn't even know how to use an ATM because he never allowed me to have a bank card." She was frank and open as she began to explain everything.

Quinn sat quietly listening to her as the coffee went cold.

Chapter Forty-Nine

"When you gave me those bags full of clothes that you got for me at the mall, do you remember?" Quinn nodded, she still had them. "It was the sweetest thing anyone had done for me in a long time, but it also made me realize that something as simple as picking out clothes for myself, I couldn't do. I was going to end up relying on you. I didn't want that for you, and I didn't want that for me either."

"I would never have become him," Quinn said sadly. Her eyes wide with fear that she would ever think that of her.

"Oh God Quinn, I know that honey, I do," Natasha said, her left hand rising up to cup Quinn's cheek in her palm before slowly withdrawing and continuing to talk. Quinn missed her touch immediately, but the warmth of being her honey melted her a little more. "It is difficult to explain."

"Try, please," Quinn said, gently shifting her position to move a little closer. When Tasha didn't move away, she breathed easier.

"When I left here, you, I found a therapist in a live-in facility. She helped me get to a place where I could deal with my finances, and my divorce, and get all of my ducks in order. And then she helped me find myself again. For a long time, I didn't like myself, I didn't like the weak pathetic person I had become. It was easier to not think of you. To imagine that you were better off without me, you just didn't know it yet."

It was becoming overcast as they sat there, the sun hiding behind a white cloud. The wind picked up too and Quinn was reminded once more of the first time they'd met, in this spot, right here. Waiting for the storm that was brewing.

"Can we - can we go inside?" Quinn asked. Her arms prickling like gooseflesh, she rubbed them both briskly.

"If you want to, I don't want you to do anything you're not comfortable with Quinn." She smiled and watched as Quinn stood up and walked towards the house.

Stopping after a couple of steps, Quinn turned to make sure that Natasha was still there and following her. From her periphery, she could see Caroline waving at her. She waved back quickly before turning once more to check that Natasha was still there.

When she got inside, she headed straight to the kitchen. Found a bottle of wine and held it up.

"Want one?"

"No, thank you, I can't."

Quinn noticed that she blushed a little, but didn't push it, instead she poured herself a glass and then moved toward the coffee machine.

"Can I just have some water?" Tasha placed her hand on Quinn's arm to stop her from going any further with coffee.

"Sure." Quinn swiveled around and opened the refrigerator door. There were several small plastic bottles of water neatly on a shelf and she took one out, twisted the cap loose, and passed it to Tasha. They both took a sip of their drinks, eyeing each other in the silence. "Let's go sit in the..." She waved a hand towards the lounge and without another word, walked through and waited for Tasha to join her. When she did, Quinn took a seat and continued to sip at the sauvignon.

"Would you like me to continue?" Tasha asked once she was comfortable. She looked happy; Quinn noted. Her eyes sparkled in a way they never had before. Even in those moments when they were together, and the world was locked outside, the likes of Nick Miles a painful memory they could block for a few hours, she never looked this happy. And Quinn was glad, she wanted nothing but happiness for her. So, she sat back and tried to relax, ready to listen to Tasha's story.

"I need to understand why you did what you did?" Quinn said, still trying to get her head around the whole Hatless persona.

"Why I contacted you?" Tasha asked for clarity.

For a moment, Quinn considered it. "Why you pretended to be someone else and by doing so, tricked me into sharing my thoughts."

Tasha glanced at the floor briefly, before gathering herself, and looking back at Quinn. "I understand why you would feel that way. I didn't set out to," she said leaning forward and resting her elbows on her knees, her chin sitting perfectly in her palms. "I thought... I just wanted to know that you were okay, that you were happy. I read an article that said you had returned to the show and...so I signed up to Twitter and would just read the tweets from the live sessions. It made me feel closer to you somehow." It was obvious to Quinn that she was being honest. Not that she would ever doubt that. "Then one night I just couldn't stop myself. I never dreamed you would actually reply or that you would follow me back and start talking to me. At first, I was so happy, to just have those small moments in time with you but then... then we started to really talk, and I couldn't stop myself. I hated myself for it, for lying to you. Susie, my therapist, told me that I needed to be honest with you, but I was nervous, and the more I tried, the more I worried that you would hate me."

"I would never hate you. Don't you get that? Why is it so hard for you to understand that I love you?" Quinn said, more loudly than she intended. She panicked that her reaction would have Tasha squirming in her seat, but to her amazement, Tasha just sat back and remained silent until Quinn calmed again and sat back herself.

"Because until you, nobody ever had loved me, not really...not the love that I wanted to feel," Tasha answered, tears welling in her eyes as she spoke. "And I didn't know how to accept that, or how to embrace that, because it wasn't what I knew, and it made me uncomfortable. Until you, all I knew how to handle was control, aggression, and violence. I didn't know what love was, can you understand that?"

Quinn nodded but remained silent. She understood the words she was using, but she didn't understand them. How could she?

"My perception of love was to do as I was told. It was to allow someone else to have total domination over me. That was all I knew, and then you came along, and suddenly I was confused. Why would you give me choices? Choices that I didn't know what to do with. You would hug me, love me, and all the time I was expecting you to hit me, and knowing that you wouldn't, was just very confusing. Why would you defend me and risk your own safety to do so? I didn't understand it because until you I had never had it."

"I would have -"

"You would have what?" she questioned with a raised brow. "Quinn, you would have put me before everything. You would have done all you could to rescue me, and I wouldn't have been able to accept it. I'd have pushed you away in the end because I needed to take charge of my own life. I couldn't be rescued, I needed to learn to do that for myself. And I am still learning, this is an ongoing process that could last for years. You would have been unhappy, and you would have accepted it, and that wasn't fair."

Quinn wanted to argue, but she knew Tasha was right, that's what she would have done.

She continued on. "When Nick would hit me, he would spend hours telling me that he had to do it, that it was because he loved me. He would tell me that it was my fault, that if I loved him, if I just did this, or did that then he wouldn't have to educate me. That was all I knew of love... until you." Her voice softened as did her eyes as she looked at Quinn. In that moment, Quinn saw it. The love she had yearned for.

"Why did you decide to finally meet me?" Quinn finally asked, she didn't want to hear about Nick anymore, not right now. She had witnessed for herself just a smidgin of what that had been like, she didn't need a recap.

Tasha thought for a moment. Every move, every word, was thoughtful, Quinn considered as she waited for the response.

"It was something you said. I talked it through with Susie and I realised that I wasn't being fair. You said something about waiting, and I asked who you were waiting for, because I selfishly needed to hear you say it was me. But you replied that you were waiting for..."

"A ghost, someone that doesn't need me," Quinn answered for her, remembering the conversation.

"Yes. But I did need you. I just hadn't realised you were still waiting; I'd hoped and wanted you to be, but I wasn't sure, and why should you be? But talking it through with Susie, I realised how unfair it was to have left the way that I did, with no real explanation, to not have updated you to my situation."

"Honestly, until that conversation, I hadn't realised that I was waiting for you. At first, yes, I waited and hoped you'd come back, but as time went by and there was no contact from you, I kept telling myself that I needed to get over it and move on. But I couldn't."

"Susie made me realise that after all the years of control Nick had over me, I was now controlling you."

"I don't understand, how?"

"Everything I had done had left you in limbo, I shouldn't have told you that I would return. I should have just ended things and made sure that you were free in your heart and mind to move on when you were ready, but I didn't. Mainly because I wasn't thinking straight enough to do that, but also, selfishly, because I wanted you to wait. But talking it over with Susie made me face the choices I'd made, and I hated that I had done that to you. I loved you, and I finally understood what that meant, and what that felt like. I finally understood what it meant to have someone like you love me." She stood and crossed the room. Kneeling in front of Quinn she took her hands in her own, interlocking their fingers as she spoke again. "Quinn? I know that the way I have dealt with things hasn't always been the best way to have gone about it. I understand if you want me to leave, if you want me to walk away so that you can stop waiting, then I will, because that is the least you deserve. But I want so much to spend time with you, learning about you from a place of safety, not fear."

"I searched for you," Quinn said, needing her to know how hard this had been for her.

"I know you did, but then you stopped. You set me free to find myself, and I love you for doing that for me."

Quinn had held it together until now, but the tears finally fell as she sobbed. Warm arms wrapped around her. Fingers stroked at the back of her head and words were whispered, but she couldn't recall what was said. She didn't recall anything of the rest of the evening falling asleep still wrapped in Tasha's embrace.

~***~

Sitting up with a start, Quinn looked around the darkened room. Had it all just been a dream? The other side of the couch was empty. The curtains were still open. It was silent as she listened for any sound, anything that would alert her to someone else in the house. But there was nothing.

Getting up, she stretched her long limbs and ran fingers through her hair. Her eyes were sore, evidence that the crying part was at least real. Wandering into the hallways, she timidly called out for Tasha, feeling a little ridiculous and even more convinced that it had all just been a dream. With no response, she moved faster, checking each room, but nothing. She wasn't there. Panic set in as Quinn felt the pain of her leaving again. Her back hit the wall, and she slid down until she felt the floor beneath her, her legs pulled up instinctively to her chest, where she wrapped her arms around them and tried to breathe. She had no idea how long she sat there, only the numbness and the ache in her bones and muscles gave any indication of time. And then she heard it, the sound of a key turning in the door, and the door opening slowly as a hand pulled the key back out and pushed.

Tasha walked in nonchalantly carrying a takeout bag.

"Hi. Sorry, you were sleeping so..." She held up the bag as evidence. "I had to go home for a little bit, and I didn't want to disturb you, did you see the note by the TV?" Quinn shook her head, why hadn't she thought to look for one? "I grabbed some dinner on the way back. What are you doing down there?"

"I don't know... I thought...I wasn't sure if I'd been dreaming, or if you'd left me again and...I didn't see the note."

"I'm sorry. I should have woken you." She helped Quinn to her feet and leaned in to kiss her cheek. "I wouldn't leave you like that."

"You did last time," Quinn said following her into the kitchen, unable to forget that feeling of being abandoned.

Tasha placed the bag down on the counter and pulled Quinn into her arms once more. "I'm sorry, Quinn."

Chapter Fifty

Standing together, plating the take-out so that they could sit down and eat. Natasha's arm brushed against Quinn. They worked in a comfortable silence, but Quinn's mind was racing with unasked, and answered questions.

"Was it you who I saw?" Quinn finally asked, turning slightly as she piled rice onto the plate. Tasha looked confused, so Quinn clarified, "On the beach, all those times I thought I saw you, was it?"

Tasha glanced away, her cheeks blushing instantly as she placed the carton of noodles down and gripped the worktop.

"Yes," she said, still unable to look at Quinn. "I mean I am not sure when you saw me, but yes I have sat on the beach outside your home."

Quinn listened; her sanity at least was no longer in doubt. "Why?"

"I used to come when I thought you would be out." She smiled shyly. "Ridiculous, I know, but I would pretend that you were sitting with me or had popped inside for more coffee." This time she chuckled. "And sometimes I would come hoping you would be at home and catch me. That you would come outside and wrap me in your arms, and I'd finally feel safe. Then I'd remember how unfair I was being, and I would leave quickly. I never knew you had seen me." She paused, then turned fully towards Quin and said, "I'm sorry."

"It's okay, I just thought I was going crazy," Quinn admitted. "I'd look up, and there you'd be, and then instantly, you'd be gone again. Like in the movies when there's someone on a street corner and then the bus passes and they're not there. In my heart, I knew it was you, but I couldn't trust myself." With everything divided up and plated as equally as they wanted, they both walked through to the lounge and sat down with plates on their knees. "But you knew that I wanted to meet you. I kept asking you to meet me."

"You were asking Hat, not me. You didn't know it was me. And that scared me, what if I turned up and it wasn't me that you wanted. I didn't know how you felt about Hat, but it was her that you were expecting."

"But you are her, whatever I might or might not have felt, it was still you I was feeling it about."

"You're right, and that's why I decided that enough was enough, you deserved to know the truth and I came here to tell you. I knew you were home because of the selfie you posted, and so I drove over. When I walked onto the sand I could see you in the water on your board, I was going to call out to you but." She shrugged her shoulders and with a small curve of her lips added, "You just looked so peaceful out there." She grinned as Quinn tried to catch a falling prawn from her fork. It landed on her plate, and she stabbed it once more with her fork and tried again. "I panicked. I ran through my head all the things that I needed to tell you, and I convinced myself that you didn't want to hear. So, I left and sat in my car arguing with myself."

"You drive a red sports car?" Quinn asked and Tasha nodded quizzically.

"Yes, how did you know?" Her head titled to one side, just the way Quinn remembered, and it made her smile.

"Because when I looked up, and saw you, I paddled for all I was worth to get back to shore. I dumped my board and ran up the sand, down the alleyway and out onto the street, but I couldn't see you anywhere...it was deserted, except for this little red sports car that pulled out and into the traffic."

"I am so sorry, Quinn, it was cowardly of me."

"I just wish." What did she wish? She put her fork down and looked at Tasha, those green eyes that drew her in all those months ago were still doing it now. "I just wish that..." Struggling to find the words she needed, the words that matched her feelings, she looked away. She felt the touch of soft fingers taking her hand. "I just...I don't know what I am supposed to be feeling. Part of me is so happy that you're here and yet, I can't help but feel anger, does that make sense?"

"I understand," Tasha said. Her fingers squeezed gently before withdrawing back into her own lap. "Do you want me to go?"

"No," Quinn said. "No, I don't know what I want but I don't... I don't want you to leave. I never wanted you to leave."

"Alright." Tasha smiled, continuing to eat.

"Unless...Do you? Do you want to leave?" It had suddenly occurred to Quinn that maybe this was just as difficult for Tasha too. Maybe she needed some space and time again.

"No, I never *wanted* to leave before," she answered, placing her plate down on the table. "And I don't *want* to leave now. But I will go if I am making you uncomfortable or hurting you."

"Would you please stop talking to me like a therapist?" Quinn said suddenly, placing her fork down with a clang onto her plate. With her hand now empty, and restless, she ran it through her hair before finally, dropping it into her lap. "Sorry. I didn't mean to..." She placed her plate on top of Tasha's and sat back again.

"You didn't scare me; I don't mean to talk to you like a therapist. How would you like me to speak to you?"

"Oh, I dunno, like maybe..." Quinn stopped speaking, calming herself until she was able to say. "I want to kiss you; I want to hold you. I want things to be simple and easy. I want to take you to bed and show you..." Before Quinn could finish, Tasha moved, climbing into her lap and staring into her eyes.

"Do not think that I don't want that?" she said, as the tip of her nose nuzzled against the side of hers. "I want more than ever to make love with you. To let you hold me once more." Quinn sucked in a breath as she felt the heat between them. Their lips were barely apart. "But I am not going to do that. I want to do this properly." She pulled back, staring into Quinn's eyes once more.

Quinn's brow furrowed. "What does that mean?"

"I would like to go on a date, I would like to spend time in the open getting to know you properly. No more sneaking around, no more fear. Just you and I falling in love again." And then she leaned in, lips connecting. It felt like forever, and felt like too soon, all at once. Over way too soon in Quinn's opinion, but the electricity she felt pouring through her nervous system was enough to leave her speechless. "But also, there are more conversations to be had, and we need to process each part and to make sure that we are both okay with things. Being with me isn't as simple as you hope it will be," she explained.

All Quinn could do was nod her head. She didn't need simple. She needed Tasha.

Chapter Fifty - One

"I wrote to you," Tasha said as they lay together, entwined on the couch. Fingers interlocked. "I wrote a lot while I was away."

"I didn't get -"

"No, I didn't send them. It seemed somewhat cruel to... I would write them and then burn them. I guess, I just felt better knowing that I'd told you. Ridiculous really, but at the time it was...cathartic I suppose." She let go of Quinn's hand and started to run her fingers through her hair instead. "Therapy is such a strange thing." Her smile was there, wistful, and reflective. She looked away to gaze longingly out of the window. Her memories took her somewhere Quinn was yet to visit. When she turned back to Quinn, there was a steely resilience in her eyes. "Do you know why I used to sit on the beach? At the start, when you first met me." Quinn shook her head; she had some ideas of her own, especially at the time, but had never voiced them. "My life was so unimaginably miserable. For twenty years I had endured a life, I never lived it. I used to sit on the sand and contemplate if anyone would miss me." In those words, all of Quinn's worst fears were confirmed. "I was considering how easier it would be if I just got up and walked into the ocean...and I think I would have. I think had something miraculous not happened, I would have done exactly that."

"What stopped you?"

Her face lit up. This smile only for Quinn. "You did my love, it was you."

Quinn sat up, twisting around until they were face to face. She felt the hot sting of tears prick at her eyes as she listened.

"I'd sat in that exact spot for two or three days before you ran past the first time. Too cowardly to actually do what I'd gone there to do right away. So, I kept coming back, gradually building the courage it would take to say goodbye to this cruel existence I'd been living...and then you appeared. I remember thinking, as you ran past me, that you were the first person that really looked at me." She held up a palm as Quinn went to interrupt. "It was just a moment, a split second where our eyes met, and I felt..." Her eyes closed as she thought back to that moment in time. "I felt confused." She laughed a light chuckle that brought a small smile to compliment it. "And then you brought me coffee and a blanket. It was the simplest of things and yet, it meant more to me than if you had laid down gold bars and silk."

"I think I always kind of thought that the reason you were there was to do that. But I didn't want to think about it, so I pushed it away." Quinn pulled her close. "I am so glad that you didn't," she whispered against her hair as she placed a gentle kiss.

"As I said, therapy is a strange thing. For a long while I hated you." She saw the look of utter horror that registered on Quinn's features and quickly kissed her lips. "Oh, please don't be upset. It's a process. I had to go through my feelings one by one before I could even begin to understand myself and strangely, Nick wasn't the first thing I needed to deal with. It was you. I hated that you had made me feel something. I blamed you for the situation I was in. Without you, I would have just killed myself and not had to go through with all this painful therapy, or I could have just stayed with Nick and let him eventually kill me. But you changed everything. You showed me what I could have, and I wanted it so much, so, so much, and yet, here I was stuck in an institution of sorts. Free from him, but nothing had changed, I was still miserable and so I projected all my problems onto you for a while." The tears Quinn had been fighting back, finally broke the dam and Tasha smiled kindly as she wiped them away with her sleeve tucked over her thumb. "And then I understood, that it wasn't hate that I felt, it was sadness. I was grieving a loss. A loss that

I had created. I was angry with myself that I wasn't a normal and capable person that could enjoy being loved."

The clock chimed. On the hour, nine gentle dings indicating that it was 9 o'clock already. The hours had passed by so quickly, and yet, Quinn felt as though Tasha had just arrived. It was all so surreal. She felt as though she were floating around the words as one by one, they penetrated Quinn's flesh and hit home in different parts of her psyche. Some wounding, others healing, but all of them needed to be said and heard.

"It's getting late, I should go," Tasha said gently.

"What? No, why? It's just nine. Stay, please," Quinn implored. Ready to fall to the ground and beg if she had to.

"Quinn, I'll be back. Maybe tomorrow we can..."

"No, you won't. You'll walk out that door and I'll never see you again. You'll leave me and..." Quinn sucked in a breath and grabbed her hair as she tried to rein in the fear she suddenly felt. Tasha sat silently, allowing her to get it out. When she was ready, and feeling calmer, she explained. "You always leave me and I never...I never know when you'll be back. If you'll be back...I have no way to find you. You just...it isn't fair Tasha; I have nothing of you except what's in here." She beat her chest with her palm twice.

"You're right." Tasha smiled, picking up her bag. She delved inside and found a pen and a small notebook. For a moment, she scribbled several things down, before handing it to Quinn. "My address, telephone numbers, and email. I'm not leaving you Quinn unless that's what you want me to do, but I need to go right now, and you need some space to process everything. Can we meet tomorrow?"

Quinn nodded.

"Alright, goodnight, darling. I'll see you tomorrow," Tasha said, kissing Quinn on the cheek.

Chapter Fifty-Two

At 4 a.m., Quinn found herself staring up at the ceiling. The sleep earlier, plus the fact that her mind was in overdrive, meant that she couldn't sleep. Throwing her legs out of bed with a sigh, she got up and pulled on her running gear.

Outside it was silent, the moon lit up the path ahead as she immediately began to pound against the sand. It was cool in the night air, and as she got closer to the water's edge, the wet sand flicked up and soaked her legs. At any other time, she might have noticed the numbing feeling as sand stuck to her skin, penetrating the coldness into her bones. But her mind was too busy to think about something so trivial.

She'd never felt like this in her life before. A sense of elation mixed with confusion and, if she were honest, a little anger still. Natasha was back. No guessing, no hoping, no figment of her imagination. She was back and, in her arms, again, but still, there were so many questions. And all of them were running through her head at once.

When she reached the point at which she usually turned around, she considered just how easy it would be to keep going. Keep moving until she physically couldn't move any longer, and maybe then, her body would be so tired that her brain would shut off. Common sense took over, however, and she did an about-turn and headed home again.

In the dark, she pulled off her clothes and walked into the shower. Sand flushing away as she stood motionless under the spray, letting the water warm her bones and muscles until she felt more relaxed. Once she was dried off, she fell onto the bed, and slept fitfully.

Subconscious took over from the conscious mind, and dreams, vivid and wild now invaded the space that her waking thoughts had held hostage all evening. Natasha in bright color, dancing around on the sand, twirling and spinning, getting further away with each twirl and no matter how fast Quinn tried to run, she couldn't catch her. "Don't leave," she screamed, but the retreating Natasha just smiled at her and kept moving, further and further away.

Quinn woke with a start. Sitting up quickly, she glanced around the room and tried to ground herself in reality. It was just gone 8 a.m. according to the clock by her bed. She looked around for her phone but didn't see it. then she remembered plugging it into a charger downstairs. Grabbing her robe from the back of the door, she pulled it on and headed down to retrieve it.

She checked her messages, nothing that she couldn't respond to later. Nothing from Natasha either. The dream had left her feeling antsy. She put the phone down and went to the kitchen instead, starting the process of making some coffee. Caffeine was going to be needed today.

With coffee in hand, she headed back into the lounge and looked at her phone again. Still, nothing from Natasha, not that she was seriously expecting there to be. She scrolled absently through her old messages, stopping when she got to Caroline.

Rattling off a quick text to see if her friend was free, she stood at the window peering out, sipping coffee until the beep alerted her to a reply,

Caroline: Yes, coming over?

Quinn: That would be great. An hour?

Caroline: See you then.

~***~

By the time she got through the traffic and arrived at Caroline's, it was nearer an hour and a half, but her friend didn't complain. She opened the door and invited Quinn in with a smile and a hug.

"You look like you've been up all night," she stated as Quinn passed her and stopped, waiting to be directed to wherever Caroline wanted her to go.

"Feels like it," Quinn replied with a half-smile on her lips. She followed as Caroline beckoned.

"I've just made some tea, but maybe you'd prefer a coffee?" She chuckled, leading them into the kitchen. It was a nice house. Modern and stylish. Much like Caroline herself.

"Actually, can I get some juice or water?" Quinn asked, taking a stool at the large island that dominated the center of the room. "So, you were right."

Caroline turned to glance at her as she opened the refrigerator door. "Was I? When?" With orange juice in hand, she narrowed her eyes at Quinn. "I mean, I usually am, but I don't know the context to this, so..."

Quinn smiled. "My online friend, it was Natasha."

Caroline said nothing at first, but the smirk that appeared on her lips was enough of a "told you so".

"So, that's a good thing, right?"

Quinn nodded. "Yep. It is."

"And yet, you're here, looking pensive and like you haven't slept..."

"Right again." Quinn grinned. "I am happy, she's back and she wants to see me, and work things out. I'm just...that's the thing, I don't know what I am .... I've been waiting for this for almost a year..."

"But?"

"I feel like there's something else; I'm missing something. And I can't put my finger on it. I can't work out why I am not jumping around for joy? I should be happy, right? And yet, I feel...anxious."

Caroline poured herself some tea and then took the stool next to Quinn. "I think it's totally understandable. This has been as traumatic for you as it was for her." Quinn went to interrupt, but Caroline held up a finger. "I'm not saying that what she went through was the same. But the impact of her leaving you the way she did, after everything that happened, means that it was equally traumatic for you, and now, all of this cloak and dagger chatting behind a screen, pretending to be someone else? That's all quite overwhelming to suddenly be faced with the reality that it was her all along. You have every right to feel somewhat angry at that deceit."

"I guess I also feel a little foolish. She just turns up pretending to be someone else. How didn't I know?"

"Why would you?" Caroline tossed back before Quinn could dive down that rabbit hole. "What is it that's really bothering you?"

"That she will leave again. That I'll let her back in, fall more in love, and she will leave again," she admitted, looking away. "I'm being an idiot, aren't I?"

"I wouldn't say that. But I do think you're being given the chance to have the kind of relationship that you wanted all along and you'd be an idiot if you'd waited all this time, just to throw it all away now." She reached out, placing her hand on top of Quinn's. "Okay, listen. Just for a moment forget all of that. When you saw that it was her, were you happy?"

Quinn nodded. "Yeah,"

"And are you still attracted to her?"

Smiling, Quinn nodded again. "Yes. Definitely."

"And she apologized and explained herself?"

"She did, yes. Though I still think there is more she isn't telling me just yet, but yeah, she was contrite."

"Well, it would seem to me that your dreams were answered, and now it's up to you whether you enjoy it or make mountains out of molehills."

Quinn swallowed the last of her drink down. "I guess I'm going to enjoy it then."

"Atta girl." Caroline grinned, raising her cup to salute the plan.

Chapter Fifty-Three

Leaving Caroline's, Quinn felt the smile appear back on her face. There was a lot to talk about still, but Caroline was right, this was the opportunity she had been pining for all this time. As she climbed into her car, she tapped out a quick message and sent it to Tasha.

Quinn: La Greco, 2 pm?

If Tasha agreed, she had 40 minutes to get there. A minute later and she had an affirmative in reply. Grinning, she set off back towards the beach.

When she arrived, she found Tasha already waiting for her at the bar. She looked great and Quinn was beginning to realize that this was how she should have always looked. Her hair was swept up in an elegant chignon. Gentle wisps hung loosely to frame her face. Her face was sun-kissed and blemish-free. She looked happy, and as she turned and caught sight of Quinn, the grin widened, and Quinn couldn't help but return it.

"Hey, thank you for meeting me," Quinn said, greeting her with a kiss on the cheek. The barman was already hovering for her order. "Actually, I took the liberty of booking a table," she said to Tasha. "Are you hungry?"

"Yes. Let's eat."

"Shall we?" Quinn gestured towards the tables and then led the way to one that overlooked the ocean. The scenery outside was beautiful, but she only had eyes for the woman now sitting across from her. "What would you like to drink? Wine?"

"Oh, no I think I'll stick to something light...sparkling water?" she said just as the waitress appeared. Quinn eyed her for a moment, that was the second time she'd turned down alcohol. Not that that was a problem in itself. Quinn wondered if it was something to do with her therapy. Abstaining from certain substances.

"I'll have the same," she said, closing the wine menu and handing it back to the waitress.

"So, how are you?" Tasha asked once the server had walked away and left them to their privacy. Her eyes never left Quinn's as she waited for the answer.

"I..." She was about to say that she was fine, that all-encompassing answer that anyone wants to hear when they ask the question, the answer that allows the asker to not worry any further about you, but that wasn't how Quinn felt and she decided that if they were to move forward then she needed to be honest from the start. "I'm conflicted," she finally verbalized an honest answer. "I've spent so long now wondering and hoping for exactly this. That I would wake up one morning and find you sitting on the beach in *your* spot." Her smile faltered slightly as she listened to me. "But the thing is...I never really expected it would happen. I'd convinced myself that...you were gone, and I needed to deal with that. So, I tried to move on...I tried to open my mind to other possibilities. I tried to let someone else in and that someone else turned out to be you." She laughed at the irony of it all.

"I'm sorry Quinn."

"You have to stop doing that." Tasha frowned at her, but Quinn continued, "You have to stop apologising for everything. I accept you're sorry, I do. I understand why and I know that things were difficult enough for you," Quinn explained, but she was cut off.

"Yes, they were, but I didn't realise until recently just how difficult it was for you too. My therapy was, in many ways, selfish and it had to be, I had to think about myself and...it was difficult yes, but..." She reached across the table for Quinn's hand, linking their fingers together. "I wish there had been another way."

The moment was interrupted when the waitress reappeared to take their order. Moussaka for Quinn and a Greek salad for Tasha. So simple, so easy. They both took a moment to sip their drinks and admire the view. It had been sunny that morning, but now, as they looked out to sea, the dark clouds were rolling in.

Another storm was brewing on the horizon.

"This counts by the way," Quinn said, breaking the silence and grinning at her. Tasha tilted her head slightly and narrowed her eyes, confusion etched across her face.

"What does?"

"This...lunch. I'm counting it as a date." It took a moment for the words to register with Tasha, but then she grinned as she understood. "No more sneaking around," Quinn insisted.

"No more sneaking around," Tasha agreed, their hands still linked, she squeezed Quinn's fingers. "I like that plan."

When the lunch arrived, neither woman withdrew their hand. They chatted easily, eyes on each other as slowly the food disappeared from their plates. It was comfortable and Quinn was as relaxed as she had been for a long time. But gradually, she began to notice how quiet Tasha had become.

"Are you ok?" she asked tentatively.

Now, Tasha released her grip on Quinn's hand and sat back in her seat. "I'm fine." She smiled a little nervously, "Quinn, there is something else that you need to know, that I need to tell you about, but it's easier if maybe I just show you." She clasped her hands together and began to fiddle with the ring she wore on her right hand.

"Sure, this sounds ominous." Quinn placed her fork down on the edge of the plate. "Should I be worried?" She tried to smile, but the butterflies of anxiety appeared and put her on edge again.

"I hope not. I'm sorry if I've worried you, that wasn't my intention, but it is important. Will you come to my place later, and we can talk about it then?"

"Yeah, of course."

Tasha smiled more confidently now. "It's really not something to worry about, it's just important, for us both moving forward."

Quinn nodded. "Okay." She breathed in and pushed the anxiety away, she trusted Tasha, and that meant that whatever this was that she needed to share, it wouldn't come between them. "Dessert?"

Tasha's new house was up in the hills. One of those gated communities where the rich and famous lived hidden away from the rest of the world. Big iron gates stood proudly in front of Quinn's car as she pulled up to a small sentry box. A uniformed guard sat ready to lift the barrier and open the gates if Quinn passed the entry test. He used his hand in a winding direction to indicate that she should open her window to talk to him.

"Good afternoon, ma'am," he said politely, adding in a friendly smile as he quickly glanced around the car for anything untoward.

"Hi," she read his name badge. "Jorge, I am here to see Natasha Miles. Quinn Harper."

He glanced down at his clip board and marked something off with his pen before he smiled at her again. "Ok, just give me a minute." He walked around to the front of the car and jotted down the number plate details. When he was satisfied that he had completed his tasks, he came back around to the window. "Thanks for your patience. Ms. Miles has indicated that you would be visiting." He lifted the barrier and then leaned into the box to press a button that opened the gates. "Ms. Miles' home is on the left about a mile up, please drive safely and keep to the speed limit. Have a nice day," he said as he picked up a phone, to alert Tasha to her impending visitor no doubt.

"Thank you very much," she replied and moved forward and through the gates. Passing homes that wouldn't look out of place in Beverly Hills. Each one with its own set of gates and a wall of brick or bush surrounding it for privacy. Just like a regular street, the numbers were painted on the kerbstone and Quinn counted them off as she got closer to the house that was now home to Tasha. The gates were already open, and she swung her car onto the drive and got her first glimpse of the impressive house with its fountain out front in the center of the drive. A Spanish style villa painted white with yellow framework and shuttered windows. The little red corvette was parked to one side and Quinn pulled up next to it just as the big double doors to the house opened, and out walked Tasha. The sight took Quinn's breath away as she studied her for a moment. She really did look well, healthy, and happy. Honey blonde hair that had earlier been worn down, was now up in a high ponytail. Showing off a long neck and collarbones that peeked out from beneath the yellow blouse she now wore. Buttons down the front and hanging loosely over short legged white pants. Accentuating her tanned skin. Topping it all off, were the three-inch heels that Quinn knew would put her mouth in exactly the same place as her own when their lips met.

Quinn climbed from the car, not bothering to take the keys or lock it. She took a few quick steps and within seconds was face to face with Tasha. In one swift move their lips met and Quinn's hands reached down and lifted Tasha until her legs wrapped around Quinn's waist, and warm palms clasped her cheeks, and Quinn carried her into the house, still kissing.

When Tasha pulled away, breathless and grinning, it took all Quinn had in her to not press their lips together again. "Hi," she said staring into green eyes that sparkled back at her.

"Hi," Tasha replied. "I can't believe you're here." Her palm stroked Quinn's face and she melted into the touch.

"I keep pinching myself, thinking I'll wake up soon and you'll be gone," Quinn admitted. It was a fear that would sit with her for a while, she knew that, but also one that would dissipate in time.

"I'm here." She wiggled and Quinn put her down onto her feet again, her arms wrapping around her instead, needing to keep her close for just a little longer. "I want you here too."

"I'm not going anywhere," Quinn assured.

Tasha took a step back. "I hope not." Her eyes looked sad, and Quinn couldn't understand what could be so terrible that it would cause Tasha to think she wouldn't hang around once she knew.

"Tash, just say it, whatever it is you're holding back, just say it."

"I just..." She turned and looked up the stairs. Wide steps led to the next floor with huge paintings hanging on the wall. She reached out and took Quinn's hand. "Come with me."

The move surprised Quinn, why did they need to go upstairs? And then it hit her, maybe there was something physical that Tasha needed to share; a scar that worried her maybe? So, she let herself be led. "You know, if you just wanted to lure me here to get me into the bedroom, you could have just asked," she joked nervously halfway up the stairs.

Tasha laughed, stopping one step higher. She took Quinn's face in her hands and kissed her again. "Please never stop making me laugh."

"I'll do my best." Quinn saluted as Tasha took her hand once more and led her up the last few steps. At the top, there was a long hallway, left and right. Identical doors dotted the walls, at least six that Quinn could count before they stopped in front of one.

Tasha reached for the door handle, but then stopped, and turned back to Quinn. "I'll understand if you can't..."

"If I can't what?"

"Do this with me." She smiled sadly and then looked away, back at the door and the handle that she turned slowly. She walked in, and for a moment, Quinn lingered outside. Questions flooded her mind, and she needed a moment to ground herself and prepare for what was obviously a big deal. When she finally breathed deeply and settled, she took a step forward and entered the bright room. Her eyes scanned around until finally, they laid on Tasha. She was standing in front of the window, illuminated by the sunlight that shone brightly through, and in her arms, over her shoulder lay a child. A baby really. She had a child.

Next to her was a crib, and as Quinn looked around the room, she saw toys and bookcases, a rocking horse that was far too big for this baby, but in time would be the perfect plaything. She was speechless.

"Her name is Amelia. Amelia Quinn Walker. My maiden name," Tasha explained as Quinn stepped forward again. She looked proudly at Quinn. "I..."

"She's beautiful," Quinn said before Tasha could get any "buts" into the conversation. Of all the reasons Quinn could imagine not being with someone, this wasn't one of them. "Amelia..." As Quinn spoke the child's name, small eyes opened and stared at her. Green like her mother's. Tiny fingers that opened and closed. "Can I?" Quinn asked, stroking the wispy fine blonde head of hair.

Tasha beamed a smile that made Quinn's heart melt a little more. A smile of acceptance. She passed her daughter to her lover and watched as she settled into Quinn's neck and nuzzled contently with Quinn's gentle palm resting against her back. "She likes you."

"Of course, she does." Quinn smiled, her other hand reaching for Tasha. "But...how?"

Tasha's eyes closed and she took some calming breaths before taking Amelia and kissing her head. Gently, she placed her back into her crib and for a moment they both stood there, looking down at her as little legs kicked happily.

"She's my miracle," Tasha whispered, her head against Quinn's chest. "I have no idea how she managed it, but she's a fighter."

"I want to hear everything," Quinn said, kissing the top of her head.

There was a small knock on the door, and a woman half Quinn's age popped her head around the door and smiled at them both. "Ms. Walker, I'm back."

"Thank you, Robin," Tasha said once she had turned to face the door. "We're going to go downstairs, she's just woken, but I expect she will nap a little longer."

Robin came into the room and over to the crib with confidence. This was a woman who was used to being here. "No problem, I'm sure we can find something entertaining to do if she doesn't." She smiled down at Amelia. "Maybe a walk?"

"Thank you," Tasha repeated, touching Robin's bicep as she led Quinn away from the crib, and out into the hall again. "Shall we get a drink?"

Suddenly it hit Quinn. "This is why you've not been drinking."

"Might have something to do with it, yes."

Chapter Fifty-Five

They sat together on a plush cream-colored couch surrounded by pillows in a room that was twice the size of Quinn's living room. Tall windows looked out onto a garden full of flowers and trees. The ocean in the background. From here, Quinn worked out where her home would be.

"Sometimes I'd sit here just looking out, knowing you were there," Tasha said, as though she could read Quinn's mind.

"How long have you been here?" It bothered Quinn that she had no idea about the last months. All she knew was that Tasha had gone. But gone where? And when did she return?

"I bought the house last year, not long after I left. My therapist helped me to realise that I needed a lawyer and speaking with them, helped me realize what I needed moving forward. I didn't have to speak or see Nick again, but there were things we needed to arrange."

"Like a divorce?"

Tasha smiled up at her. "Yes, like a divorce. But practical things like where would we live, what would I need for Amelia? How would I pay for it all? The lawyers dealt with it. We have several agreements."

Quinn twisted around a little. "Like what?"

Tasha sighed. "Well, firstly, he doesn't have access to Amelia unless he completes several anger management courses and agrees to see a therapist of my choice, even then it would only be with supervised visitation. He didn't want to sign it. I think he wanted to try and use Amelia to get to me, but he didn't want to go to prison either, so I agreed not to press charges if he signed the paperwork."

"He doesn't deserve to be anywhere near that child," Quinn stated.

"So far, he hasn't attended any of the courses laid out, or even inquired about seeing her, so for now I hope that that continues, but I am not concerned with that." She kissed Quinn's bicep before continuing.

"Why not just have him sign away his rights to her completely?" Quinn quizzed. It was the obvious opportunity.

"Because I didn't want to take that away from her. In time, I will tell her the story of how she came to be and leave it to her to decide if she wishes to have anything to do with him. And if he chooses not to put his daughter first, then that's on him. When Amelia is older, she will be able to make up her own mind about her father, knowing that her mother never stopped him from seeing her."

"I guess that makes sense. You were always too good for him, you know that, right?"

"I do now." Tasha grinned. "Obviously, the house we shared wasn't somewhere that I wanted to live. I also don't want him to know where we live. So, I signed a non-disclosure agreement in return for an obscene amount of money, and multiple assurances that he will not contact me. Any breach will make our agreement null and void."

"So, he won't risk anything if he wants you to keep your mouth shut?"

"Pretty much sums it up. It means that Amelia is taken care of, and I can put that part of my life behind me and start building a new future life...with you?"

Stretching her neck, Quinn leaned down and found willing lips waiting for her. "I like that plan. I like it a lot." Kissing Tasha felt to Quinn as though this was what she had been waiting for her entire life. Kissing, in general, had always been good, really good, but this felt different. When they broke apart, it still felt like they were connected. "Tell me about Amelia," she whispered against Tasha's lips.

"As I said, she's, my miracle. It wasn't often that Nick and I were intimate. On occasion though, it happened. More from not wanting to set him off I suppose, but I was a willing participant," she added quickly before Quinn got the wrong idea. "Christmas Eve, he surprised me with a very thoughtful present, something he hadn't done for years. He was charming and..."

Quinn touched her arm. "You don't have to justify anything to me."

"Okay, I just..." She smiled and nodded an understanding. Quinn didn't need or want to know the details. "I was three months pregnant when I left. How she withstood that last...the last time that he beat me, I'll never know, but she did. She was born at the end of August, a little early. The doctors were amazed. They'd told me to expect a premature arrival, after the trauma of everything, but I went to almost full term with her, and she was born healthy. All her fingers and toes, and she smiles and laughs. She is the complete opposite of anything she was created by."

"It must have been difficult, being pregnant and still trying to go through the therapy?"

"It was, but in some ways having her growing inside of me, it gave me something else to keep going for. I already had my hope to come back to you, but I knew the risk would be that you'd meet someone else, and forget about me...but with her, she was part of me. She relied on me. I had to get better, to find my way, because of her."

"She's beautiful, she has your eyes."

Tasha grinned. "Yes, she does. She has Nick's nose and ears, but I can live with that. She's mine and the love I have for her is...nothing I ever imagined. I always used to chuckle when women said that, but it's true."

"She's a lucky little girl to have such an awesome mother. And you gave her my name?" Quinn choked up, nothing about this was anything she had expected, but if she had, it still wouldn't have occurred to her that someone would use her name for their child.

"I did, I wanted her to know you even if she never got the chance to meet you. She would one day ask me about her name, and I would be able to tell her that she was named after the most amazing woman her mama ever knew, that she was someone with so much love inside her that I thought I might burst just being in the same room with her."

The emotional dam erupted, and Quinn wiped her eyes. "Really? That's..."

Tasha stroked her face; their eyes, both watery and filled with all of the emotion they'd been holding onto these past months, stared into each other's. "I love you. I have loved you for a very long time and don't think I'll ever love anyone else the way I love you, but I come as a package."

"And you already know me well enough to know what my answer will be."

"I hoped that I did..." She whispered against Quinn's lips as she climbed into her lap, straddling Quinn's thighs before pressing their lips together. "I want you so very badly."

"Not as badly as I want you." Quinn smirked.

"My bedroom is just upstairs."

Chapter Fifty-Six

Tasha clung to Quinn. Her smaller frame light enough that Quinn could carry her, legs wrapped around Quinn's waist, her arms around her neck, fingers entangled in Quinn's hair. Her face buried into the crook of Quinn's neck, kissing, and sucking at the skin available.

Step by step, Quinn climbed the longest staircase of her life. Carefully taking one step at a time until, once more she reached the top. She turned in the hallway the opposite way to Amelia's room, and in eagerness, opened the first door she came to.

Tasha giggled as Quinn came face to face with shelving, buckets, and mops.

"Closet. Try the next one," Tasha murmured against her ear, sending a shiver of excitement rocketing throughout Quinn's body. "There's at least a bed in there."

Quinn all but growled as she continued down the hall to push open the next door. She kicked it shut behind them just as Tasha's mouth moved from her throat to her mouth. The muscles in her arms began to shake and Tasha slid effortlessly from them. With her feet on the floor, her hands grabbed at Quinn's shirt, pulling her forwards, towards the huge bed.

With her fingers shaking, she unbuttoned the blouse Tasha wore, pulling it apart and off of her shoulders just as quickly as Tasha lifted the hem of Quinn's shirt and tugged it up and over her head. They barely took a moment to stare at one another before their lips crashed together once more and Quinn pushed gently until Tasha fell backward onto the bed.

Now, as Quinn stood before her, she took it all in. The beauty of her. The need and want for her. Leaning forwards, she pulled at her pants until they slid away from her body, landing in a heap on the floor beside the other discarded fabric.

As Quinn hovered above her, she noted her skin. Blemish and bruise-free. Small scars that were now barely visible white lines. So very different from the last time they had shared themselves with each other.

Tasha watched her curiously as she made her inspection.

"Have you finished?" she asked, smiling.

"Yes. You're really...okay." It was a statement, not a question.

Sitting up in just her underwear, perched on the edge of the bed, she reached for the button to Quinn's pants. "I'm not broken anymore, Quinn." She stared up through hooded eyes and yanked enough that Quinn's trousers fell by themselves to the floor. She kicked them off as Tasha scuttled backward, holding Quinn's hands, and pulling her along with her. "You told me once that you wanted to show me."

"I was so naïve to think I could solve everything for you," Quinn admitted, holding her body weight off, she reached a hand up and pushed aside a strand of hair that fell across Tasha's face.

"Without you, I would never have had the courage to solve everything for myself."

"But I was so selfish. I wanted to be the one that made you better. I never understood why you wouldn't let me."

"It was never wouldn't, I couldn't. There is a big difference sweetheart," she said, kissing the corner of her mouth.

"I know that now," Quinn acknowledged, turning her head to meet wanton lips fully. Tongues engaged in a battle of wills as each tried to outdo the other with an expression of want and need. But when Tasha took control. Flipping their positions, Quinn already knew she would let her win every battle from here on out.

"I told you, I'm not broken." Tasha grinned down, pressing her supple thigh between Quinn's legs. Quinn's hands pinned beside her head.

Unbridled passion released as she took control. Quinn was in awe of the way she had built her confidence these past months. Tasha was now the one taking charge, not asking, unafraid, it was hot as she leaned forward, kissing Quinn as her hands explored every inch of the person she had been consumed with since leaving behind her old self.

"Maybe it's time that I showed you how you should be loved," Tasha said, looking deeply into Quinn's eyes as her fingertips found a taut nipple. She smiled at the small hiss and gasp that slipped from Quinn's mouth as her body arched into the touch. "Hmm, like that, huh?" she smirked and repeated the move. "What about if I do this..." Her voice was low and husky as she moved away from Quinn's mouth to use her lips elsewhere. Encompassing the nipple and sucking, teeth nibbling until Quinn groaned and squirmed.

"Fuck." She'd had that move pulled on her many times, but it had never invoked the reaction her body was having right now. Her hips moved involuntarily against Tasha's thigh, desperate for any relief from the sensations pulsing through her clit. And as though Tasha could read her mind, she felt her lover slide down her body, settling herself between Quinn's thighs, and when that mouth wrapped around her once more, Quinn felt herself float away from herself, as though she were able to see them both from above. Her naked body writhing beneath her lover's tongue as she was swept up and away in a glorious eruption of sexual awakening that she was sure, she would never find again.

"I love you," Quinn said between gasps. She felt the momentary pause as the words hit Tasha's ears. Then she understood the movement of a smile against her skin and relaxed back into the feelings that Tasha was eliciting from her.

Tongue replaced with fingers while Tasha moved slowly, kissing her way back up to find Quinn's eyes searching hers. "I love you too," she said before leaning down to kiss Quinn's mouth while her fingers found the depths of her, and slowly, intently, and with every ounce of love within her, Tasha showed Quinn what it was to be loved.

~***~

"Do you think maybe we should get dressed?" Tasha asked as they lay together in a hot and sweaty mess of ecstasy. Frenzied lovemaking had turned into something slower, emotionally charged, and accepting, before finally, they'd both collapsed against one another and caught their breaths.

"No. I don't ever want to wear clothes again, I want to spend my entire life right here with you, naked!" Quinn laughed, grabbing her around the waist and tickling her. Tasha wriggled and giggled before turning the tables and coming back on top. She leaned down, kissing Quinn until her fingers stopped all movement.

"Worked out how to stop me already, huh?" Quinn laughed some more.

"I've always known," Tasha cooed, combing her fingers through Quinn's messy hair. "I want to get dressed and take you out."

"Like a date?"

"Yep, exactly like a date."

"What about Amelia?"

"She can't go, she is far too young for dancing all night..." Quick as a whip, Tasha answered, smiling at her as she stared down from above. "Robin lives in, she won't mind watching her for me. She knows all about you and how important this is to me."

Quinn felt herself fill with more emotion at that, to be so important that people knew about her before they had even been introduced.

"Alright, I'll let you take me dancing, on one condition."

"What's that?"

Quinn sat up, wrapping an arm around Tasha's waist, and pulling her closer. "You take me home to get changed into something more appropriate for dancing in."

Climbing from her, Tasha walked naked across the room. "I guess I can do that...but I have a condition too."

"What is it?" Quinn smiled, watching her as she reached the doorway to what must be a bathroom.

"You join me in the shower."

Quinn didn't need to think about it. She would have followed this woman to the edge of the Earth if she had to.

Epilogue

The van had arrived before Quinn. Already her boxes were being unloaded and taken inside. All under the strict direction of Tasha. She stood at the back of the vehicle, baby in her arms and ordered the three men carrying boxes to take them to whichever room was appropriate.

As Quinn pulled up alongside the Corvette, Tasha smiled and waved. She was in her element, Quinn thought as she studied the scene. Grabbing her laptop bag from the passenger seat out of habit, she climbed out and wandered over to where all of the action was taking place.

"Are you sure you don't mind dealing with all of this?" Quinn asked as she reached Tasha, kissing her quickly on the cheek before turning to Amelia and making baby noises and kissy sounds at the giggling child.

"Of course not. We're having fun, aren't we Amelia?" She smiled as the three men reappeared ready to take the next boxes. "All done on your end?"

Quinn nodded. "Yeah, I left the cleaning crew there, it's all ready to close up, or rent out."

"I have to admit, the idea of a beach house is appealing. Especially as Amelia grows."

"Then let's keep it as that." Quinn kissed her again. "I need to head off, but I won't be long. Just a few rewrites before they finish filming. Honestly, they could do this without me, but I guess I am in charge." She winked. "I'll see you tonight...at home."

"Can't wait. I'll have dinner ready for seven, so if you're going to be late, let me know?"

"Sure will." She kissed them both and headed back to her car.

~***~

Returning home, she liked the way that sounded in her head. She was returning home, to her family to have dinner together. They'd done that a lot recently, but the idea of Quinn moving in had only been broached a month ago. Amelia had just turned one, and she and Quinn had already bonded. When Tasha asked her to live with them, she hadn't hesitated in agreeing. It just made sense.

She'd had a key for a while too, but this was the first time, she would open the door with it and walk into her new home. She grinned as it turned in the lock and the music from inside could be heard at a distance. Tasha was in the kitchen, and Quinn imagined her dancing around, singing as she boiled and fried, or whatever it was she was doing in there. It smelled delicious though.

Quinn placed her bag down, kicked off her shoes, and walked down the hallway, down the three steps, and into the kitchen. The music was louder, and now she could hear Tasha singing along quietly. Amelia would be in bed, sleeping like an angel with Robin down the hall listening in until 9 p.m. when she would be off duty and Tasha and Quinn would take over. It was a neat arrangement. Robin had been a godsend to Tasha in those early months. She lived in, and although she had set hours, she was much more flexible than many nannies would be. She was almost part of the family too, and Quinn liked the easy-going young woman. Especially right now, because it meant she and Tasha could just enjoy a couple of hours to themselves.

"I'm home," Quinn said, Tasha had come a long way but anyone sneaking up on her could still trigger a reaction. So, Quinn made sure never to do it.

"Hey..." Tasha said turning with a wooden spoon in her hand. "Come try this?" She blew on the spoon several times while Quinn crossed the room.

Leaning down, Quinn let Tasha feed her. "Oh, that is...wow."

"It's a new recipe I'm trying," Tasha announced proudly. "Tuscan chicken."

"It's delicious."

Tasha put the spoon down, and slid her arms up and over Quinn's shoulders, wrapping around her neck. "So are you." She smiled into the kiss.

"Hm, wanna skip dinner?" Quinn joked.

Laughing, Tasha untangled herself. "No, but afterward I am expecting dessert. Oh, come see what I did?" she took Quinn's hand and dragged her out of the kitchen and along the hallway to the lounge before she had any chance to question things.

In one corner, there was a glass cabinet, that used to hold photos, and small ornaments, that Quinn could now see were dotted elsewhere around the room, inside the cabinet, however, were her awards. Lit and proudly displayed.

"I think it's time we started to appreciate them, and your success, what do you think?" Tasha said linking her arm through Quinn's.

"I don't know what to say?"

Reaching for her face, Tasha brought her eyes to Quinn's. "You have given me so much. And I appreciate that you don't want the entire world to know how awesome and amazing you are, but in this house, our home, that will never be in doubt. Our friends, and our daughter, will all know just how talented you are. Your light needs to shine, sweetheart."

"I have everything I need, right here, with you and Amelia. Anything else is a bonus, I don't need these trophies to prove anything, but I do kind of like them on display." She winked. "But on one condition."

"Name it."

"When Amelia is old enough and wants to play with them, she can. They're not going to become a shrine that can never be touched."

"Alright, I'll agree, so long as you can meet my condition?"

"What's that?"

"You win a few more. Fill it up."

Quinn laughed, leading her back out of the room and towards the food. "I'll do my best. Speaking of which, I've got this great idea for a film...it's about this gorgeous doctor who's married to a complete asshole, and then she meets this awesome writer, and they fall in love..."

The End.

If you enjoyed this book, or any other of Claire's books, then please consider leaving a review.

Many thanks!

UK Readers

https://www.amazon.co.uk/default/e/B074G45R1C

US Readers

https://www.amazon.com/Claire-Highton-Stevenson/e/B074G45R1C

French Readers

https://www.amazon.fr/l/B074G45R1C

German Readers

https://www.amazon.de/Claire-Highton-Stevenson/e/B074G45R1C

Australian Readers

https://www.amazon.com.au/s?k=Claire+Highton-Stevenson

If you want to know more about Claire, you can follow her on Social media.

Facebook: https://www.facebook.com/groups/ClaireHightonStevenson/

Twitter: https://twitter.com/ClaStevOfficial

Instagram: https://www.instagram.com/itsclastevofficial/

Tumblr: https://www.tumblr.com/blog/itsclastevofficial

Blog: https://wordpress.com/view/itsclastevofficialblog.com

Website: http://www.itsclastevofficial.co.uk

Why not sign up to Claire's monthly newsletter?

Subscribe here: https://mailchi.mp/761fcafef004/stranger

Printed in Great Britain
by Amazon